Praise for *ROSANNA*

'This is a lush and beautifully written novel. As her therapist uncovers what Rosanna is hiding and why, an evocative climax builds to a rewarding finish. The author has captured the energy and emotional tension of intertwining relationships. The Australian threads which are woven throughout the book – the places, people and landscapes – are beautifully described. I absolutely adored this book.'
Vicki Bennett, Author

'Captivating and real, a beautiful story about healing, found family, overcoming trauma and tragedy, and the importance of the good things that can be found in life.' *Nita Delgado, Editor*

'*Rosanna* is set in a small rural town in the magical forests of the Northern Rivers region of NSW. Underlying this natural beauty is a disturbed and destructive underbelly that reflects a shameful era of neglect, abuse and violence in Australian family culture. Annie O'Moon-Browning's subtle and sophisticated debut novel weaves the story of one woman's triumphant healing journey back to herself. *Rosanna* is an important read.' *Dr Nici Buirski*

'*Rosanna* is a raw and healing tale of Rose's journey through love, trauma and loss as a young girl and free spirit in Nimbin, New South Wales. *Rosanna* explores the deep, spiritual enchantments of Australian nature and its connection to the complexities of human experience.'
Beth Falzon, Reviewer

'Some novels are woven with magic. *Rosanna* is one of them. O'Moon-Browning writes as if the earth itself composed a melodic symphony and she stood as the sole enraptured listener to write it for the rest of us to hear.' *Paris Thompson, Editor*

Praise for *ROSANNA*

'Rosanna's life has not been easy. The richly descriptive prose journals her path through hell and back during the post-Vietnam hippie era of northern New South Wales and southern Queensland. Rosanna survives and ultimately thrives, not just through her own strength but through the love shown and shared with a wonderfully eclectic cast of characters. This book has many twists and turns, mystical allusions and historical referencing, so read it slowly to savour the difficult but intriguing mystery and ultimate restoration of her life.'
Dr Margaret Matthews

'I loved the vivid, descriptive prose of O'Moon-Browning's skilfully crafted novel about Rosanna's life journey which follows the changing face of Australian history in the counter-culture. It is a beautifully written debut novel that I could not put down.'
Cathy Scully, Karuna Biographer

'An engaging novel of a young woman's traumas and journey to healing, revealed through conversations with her therapist. Vivid descriptions of life and landscapes in 1970's and 1980's northern New South Wales and Brisbane.'
Suzy Teo, Director Union Society Brisbane

'The author has lovingly and cleverly crafted two women's colliding stories within the complexity of experiences that builds the human spirit. Certainly, Rosanna appears the star of the show, but in my view the therapist should be receiving more attention by reviewers. How the author has expertly unveiled character as much in what isn't written, as through what is written, is, to me, the true star of this surprisingly sophisticated debut novel.'
Cate Sawyer, Author

ROSANNA

Annie O'Moon-Browning

HAWKEYE
PUBLISHING

First published in Australia in 2024 by Hawkeye Publishing.

Cover Design by Eli Southward and Annie O'Moon-Browning

Author's Dedication
This book is dedicated to all women, especially those who fight injustice, and those who understand the power of their stories. To my beautiful parents, and Auntie Helen Martin, whose passion for books inspired this one.

Acknowledgment of Country
This novel was written on the unceded, sovereign lands of the Turrbal, Jagera and Bundgalung Nations. I would like to pay my respects to their elders past, present and emerging. I acknowledge First Nations peoples and recognise and honour their spiritual connection to Country, community and culture. And not least the healing possible in the sharing of story across time and generations.

A catalogue record of this book is available from the National Library of Australia.

ISBN 9781923105096

Proudly printed in Australia.

www.hawkeyepublishing.com.au
www.hawkeyebooks.com.au

1

Nimbin, December 1977

CONCENTRIC rings spread outwards from my son's hands as he lay flat on the ground, his little belly pressed into the soft fragrant earth. Small fingers dipped into the river's clear water and trailed, chasing filaments of leaves floating just below his grasp. Matted with dirt, his hair hung over his forehead as he peered into the dark depths. Body grubby with filth from the night before, Christian's face shone with a luminosity that belied our plight. Overhead, dark limbs of an ancient oak tree stretched around him, protective, shading the heat of the noon sun.

He watched the stream with intensity, its shining transparency magnifying his fingers as they danced beneath its surface. Crystal clear images of the overhanging trees reflected a melody of gentle movement that began with his dabbling fingers disturbing its depths.

I sat with my back against the gnarled trunk, my breath steadying as I watched him. My body throbbed. Fatigue a deadening blanket. The pain in my heart, a repetitive beat against my chest.

'Can we Mumma, can we?'

Christian looked up at me, eyes the colour of a darkening sky. Long lashes swept across his cheeks as he blinked, watching me, playing with my heartstrings.

We had arrived early at that secret refuge after clambering along the waterway just out of our village. The night before, our resting place had been under the old bridge in front of the Butter Factory. Christian had slept in my arms, my body huddled against the irregular, hard surface. It had been a sleepless night; the notion of safety abandoned me. Fear woke me whenever I began to drift into an exhausted slumber.

It was mid-summer, but I was chilled to the bone. Even the warmth of my child could not stop my shivering. I thanked God the rain had held off.

I was seventeen and Christian was three years old.

I'd brought nothing with me. My clothes clung, sweat and patches of blood soaking into them from the cuts on my arms and legs. I reached up in the darkness and traced lacerations in my cheeks. The bone above my eyebrow throbbed; a swollen lump covered in dirt and blood closed my vision to a slit. My mouth was filled with cracked teeth. Bitterness knifed into my temple as my head pounded like a fist on a pub bar.

In the still night, the stagnant air below the bridge stung my nostrils. The ground was damp; the underside of the bridge was covered in moist moss. I found a long ledge, where we crawled into safety, away from the river. It smelt musty and a chilled fog covered our bodies. As I looked down, the ink-black current seemed to slow, just as time had during our flight. Here, I felt I could keep watch throughout the night.

Cradled in my arms, Christian quickly fell asleep. A few mosquitoes whined around us, stinging my numb flesh, until the smell of beer and stale sweat reached me in the middle of the night. Terrified, I held Christian close, pressing my body into the ledge.

'Who is it?' I stammered. 'What do you want?'

'This is my place, you hear me, my place.' He eyed me suspiciously, then pushed past and squatted beside us.

Perhaps it was the pathos of a bloodied teenager with a sleeping child in her arms, in a starless night, hidden in an obscure place, that struck a chord within him. Or maybe, I offered no threat and human kindness found its way into the old man's heart.

A wizened hand extended, offering a partially eaten meat pie in a crumpled paper bag. Taking it uncertainly, I ventured a small bite. It was still warm and tasted good, so I pocketed it for Christian's breakfast. I felt grateful and a little safer as the old man shrugged, turned his back, curled up on the filthy ground and instantly fell into drunken unconsciousness.

I awoke at dawn to Christian wriggling out of my arms. He crouched, looking out at the road. No cars had driven over the bridge during the night and a silvery mist enshrouded us, protecting us from inquisitive eyes.

'Where are we, Mumma?' he asked sleepily, rubbing little fists into his eyes.

My body ached as I stood and grasped his hand, mind suddenly alert with the urgency to get away from that place. The old man snored, sprawled out on his back, completely at home. Carrying Christian, I stepped around him and dropped onto the bank below.

'Let's go exploring,' I said quietly. 'Want to go fishing?' I asked, putting him down.

He smiled and skipped off. I followed him warily, keeping an eye out for anyone who might recognise us. Every part of me fought the internal anarchy that threatened to immobilise me.

'Come on, Umma!' Christian's urging jolted me. 'Come on, I wanna see some fishes.'

I followed him, rock-hopping slowly, skirting large logs and deep pools. I helped him climb over huge rotting fallen trees and carried him past moss-laden embankments. He felt so small in my arms as his exuberance bubbled up, filling the dawn with the delight of his innocence.

He squirmed down to chase the dragonflies that flitted across the crystal-clear surface of the stream.

'Can we go home now, Umma? I'm hungry.'

He was lying on the bank, watching the brook flowing gently past. I handed him the partially eaten pie, which he devoured noisily, congealed gravy running down his chin. Then, humming sweetly, he turned back to watch the water, toes dangling into its cool reaches.

'Oh look, Umma,' he cried. 'Fishes. Come here. Help me catch some please?'

The silvery flanks of a brown trout glittered under the surface as it glided closer to the embankment. Christian's keen eyes, trained by many hours of playing and learning to fish with Sarah's dad, gave him an ability to see under the surface with uncanny clarity.

My breath caught in a lump of sorrow.

…Butterfly wings… Soft breath…

Rose. Go upstream, Rose… Pools of love shone in her emerald-green eyes.

'Look, Umma. Look!' Christian called, pointing into the depths below.

Tears gathered behind my eyes as he dangled his fingers beneath the surface, leaning closer to the fish.

At least we won't starve, I thought, wiping my nose with the back of my bloodied knuckles. I wondered if he'd been taught to catch fish with his bare hands. Squatting down, I drew him to me, wrapping my arms into a full circle of protection. He squeezed back with a ferocity that took my breath away. Then pulling away from me, his grubby fingers traced the dirty tears that ran down my puffy face.

'Watsa matta, Umma?' he murmured. 'I love you, Umma. You'll be okay, you're with me now,' he chirped, arms around my neck, hugging me tightly.

I buried my face in golden locks, breathed in his little boy smell, hot tears springing from my tightly closed eyes. I held onto him for an eternity as my chest heaved and shook. Christian was quiet as I wept, he momentarily the parent, me the child.

'C'mon, Chris,' I said, finally finding strength. I pointed towards the densely forested wilderness.

'Let's go that way.' I knew that if we followed the course towards the mountains, we would be less likely to be seen. Its thick foliage hiding us from prying eyes. Danny had spoken of a community living further up.

You'll be safe there… hidden, his voice soft.

Through the fog in my brain, I wondered if the longhaired women in flowing clothes and the bearded men in their plain rustic tunics lived up there. A familiar longing drummed an aching cadence in my heart as I remembered Sarah speaking of them.

An angel's touch. Tinkling ethereal laughter rings into a glade. That pain. That indelible imprint on my soul.

Sarah. SarAHHH! Beyond the turmoil, I felt her touch.

Follow the river, Rose Petal. Follow it… Lips as soft as silk, a caress, then gone.

Fatigue wracked my bones as my feet stumbled along the rocky tangled embankment. I tried to steady my breath, but his voice rose up, breaking through her love.

Fuckin' trash. Pot smoking hippies… fuckin' bitch.

Dark images flashed; my hands involuntarily rose to block my ears.

… Run, Chris, RUN…

Bile stung my throat. Sweat and dirt smarted my eyes as I shook my head trying to clear my thoughts. Nausea overwhelmed me and I sank to a squat, holding my head. Mouth dry with fear.

'Umma, want a drink?' his voice called me, cracking the illusion. I glanced up. My son's eyes were filled with apprehension. I nodded numbly as his small hand took mine and guided me into the cold current. He splashed me gently until my senses re-formed and the voices dimmed. I scooped the clear liquid into my mouth, drinking deeply of its sweetness.

Christian crooned, softly patting me.

'It's okay, Umma,' he soothed. 'Wanna have a swim?' His eyes shone with love. I tugged off my boots and stripped down. Venturing into the stream, I rubbed dirt and blood from my body before plunging deeper.

Complete silence.

Only my heartbeat.

Cool healing surrounded me as I sank towards the rocky bottom. The icy mountain-fed river cleansed my lacerated, bruised flesh. I lay there, submerged. Hidden from my world. Until my lungs burned and the muted call of my son drew me back to its surface.

I dressed quickly. Taking Christian's hand, we headed deeper into the wilderness.

2

Nimbin, 1971

I had escaped from the sounds of them fighting, their voices still echoing in my ears, their discord a routine intrusion into my child's world. His vulgar belligerence and venom filled me with fear. Her pitiful retaliation, a deepening betrayal.

This time it was mid-afternoon.

He had come home early to attend to *business*. I didn't know what that meant but it always produced tears for her. Oblivious to me as I hid in the garden outside, his cursing and her pleading provided me with the opportunity to flee.

My breath came in short gasps as I slid and scrambled over rocks and rotting logs. Everywhere there were shallow pools. Fungi and lichen grew on fallen forest giants. A proliferation of plant life, filled with mystery and wonder, greeted me. The floor beneath my naked feet was strewn with rotting leaves. Twigs and ferns hidden behind rocks, alive with dark green moss, perfumed the air. Drops trickled over shiny boulders, gathering in leaf-filled faerie hollows, perfect basins of sweet fragrant moisture.

Huge, black mushrooms clung to the trunks above me; colossal growths amid staghorn that spread their green wings, wrapping themselves around massive buttresses, reaching for the heavens. My head spun, adjusting to the dim light. Dense undergrowth parted beneath my hands as shapes emerged around me. Enormous trees towered over me, leaning inwards, their long, gnarled arms reaching out to touch me.

My toes bumped against hard rock and soft soil. The knee I hurt whilst escaping no longer stung, as I pushed deeper into this land of magic.

Suddenly, the ground opened under my feet. Small pebbles scattered as I tumbled over and over. I seemed to float as I fell, my mind rising above me as my body toppled. Leaves protected me, cushioning my fall. I caught glimpses of a blue sky as I levitated above the rainforest in that brief descent. I came to rest on the soft earth below. Flat on my back, winded from the impact, I gasped for air, senses reeling, wondering which bone was broken in my small wiry body.

A thundering sound filled my ears.

It was then that I heard a soft low chuckle. I looked up. Standing over me was a giant of a man. His face was covered with a thick rust coloured beard and his cornflower blue eyes twinkled at me. His bushy eyebrows wriggled as he smiled. Shiny gumboots rose up from the earth, holding massive legs. He wore brown pants torn at the knees and an open shirt, with a fishing rod slung over his shoulder. Large, hairy hands held what looked like wire cages with hooks in them.

'How the hell ye didn't kill ye'self, I don't know,' he drawled, reaching down to help me up, his thick, lilting accent unfamiliar to me.

'What was ye thinking of, littlun?' he asked. 'No one comes down here, 'cept me and my fish traps.'

He dusted me off then straightened, looking at me.

'Hmm, yer a scrawny one, that's a fact,' he exclaimed. 'You okay?'

My attention focused past him on a vista that took my breath away. I had never seen anything so beautiful. A wide gorge filled by a rushing cascade thundered over a rocky outcrop. At its far edge, a torrent disappeared into thin air, forming a foaming, booming waterfall that plunged into a pool hundreds of metres below. I pushed past him, scurrying over to the rock-strewn edge.

'Careful there,' he warned. 'It's slippery.'

Throwing myself onto my belly, I gazed forward into the cool spray. A rainbow arched over the top of the surging current, its multi-hued tones shining above the forest below. He watched me silently as my heartbeat slowed and my sight cleared. No words were needed to explain our extraordinary meeting.

I lay there for an eternity, excitement grasping me from within. The man wove threads through hooks and tied them to fishing tackle. He seemed to be waiting for me to come to my senses. But my voice lay mute as my rich inner world opened up to absorb the intense beauty.

'Yer know, there's good fishing to be had in this part of the woods,' he finally said. 'Wanna look?'

He strolled up-stream towards a deep, crystal-clear pool. Untangling his tackle, he bent over and lowered a wire cage into the shallows, watching it sink below the surface and settle on the water's bed. I turned back to the vista as he moved wire baskets and fixed fishing lines, securing them to fallen logs on the bank.

'Yer know? I used to come here as a young-un too. Loved fishing. Watching that there waterfall. Many folks can't find their way in here,' he said. 'Or their way out,' he grinned.

'Yer lucky yer got here in one piece,' he continued. 'These woods hold many secrets. 'Tis a special place, yer know.'

I watched him, fascinated by the red in his beard and the sheer volume of hair on his face. I'd never seen such large hands before and in those few brief words, this goliath had shared more humanity with me than I had ever experienced. I was spell bound by him. A living, walking giant who was every part of that forest.

'Ah well. Better be off. Looks like rain,' he drawled. 'Yer need a hand getting outa here?' he asked, looking quizzically at me as he picked up his belongings and turned to walk away.

Reluctantly, I drew myself away from that mystery and, slowly rising, followed him.

We scrambled down into the gorge, using the plants and trees to hold us as we descended. Following the rocky outcrops on the edge of the precipice, we dropped down onto the level forest floor at the bottom of the waterfall. He continued along the creek, rock hopping in easy strides, waiting patiently for me as I scrambled to keep up with him. Climbing back out of the forest, we made our way into a clearing a little way from my home. The distant rumble of thunder signalled the gathering storm as we stepped out onto the dirt road. The village was outlined in the far distance by towering grey-black thunderheads and streaks of lightning.

He turned and held out his hand.

'Well. It's been nice meeting yer, little Miss. I'm Dad O'Reilly,' he said, taking my hand in his and shaking it.

'Guess I'll be seeing yer around, huh?' His eyes twinkled with fun as he turned and wandered off into the growing dusk.

I watched his loping stride carry him away as heavy droplets of rain began to fall, quickly soaking me to the skin. Thunder rumbled and crashed. Shards of lightning illuminated the hills around the valley. I turned and ran towards home, gratitude soaking into my bones, hoping that the rain would wash off all evidence of my forbidden journey into the forest.

The booming of the storm muted my footfall as I crept into our home. Silently I secreted my torn soaked clothing under my mattress for stitching later, then drying myself, I slipped into bed. I was hungry and exhausted, but exhilaration filled every fibre of my small body as the Irish magic of the afternoon sung its song into my future.

~

Brisbane, October 1987

I sat with my back to the door, the coffee table in front of me laden with magazines and books on art and health. The deep tan of the wooden floorboards, dull against the backdrop of French doors framing the green of the overhanging jacaranda. Some of the soft mauve florets had made their way onto the veranda, blown there by spring breezes.

Beads of sweat collected on my upper lip, gathered there from the heat of the walk along the busy road from the bus stop and up to the house. They were a visible presence of the feelings that sat in the pit of my gut, wanting to be released.

She told me that this would help to win them back. To soften the delusion. To move me on.

Auntie Mim was usually right.

Why the fuck come? What the hell am I doing? My stomach queasy with the habitual liquid of anxiety.

Brisbane's October heat bore down on the cars and road outside. In the background, the muffled growl of traffic echoed down the long corridor. The floorboards creaked under my weight as I swung the heavy front door open and made my way along the shadowy hall to the waiting room.

It was cool there; the couch strewn with bright cushions. My fingertips stroked the sofa's silky velvet. Its subtle brocade, teal and gold threads, shone in the light of the room, swimming before my eyes, reflecting images inside of me.

Soft skin… Golden strands of silken hair tickling my cheek… Tinkling laughter floating upwards…

Mumma. Can we go home now, Mumma? Can we? his voice echoed in my brain.

I can't do this, Sarah, my heart pleaded.

Breathe, Rose. Breathe… A smile lit the corners of her eyes.

Muted voices and laughter rang out from the next room. I settled into my chair, trying to control my breathing as the door opened and two people walked out. Their voices wove a melody of warmth as they embraced a farewell. The front door swung open as she spoke.

'Don't forget your canvas next week, Oliver.' Her intonation sparkled with warmth.

Footfall receded along the front path and the gate creaked open, then banged shut. I peeked as she moved with purpose towards me. Her clothing floated the scent of roses into the room. Her gaze rested on me as I ducked my head.

'Rosanna?' she enquired.

Nodding, I hunkered lower into the lounge.

'Would you like to come in?' Her voice was neutral. The last syllable inflected upwards.

'Rosanna.'

I glanced up.

'Hello,' she said, reaching out her hand. 'I'm Anna. It's nice to meet you. Would you like to follow me?'

Deep eyes met mine, reached into my core, saw all of me. Strong fingers wrapped around mine as we shook hands.

Forever sista, Sarah's voice echoed in my ears.

Anna released my grip and stepped into her room.

'Please take a seat.' She gestured to a wide cane chair plumped with a soft silk cushion. I sat down awkwardly.

My eyes traced across bookshelves filled with cover-bound manuals and texts. The scent of incense filled the room. An ancient white marble fireplace spanned one wall, its mantelpiece dotted with rose quartz, tiger's eye, malachite, and aquamarine crystals. A small Buddha statue sat in the middle of a flowered china bowl, surrounded by floating frangipani.

Vivid landscapes and charcoal nudes adorned the walls. A cacophony of colour and form. An artist's easel leant against the far wall. Tins of acrylics and oils cluttered the floor.

The window looked across a suburb with the steep streets of the inner city as rooftops. Trees dotted the rooflines. In the distance, the tall straight tower of the city's single skyscraper defined the horizon.

Stillness enveloped me as my fugitive gaze stole the vista before me.

'Rosanna,' she spoke again, 'my name is Anna. I'm to be your therapist.'

I watched her silently as thoughts spun inside my head.

Umma's hurt… Umma!

She's in dire need of help…

'What has brought you here today?' Her words broke through my daze.

Her round gentle face was framed by wavy blonde hair flecked with silver. Blue eyes gazed at me with interest. Laughter lines crinkled the corners of her eyes. Her knees were crossed and the drape of her skirt hinted at shapely, long legs. Low-heeled pumps dressed her feet. A silken jacket wrapped loosely around her shoulders and dropped to her waist, sculpting a youthful figure on a mature body.

Her gaze held mine with penetrating steadiness. Leaning imperceptibly towards me, she waited for me to respond. There was a disturbing familiarity in her look and a recognition that filled me with apprehension.

My voice choked.

'Have I seen you before?' I finally managed.

She watched me carefully.

'I'm not sure,' she replied. 'Why do you ask?'

'You look familiar to me. Are you a natural blonde?' I blurted.

Her eyes flickered. She smiled.

'That's an interesting question. I wonder why you ask me.'

Suspicion churned my guts.

'Because I have been told that I will meet a blonde woman who will be responsible for my death.' I spat out the words.

She looked steadily at me.

'Actually, my hair is natural. But I do love colour.' She gestured to her walls and smiled.

I watched her cautiously, images forming in my mind, thoughts spinning with anxiety.

'What do you do here?' I muttered.

'I help people. I listen. Sometimes, all we do is talk. But I love to paint. And to collaborate with my clients. The big thing is that my work is a catalyst for deep change. In a positive way. Perhaps your clairvoyant saw our paths crossing. That this would begin to set your life back on course. Does that sound like it could be what she meant?'

I ducked my head, unable to respond.

'Okay, I hear your hesitation,' her words soft, reassuring. 'I am here to help you, Rosanna. In whatever way I can. You are here because you want something. Is that right? Your aunt referred you, didn't she?'

My heart froze as I hunched into myself.

The room filled with silence, her gaze steady on me.

'I believe you love art?' I heard her voice above the others that growled at my guts and tore my heart from its moorings.

'Shall we start there?'

Pause.

'Rosanna?'

~

Brisbane, November 1987

I wait for her as the arms on the clock pass the hour. I make a note and walk out to open the front door.

She's pacing the footpath. The peak hour traffic loud on the street.

'Hi, Rosanna. Want to come on in?' I ask.

She looks at me. Face dishevelled with the evidence of a late night out.

Digging her hands into her pockets she pushes past me and

stomps down the hall to my room. Thongs flipping noisily.

I follow, close my office door and settle into my chair. Watching.

She's restless. Agitated. Silenced. Her first art project is strewn on the floor between us.

I wait for her to start. Looking up at me, she's on the verge of speech.

'Ever been… in one of those… real old country stores?' Short breaths punctuate her words. She gestures randomly, her brow furrowing.

'Yer know. The ones where… there's so much stuff… you can't… even see the aisles?'

She slides her feet out, parting her legs. Her hands flutter close to her inner thighs as she tries to hide the urge to touch them. Her body is taut with anxiety.

'You mean like the ones out west?' I respond.

'Yep… like that.'

'Yes, actually, I have. As a child.'

She peers at me.

'They smell dusty, ey? Stale…like old onions.' She moves in her seat, closing her legs. 'There's heaps of amazing stuff in them. I found this old photo in one… once… of this beautiful girl, with a baby. It was hidden… behind the last shelf… out the back. So dark there… Couldn't see much… But the light caught… on the glass.' A sharp gesture. 'Cracked edge to edge. Her face was cut in two.' She screws up her nose.

I make a note. *Photo? Old country store?*

'Yer know… when I was a kid… I used to hang out in one. In this hippy village. The folk there really hated me.'

'What makes you say that, Rosanna?'

Her head snaps around as she looks at me suspiciously. Holding my gaze. Searching. Dark with wariness. 'Why ask?' she retorts.

'I think it's important. For me to get to know you.'

A sharp outbreath. 'Alright. So, ya wanna know me, huh?' Defiance. Her feet shuffle on the floor, pushing the rug edge up and down. She sits on her hands then rubs her arms.

'Would that be okay with you?' I begin. She looks away abruptly.

Distracting me. Silent.

'They're narrow there. Folk don't like change… Didn't like me… And then… well… the hippies came. That got 'em…' she snorts.

'In what way?'

'Changed heaps of stuff. I liked the new way when they came. Seemed they were better than most of the others… and… I dug their music. Their dancing.' She rubs her nose with the back of her hand.

'Their clothes were different… easy… they talked to folk… like me.' Abruptly she stops. Stands. Walks to the window. Silence fills my office as I wait for her to settle.

'Where did you grow up, Rosanna?'

'Don't want you to call me that,' she mutters. 'He said that…' She ducks her head.

He? I make a note. *Said?*

'What name would you like me to call you?' I respond.

'Rose,' She spits the word back at me.

I watch her carefully.

'So where did you grow up, Rose?' I repeat.

'In Nimbin?' Her voice fractures with confusion.

'That's in the Caldera?'

'Yup.'

'Dairy country, isn't it?'

'Used to be… but the farmers wrecked that. And the Aboriginal mob who lived there.' She frowns.

'Okay. Right. Wasn't that where the Aquarius music festival was?' I ask.

Rosanna looks at me. Annoyance twinges across her broad cheekbones as she turns away. 'Yeah. That was part of it.'

'Sounds interesting. Tell me more.'

She returns to her seat, hugging shoulder blades as she stares out my window. Resounding heaviness fills my office. Her voice is distant.

'Our village was cut off from the world. 'Til '73. Farming community. Dairy… butter… Before the loggers cut most of the forest. What was left was real beautiful.' Her voice softens, a dreaminess travels its edges. 'Ya know… we never saw anyone else. A lost tourist… maybe. Without a map.'

'There's this old musty shop there.' Her eyelids flicker. Her foot reaches out. A dirty toe traces the edge of her canvas.

'Like the one you mentioned before?'

'Yeah… 'cept it smelt of herbs… not onions.'

'Was that where you found the photo?'

'Nup.' She's defensive again.

'Okay. So, who owned it?' I ask, feeling my way with her today.

She relaxes a little.

'Maureen O'Reilly. That's Auntie Mim. And Dad… they were the owners. Sarah worked most afternoons… after school… she was their stockist. She was that smart.' Rose's face draws in on itself. Her brow furrows. She stops. Silent.

I watch. Make a note. *Sarah?*

'Would you like to talk about this more?' I enquire.

She ignores me. Crosses her arms. Looks away. Rubs her nose.

I wait.

A sudden inhale. Then an explosive out breath.

'Everyone went for groceries. Sarah was on the counter… she loved the goss… she…' Her voice trails away. Shoulders hunch. Hands under knees. Eyelids snap shut, then begin to flicker.

'Rose?' I begin. 'Are you okay?'

She glances at me.

'Would you like to take a break?'

She nods. I get up to make a cup of tea and grab some art gear. When I return, she seems calmer and sips the tea slowly.

'I like herbal. Chamomile, innit?'

'Yes.' The room fills with its aroma as I wait. 'When you're ready, Rose.'

She drinks more tea. Moves to put the cup down.

'There were these new folk… Sarah told me about 'em… came in Kombis. And trucks. And beaten-up cars. There were these strange symbols. Sarah said it meant… peace.' She sits back. Wraps her arms around her chest.

'The men looked different. Beards and long hair in ponytails. Colourful bandanas… jeans. Jesus, I loved their clothes. I'd never seen a bloke in a waist jacket… or beads… or wearing leather shit. I was the only person in town with bare feet 'til them.' She stops. In the silence, my French clock ticks audibly.

A shuddering inhale.

'Yer know… I never… never… thought about clothes… Ma put me in hand-me-downs… Always torn… worn… thin… but those women… they were real beautiful… their hair… skin… I just wanted to touch them.' She rubs her thighs then slides her hands between her legs. Shoulders hunch protectively.

It's a soothing feeling that she emanates now. She's found her safety. Her voice gains strength. Flowing.

I make another note. *Ma?*

'I dreamt about me wearing their long floral skirts and flares. My feet prettied up in sandals and beads. About dancing with them. My hair flowing down my back. Not all scruffy and dirty and short.' She stops again and looks at me. Questioning. Pinched. Scared.

'Go on,' I murmur.

Rose turns back. 'They were always loving. Friendly. Called out to me. Waved. It scared me shitless. Just seeing them do it in town.' She pauses, reaching for a tissue.

'Doing what, Rose?'

'Yer know!' Annoyed at my interruption.

'Actually, I don't,' I respond.

She scowls at me. 'Whatcha reckon? Pot… drugs… getting high… God, my fuckin' head spun. Those reefers… wafting through town. Loved that smell. Loved it.' She smiles for the first time today. Body straightens. Relaxing a little.

'There was this carefreeness,' she gestures. 'They just got high on life.'

I go to speak. She's oblivious. An interplay of light and dark begins to narrow her features and harden her mouth. Her moods command my attention.

'And Pa. He saw things very diff… differently.' Her words shake. 'He called 'em trash… dole bludgers… fuckin' tree huggers. He spat at 'em…'

A tremor runs through her as she rubs her arms.

'…fucker…'

'Pa?' I ask.

She looks towards the door. Her feet move on the floor angling to stand. She kicks her brushes over. Clamps her legs together, thrusts her hands beneath her thighs, looks at her feet. The stifling feeling of quashed emotion sits heavy.

In the silence, I make a note. *Pa?*

Something stirs in my memory. I want to know more.

'What are you doing?'

I look up. She's staring directly at me. Hard. Intimidating.

'I make notes. So that I can remember what you say.'

'You didn't ask me!' She's angry.

'That's true, Rose. But I thought you would understand.'

Her face turns crimson red. My pulse quickens.

Careful!

'My job is to help you,' I continue cautiously. 'To make reports on your progress to send back to your psychologist. That's why I write.'

'Pig's arse! Who gets to see them?' Pupils dilate.

I control my voice. 'No one except you, me and the psych.'

She thrusts her hand at me, demanding. I extend mine, my notes clearly visible. Sketches and marks adorn the page. She quickly scans them. Then stops and looks at me. Staring into me. The tip of her finger rests on a doodle. Slowly, she hands them back. Her gaze is impenetrable.

'Ya bloody like to scribble, don't ya?' Her voice is hard.

This one's trouble… Move it on!

'Rose. I am going to ask your permission to write. What I put here stays between the three of us.' I watch her cautiously. There's another noticeable inhale. Her body is wound up like a clock. She fights to relax.

'Is that alright with you?'

Easy!

'No!' Her words spray pepper at me 'But. If it means I get them back, okay!' She looks at me with hatred.

I feel the depth of her anger, then steady my breath. 'Thanks, Rose. That's the way things will begin to become clearer for you.'

I wait, noting if her body language mirrors mine.

It doesn't.

She looks at the window.

'Rose. I can feel your anger. Would you like to talk more about them?' I watch her micro movements.

Eyes flicker. Close, then open. She's trying hard.

'I've got a fuckin' lot to be angry about.' Slowly trying to compose herself.

'Okay.'

A smothering, eruptive silence fills the room.

Then.

'I wanna talk about Sarah.'

'I'm listening.' Our breathing synchronises.

'Sarah said they had come for a music festival.'

'The hippies?' I clarify.

'Yup. Didn't know what that was… only music at home was the trannie… Ma used to listen to it… when Pa wasn't home… Loved the sounds of the orchestras. Thousands of miles away. Playing beautiful melodies. Sarah said the hippies… were gonna live in the forest. Have that music in amongst the trees. Couldn't understand how that was possible. My life was gutters and paddocks and… my room.' She pauses, far-away.

'Go on.'

She shakes her head, forehead creasing, and leans forward, resting her chin in her hands. 'There was lots of good. And lots of bad. But Sarah's family… they were different.'

I nod.

'I was twelve. They moved to the far end of the main street. They built The Store.' She pauses. 'Ma sent me on errands. So… I had to speak to her. To Sah. She had this amazing laugh. Like tinkling bells.' Her voice trails off into a murmur. 'Didn't talk. Sarah was really the only…' Lips tighten.

I make another note. *The Store?*

Rose leans forward and straightens her canvas. She picks up a brush and dips it into the end of a paint tube. Carefully, she prescribes a perfect golden arc onto a crazed pattern of dark lines and chaotic, vividly coloured swirls. Tiny dots that shape small circles begin to adorn her page. Linking together to form a pattern like an underground water way.

I watch intrigued, my breath quickening. There's a rudimentary familiarity about her work.

She sits back and contemplates her marks. Her breath steadies. I reluctantly pull away, stand and press play on the cassette recorder.

The Moonlight Sonata flows softly into my room.

'Hm… Beethoven.'

'Yes. You like his music?'

She looks at me. No response.

'You were telling me about Sarah,' I resume.

Her eyes flicker and drop. She chews the end of the paint brush, bouncing her legs up and down. A sullen silence fills the space.

Then. The breath. The closed eyes.

'She… she… was like… like… a beautiful bright shiny bird. Always wanted to show me around.' Rose twists in her chair, her narrative slows.

'She'd point to all the produce. All that stuff… stacked high up… just loved that smell. She'd run her fingers over it all. Like she owned it. Proud as punch of how much everything cost and what the herbs were for.'

She bends forward and places her brush back into its sleeve.

'I always felt so warm. Inside. When I…'

Rosanna stops. Stands slowly. Walks to the window. The heaviness around her is palpable.

She looks out the window. Arms crossed over her breasts. Brooding. She rubs the back of her calf with the edge of her dirty foot. Then taking a deep breath, she leans far out of the open window, hands on its sill, legs lifted.

My breath quickens perceptibly. She looks sharply at me. Brief. Intense connection. Menacing.

The pendulum swings violently, my sense of safety with it.

'Don't worry,' she scowls. 'If I was going to do it… wouldn't be here.' Cold, hard, edge. Looking back out she straightens, her profile a shadow in the approaching dusk.

'Have you ever wanted to?' I ask, controlling my anxiety.

Pause; then an imperceptible nod. I note it.

'Great view. So many streetlights. It's cool.' Averting.

She turns to look at me. Eyes blank. Remote.

'How long have ya been here?'

'A few years.' Unblinking, I hold her gaze.

'Like it here?' She turns away, eyelids fluttering uncontrollably.

'Yes, I do.'

She looks at me again. Brow furrowed. Watching me. Wanting something. Her full lips drawn in a tight straight line.

'Why do ya do this job?' she asks suddenly. 'I mean. All them people. Crazies. Coming in here. What makes ya want to do it?' She gesticulates around the room.

'It's my vocation, Rose. It also helps me with my issues.'

I wait. She doesn't reply. The muscles in her cheek contract against memories floating close to the surface of her consciousness. Her hand flicks up. A thumb grinds into a scar above her eye.

'I mean. Look at yer books. And yer art. You must have studied a lot. You've painted a shitload. Just like I… I used…' Rose stops. She's looking at the paints and canvas.

'Yes, I have,' I murmur. 'For many years.'

Her breath shakes as she thrusts her chin at the mantelpiece.

I make a note. *Used to?*

'And what's with all the friggin' crystals? I mean… do they do something for ya? Do they help? With all that art? With us? I mean…'

Her voice drops as she looks across, her eyes full, pleading with me.

'My art is my own therapy too, Rose,' I start. 'And my crystals.'

Her eyes briefly steady on me. Then flick across the room before she fires off.

'Ya know… they reckon I'm crazy… but there's energy… magic… in them there rocks… I can feel it… it's in here…' Her hand fleetingly brushes her chest. She reaches up to touch an amethyst.

'That's where it grows… where I get the…' A cracked, dirty fingernail traces the edge of the crystal as a tear drop floats, suspended in her grief, and lands softly on her breast.

Her voice almost inaudible. 'I like them.'

~

I stand at my window, gazing across the narrow steep streets of Red Hill.

Night has fallen.

I watch the movements of the locals arriving home to their small worker cottages. The streetlights flicker on. I can hear the melodic notes of a string class coming from the back of 'Four Winds'. The waft of incense from the Tibetan shop next door melds with the scent of the frangipani below me. There's a languidness to the air. Late spring is a sweet reminder of the fecundity of our sub-tropical climate.

I'm starving.

I grab my bag, carefully secure the front door of the clinic and scurry downstairs. My suburb is full of drug addicts, and I'm mindful of the Meth-hub at the bottom of my street.

I throw on a fresh frock and hurry along Waterworks Road to the Lebanese cafe. The main road is a snarl of cars and buses whizzing past, competing to be the first to get home. Dinner will have to be a take-away tonight. Jarmbi is away, out west, on the muster. I'm exhausted from the busyness of my day.

The solitude of my flat below the clinic greets me. I toss the tabbouleh and falafel into a bowl, kick off my shoes and settle onto the couch. I slowly sip on a chilled Sav Blanc as I reflect on Rosanna's story. There's something distinctly unsettling in her dialogue. An energy that is at once familiar yet intimidating.

I breathe slowly as the goodness of the languid night and the silence in my flat soothes my jarred nerves.

It'll unfold Anna… in its own way… Jarmbi's voice a soft reminder.

~

Brisbane, December 1987

Rose's hands rest in her lap. Still at last. Her breathing soft. Steady. Her eyes closed. The meditation has helped soothe the angst that walks with her through the door at every visit.

As usual, she was late. Her lack of greeting expected now. A defence against my perceived authority. Despite her dishevelled, mismatched clothes and her acrid body odour clinging like a blanket to her, she's softer.

We start simply. An invitation to relax.

She nods. A subtle indication of acceptance. Of trust. And closes her eyes.

When the music stops, I reach over to turn the switch and when I look up, she is staring at me, a blank curiosity in her eyes.

'Ya still look familiar to me, Anna,' she says softly.

'In what way?' I ask.

She continues to scrutinise me.

'I mean… yer married, ey?' She points to my ring finger.

I nod.

'Yer man. Him a black one? Yer got kids?' she asks.

I watch her carefully, taken aback by this unusual interest in me. But she looks away, suddenly indifferent.

She moves in her chair. Eyelids flicker, breath deepens. Her shoulders shrug slightly as her hands move to her hips.

'Well? What are we going to talk about today?'

'Whatever you like, Rose,' I reply.

She crosses her arms. Then her legs. Foot jiggles. A gesture now familiar to me.

'What do ya wanna know?'

I watch her. Observing the subtle changes of colour in her face. The darkening of her eyes.

'Last time you were here, we talked about Sarah's family. And about Dad.'

'Yeah? I forget.'

I change tack. 'You said you loved animals.'

'Yeah?' She looks at me, the corners of her mouth turning down. Then a restrained nod.

Releasing her hands, she leans into her chair. Reaching up, she clasps her fingers behind her head and lifts her feet, bounces her legs up and down. Indecisive.

'They were my friends, hey?' Stretching back, squeezing her thighs together.

Then. That punctuated explosion of breath as she bends forward and sits on her hands. Hunching her shoulders. She remains motionless for a long moment, then stands. The pacing moving her energy, calming her down.

'Ya know, there was this void.' She turns to look at me. 'My animals helped a lot.' She sits back down, composing herself. Her voice is slow, reflective.

'Void?'

'Yeah. With them…'

'Them?'

Her mouth sets. Her eyes flash. A shake of the head.

Ma and Pa? Don't push this today, Anna!

She flutters through her narrative.

'The wounded and sick. Found their way onto our back porch. I was twelve. Realised there was something special going on. In my hands. Musta come from God. Or Sarah's faeries.' She shrugs.

'Hell. I did enough prayer back then. Something good had to come my way. There wasn't anyone to talk to. At home. She wasn't interested.' Her mouth forms a thin line.

'He probably would have shot them anyway…' Her face flushes as her voice trails off.

'Go on.'

She flicks the dark look at me. Shakes her head. Chasing her demons. Silent.

'I'm listening. Remember your breathing.'

'Huh, what?' Brow furrowing. Annoyed. 'Okay, okay!' Her chest lifts as she works to control her emotion. 'Ya know… animals talk. To us.'

'Yes. I've had that experience. Interspecies communication fascinates me,' I reply.

She looks at me, her eyes puzzled. Pleased. She relaxes.

'It's just that we can't hear them, ey?'

'I think that's very true.'

'We don't listen, do we?' She studies me.

I make a note. *At last. Connection!*

'I love animals. I feel sad when I hear of them being badly treated. As a kid, growing up on the cattle station, we had many animals. I used to help the stockmen look after them.'

I'm level. Observing her response. Waiting for the changes to start.

'So, he is black, isn't he?' she says, her voice far off.

I go to answer but the drum of her feet on the floor stops me.

She spins a strand of her hair. Thinking.

'So many folks treat them bad,' she resumes. 'Humans are just real dumb when it comes to that.' She screws up her nose.

I nod.

'Started hearing them. Real early on. Yer know. When I was a kid. Loved the way they talked. Never judged. Always there. For me.

'Then they started to come. Onto our back steps. Cleaned their cuts. Applied Mercurochrome. Reassured them.'

She bends, picks up a paint brush, runs the bristle under her fingernails. Her *Circles* painting lies at her feet.

'At night… had dreams that called them to me… wet noses waking me at dawn. The faeries watching me. Guiding my hands. Helping me ease their suffering. Kept them quiet… especially if he was home.'

My eyebrow rises. 'He?' I ask.

She ignores me. Absorbed in her narrative.

'It's… it's this warmth.' She holds up her hands, opening her fingers. Looking through them. Tracking the prisms of rainbow light circling my room, absorbed in her reverie.

'She called these my healing hands,' closing them she lays them in her lap.

'Who do you mean Rose?' I ask.

'Sarah.'

'Okay.'

She stops again. Far away.

'They kinda pulsate,' she shakes them. 'Then it travels down through me.' Rose scans her body, looking over her breasts and then at her hands as they flutter near her thighs. Her paintbrush drops to the floor as her heels lift and fall in a rhythm of renewing anxiety.

Bouncing up and down.

She wants to pace.

Controls it, then persists.

'…always been able to find their injuries. Underneath muddy coats. Strained joints. Pictures form in my mind you know. Stories of their hurt. And their lives too.'

'That's really remarkable. Would you say you have a gift?'

She turns to look at me. Suspicious.

'Sah said that. Dan too.' Eyes cloud as she quickly looks away.

'You were telling me about your animals, Rose.'

She hesitates. I make a note. *Dan?*

'Learnt how to dress wounds. Straighten broken limbs. Could cut splints. Strap them with old, ripped rags. Studied the vet manuals. Found them in the archives of the library. Ya know, I rarely got bit or scratched. I just felt this heat. They felt it. That was what healed them.' Rose stops. Her shoulders hunch. Fingers interlace and pull tight.

'Do you need a break?' I ask gently.

She inhales, and slowly releases it, her feelings visible.

'Ya know… could tell… way back then… when I was just a kid… the difference between an animal that was badly wounded and one that I could heal. It was really clear who was too far gone. I'd stroke them. Tell them to go home.'

'Later. I'd find them curled up under a rock. In the forest. Asleep… The faeries played their harps to them in their last moments. Gave them wings. To fly.' Her voice is clear. She's absorbed in her recollection. Steadier now.

'They looked serene. As if they slumbered into the afterlife with a clear heart. Ya know? I could feel their final smiles. Like love. From deep in them. In me!'

She holds her hands to her chest. She's quiet. Reverence fills the room.

'I always dug a grave. Covered them with soil. Marked it with a cross. Took herbs from Dad's garden. And…' She smiles.

'The leprechauns…' she glances quickly at me, crinkles form in the corners of her eyes.

She's amused!

I nod.

'They left special green stones. Laid out in patterns. On their graves. Showing the configuration of the stars. And the moon. And the sun. That had traversed their lives. It brought peace.'

Rose pauses and looks slowly at me. A light plays in her eyes. She looks completely different. She draws me forwards, towards her. This inexplicable force is magnetic.

'When he was away, my room was my haven… my sanctuary.' She straightens. 'I had no brothers or sisters. When I wasn't tending to my animals, I painted.' She glances at the oils and small canvas at her feet. 'Pictures out of the mud and leaves. Collected from our sparse garden.'

'Occasionally my teachers gave me used magazines. Pieces of left-over crayons. Old tubes of paint. I covered my bedroom walls with my art. I love clay. Love making statues. Sat them in the dark corners. Hung pieces of coloured paper in mobiles. Spent hours drawing patterns. Gluing them to my walls. My windows were mosaics.' Her smile soft.

Then, imperceptibly, a change.

'Yer know… I felt safe… in my room with my animals… by myself… until… un…'

Her voice trails off as she gazes out the window. I wait. Watching her. Tension builds quickly. It's tangible and threatening.

'Rose?' I start. Her eyelids flicker.

Beads of sweat gather rapidly on her upper lip. She continues to look out of my window. Her face unreadable. Dark colour rushes to her cheeks. Her arm muscles contract as she grips the chair.

Rose leaps to her feet.

'Fucking cunts,' she screams, kicking her brushes, scattering them across the room. Flinging the door open she flees into the dusk.

My front door slams shut. My out-breath echoing its intensity.

I take a slow deliberate breath. The tension from the session knotting my shoulders. I reach forward and right her canvas, studying it. There is something bewildering in her marks. The gestalt of the form provokes a disturbing warp in my reality. An elemental sense of time distortion and familiarity.

…He is *black, isn't he*…

I pick up the tiny photo on my desk.

What's happening, Anna?

I gaze at it. An echo forming in my memory as fragments of my past interweave into the present.

3

Nimbin, 1971

SARAH'S family lived at the far end of the village in a huge timber mansion. Our town was divided by bigotry, racism and the invisible wall of class. I had always seen her, but the circumstance of my life forbade any possible connection.

That's until they built 'The Store'.

'That's 25c for yer milk, thanks,' Sarah had said, green eyes sparkling with fun as I dug into the tattered pocket of my homemade cotton pants. I dropped the money onto the counter. Then, paralysed with shyness, I turned and fled.

'What's the matter, Rose? Cat got yer tongue?' She laughed, a clear silvery melody momentarily slowing my flight.

How can anyone be like her? Why is she speaking to me? I thought.

As I walked back to my side of town along the dirt streets with rough homes and plain gardens, I thought about Sarah. In a town like mine everyone knew everyone. It was no surprise that Sarah had called me by name. I wondered as I slowed, kicking at the dirt, how she could possibly have known how painfully withdrawn I was. Teasing in my home was an act of cruelty, verbal blows that crushed and cut. Sarah's words had not made me cringe but had touched my heart, her lightness lifting a weight from my young shoulders.

The following day I saw her at school.

She waved but I hastily turned the other way, trying to hide behind the bushes in the playground. She was a grade above me; one of the big girls. There was an unspoken code that the upper classes were too mature for us. Being ignored by them was normal and I was terrified of the retribution I had witnessed for speaking to a popular, older girl.

But Sarah was not a rule player and on that hot afternoon, despite my attempts at being invisible, she headed straight after me.

'Rose,' she called. 'Why are yer hiding from me? I can see yer.' She laughed, holding out a fist full of coins.

'Ya forgot yer money yesterday,' she smiled. 'Ya gave me too much.'

I reached out to receive my forgotten money muttering, 'Sorry.' Then, turned and ran out onto the street, peals of tinkling laughter following me.

'Hey!' Sarah called at my disappearing back. 'I don't bite, yer know. I need ya help with my English. Can ya come and have supper with us?'

~

The shady bull-nose veranda on the O'Reilly house was filled with laughter, strewn with toys and boxes of dress-ups. Children played through hot summer days and cool winter's evenings under its protective shell. It was a family home, surrounded by luscious gardens that fruited all year round; feeding the hordes who frequented its richness.

Sarah's mother, Maureen, presided over the kitchen. The aroma of baking bread filled her domain. Her strong, flour coated arms rolled, pounded and squeezed the dough before shaping it and shoving it into the oven. The mouth-watering, crusty, high loaves were descended upon with no time to cool; her children oblivious to her protest of bread needing to rest before being eaten.

That afternoon, Sarah had finally coaxed me into helping her. Maureen smiled at me as I stood half hidden by the corner of the kitchen. Her rowdy mob tussled and laughed, competing for their supper. I watched, hoping that I too, would be included in this feasting ritual.

'Yer gonna need some energy to teach Sarah that English, lassie,' she said. 'Would you like some?' she asked, handing me a plate with a chunk of warm bread soaked in strawberry jam and fresh butter from the dairy.

'Thank you, Mrs O'Reilly,' I stammered.

'Just call me Auntie Mimi. Everyone does around here, Rose.' She smiled as I devoured the treat hungrily, warming to this family that was so very different to mine.

The Holden FJ coughed and spluttered as it pulled into the drive. Engine still running, children scrambled out of windows and doors laughing and calling, flung open the back flyscreen and raced into the kitchen. There was little decorum as they attacked their duties with an enthusiasm that was contagious. I had never seen such motivation to do chores. I wondered if this intensity was due only to the anticipation of lunch and the desire to get organised as quickly as possible for imminent Sunday feasting.

But this was the way of Sarah's family in everything they did. They were a team. The oldest helping the youngest. The parents cheering them on with affection and guidance. It was rare to hear complaints or reprimands.

Auntie Mimi was always up early, preparing lunch. She had everything organised before the family set off for church. On their return, the house was filled with the aromas of beef stewed in a casserole, cooked with caramelised onion, carrot and crunchy capsicum. Freshly baked bread steamed on the wooden chopping board, begging to be broken into bite-sized pieces. Potatoes, smoothly mashed with fresh full cream milk and golden butter, were piled in the ceramic bowl. Beans cooked in tomato, onion and peas, stirred in with mint, wafted past my nose as I stood out of the way in the corner of the room. Roast lamb, stuffed with aromatic rosemary and basted to perfection, made my mouth water. The fragrance of fresh herbs crushed into a crunchy salad bit into my taste buds with expectation of the meal to come.

My stomach always grumbled with hunger. My eyes, as big as saucers, watched the chaos and laughter as the family tussled and competed to see who could help their mother the most. It was not only the deliciousness of the feast, it was the warmth in that house that opened my senses to what was alien in my ordinary life.

Auntie Mimi was dearly loved by her children and presided over her brood like a mother hen, calling out to them, handing them the dishes laden with food and the cutlery and crockery to be placed on the table. Scolding the older ones if they accidentally bumped the little ones. Gently patting any passing head with encouragement and love.

The noise in that dining room was deafening. I was both enthralled at the camaraderie and terrified at the same time.

Auntie Mimi had it figured that Sunday lunch was the only time I would get a decent feed. She had spoken to Ma requesting my continued help with Sarah's English and in their garden to tend to her herbs. In return, she told Ma that it was only fair I be included in at least one meal per week with her family. It was proper, she had said, that I be paid for the work I did. Ma, always wary of other families in our town, reluctantly agreed to Mimi's persuasion.

I wasn't allowed money. So, when an occasional twenty cent piece was found in my tattered shoes at their door, I looked at the coin as if it were gold. Sarah said that, as the faeries that had left it there, I had to keep it to make them happy. That I was obliged to receive this gift to make sure my herbs grew deliciously well. She said the faeries needed me in their garden and this was their *thanks*.

I listened carefully to these earnestly conveyed directions and within the enchantment of this family it all made sense. I pocketed the coin, carefully hiding it in a sock in a small box in my room, saved for the future.

During the week, after school, I taught Sarah English and tended to Dad's veggie patch. From him I learnt all the names of the unusual plants that grew in their densely laden garden. We had developed a bond, born on that afternoon when I tumbled down the embankment, landing at his feet on the forest floor.

I followed him around like a puppy, hanging off his every word, listening with keen interest to all he had to teach me. He wandered around his lush garden, pointing to and naming vegetables; explaining how best to cook them or what fertiliser would make them grow rich and strong. He collected chook poo from their coop and took the ute down to the back block to shovel cow manure into its rusty tray. This, he said, was the best food for his garden as the animals made it especially for us, chewing their grass and passing it out of their bodies as an offering from God.

He explained that there were special planting days when we would be sure that the little seedlings that grew in his ramshackle greenhouse would strike best. That their delicate roots would thrust into the fertile soil and shoots would peek up out of the ground at such a rate that they would quickly look like jack-in-the-bean-stalk plants. He explained to me how the moon affected growth. That those that bore fruit had to be planted on different days to those whose roots we ate.

And he told me that it was the leprechauns that helped his garden grow so lusciously. That they watched over it, allowing the little coots and insects to take their fill. Just enough so that we too, had plenty to eat.

One morning, after a rare sleepover, Dad woke me at dawn. We slipped out of the house, heading down the path towards the veggie patch. He had a vegemite jar of soaked broad beans in his hand. I sleepily rubbed my eyes as I followed.

The early sunrise shone through the dewdrops on the lettuce and kale leaves, scattering fractured mini rainbows onto the earth around them. The small golden marigolds nodded to us as we passed. Secret whispers of sleepy birds opened my ears to a deeper charm. I began to see small shapes scurrying in amongst the plants. Hidden smiles and just audible whispers followed me as I crept down the soft earthen path, entranced.

The daybreak and the feeling in that garden brought me to a standstill. I stood, bare feet rooted to the earth, the garden shining as I had never seen before. My other life receded as my face shone in awe.

'Can yer feel the wee leprechauns?' he said tenderly. 'They're gettin' tings ready for our planting, lassie.'

We watched, waiting, and then, as if an invisible hand had reached out to both of us, set off in unison making our way deeper into the garden.

A newly laid bed awaited our "broadies" planting. Squatting on the ground, Dad leaned forward, his large hairy fingers poking small holes into the rich fragrant earth, creating long lines in the soil.

'Here, wee Miss,' he said softly. 'Do it this way. Make them straight so the plants will grow tall and strong.'

I knelt, reaching out to part the soil with my fingertip. Pressing down into the earth, feeling through fertile crumbling loam, I dug small holes one after the other until the garden bed was covered with them. Sitting back, I looked up smiling as he watched me.

'To be sure, yer a fine little garden gnome,' he said, his blue eyes twinkling. 'Now we have to wait.'

The sun had climbed a little higher as I had worked.

'The leprechauns will be off to bed soon and then we can plant them… after they have gone,' he whispered, holding up the jar of soaked broad beans.

We sat in companionable silence, the air still and fragrant around us. The dawn light peeked into the depths of the garden with the first rays of sun touching the earth in front of us. Dad handed me a palm full of moist beans, then turned and dropped his, one by one, into the little holes I had dug.

'Follow me, lassie,' he said and together we planted all those broad beans into a verdant soil filled with love and steeped in Celtic folklore.

Years later, I came to understand that the rich Irish brogue in Dad's voice carried the magic of a millennia of Celtic superstition. It was his reverence for the earth that had made its way into my spirit.

~

Brisbane, December 1987

The stench of her body is overpowering today. Tobacco clings to her breath. Her hair hangs in matted locks down her back. Her clothes are filthy. She looks the worst she's been.

I sit quietly as she manages to settle into her chair. She can't meet my eyes. I wait.

'Yer know what? There's no winners in war,' her voice rasps. 'No one.'

I spoke with her over the phone after her last sudden departure from my office. I asked her to think about her family. To bring these thoughts into our next meeting. She agreed. There's no apology. I don't expect it. No matter what happens, the sessions have to continue.

'That war. It was so fucked. No one wanted it. I didn't understand anything about it… 'cept that… when he came home it was hell.'

She shuffles her feet. Holds her head.

'Got any Panadol?'

I nod and stand to find it. When I return, she is lying on the floor in a foetal position, a sketch clasped in her hand.

I lean forward and hand her the painkillers.

She sits, takes them in one gulp and hugs her knees into her chest. Sitting motionless.

'Rose. It's fine if you prefer to stay there.'

She doesn't reply. Just starts rocking herself, back and forth. A rhythm of protection. Crushing her art in a tight fist.

I wait.

'I wanna start this. Hafta, I guess? It's fuckin' hard to talk about that war. About them,' she manages.

'Ma and Pa?'

She looks up at me. Eyes blank.

'Know anyone who went?'

'Yes, I do. Many men and women.'

'And their kids… they all as fucked up as me?'

She's direct today. Needs a straight answer.

'They all have big trauma,' I reply softly.

She looks away. Then struggles heavily to her feet and moves back to her seat.

'What do ya wanna know then?' She's defensive.

'Let's start at the beginning.'

'Okay.' She hugs herself. '*You* start. You tell me. *You* tell me what you know.' Emphatic.

I look at her, collecting my thoughts.

'Many people have told me their stories and there isn't a pretty one, ever. It was a war with no sides, front or back. Our soldiers were on 24-hour alert from the moment they landed. They couldn't trust anyone and few volunteered. It was a disputed, unpopular war. When it was over, our soldiers returned, often sick with syphilis and gonorrhoea. They all experienced terror and many were drug addicted. There's trauma and horror for them. It makes them mad and brings craziness into their homes and careers.' I pause, watching her carefully. She looks away, her features hard. I continue. 'My former husband fought. He did three active tours of Vietnam, the first was when he was fifteen. He told the Government that he was eighteen and they believed him. They wanted cannon fodder. Our young men were their sacrificial lambs.' I look at her. She's staring at me. Motionless.

'Did ya ever feel safe with him?' Her eyes bore into mine. I feel her perceptiveness.

'No. Actually I didn't. The war created a ticking time bomb in him. It made it impossible to trust him.' I stop. Watching for her response.

'Pa was in the Tet Offensive.' Her voice was grim.

'That was one of the most horrific battles in the Vietnam War, wasn't it?' I reply.

She nods.

'He told me he was one of the last to leave. Left the Cong rejoicing in the streets. Watched them from the boat.' Her face expressionless.

'Yes, my ex told me many Australian soldiers felt our government betrayed them. Also, their friends, the South Vietnamese. Did Pa ever talk about that, Rose?'

'Nup. He didn't.' Abruptly she turns, facing away from me. 'He came home permanently. When I was twelve,' she mutters. 'Brought that vile war with him.'

'Okay. So, you were still young?'

'Yer know. He never seemed to regret the shit that happened. He reckoned he was a hero.' She snorts with derision.

'What was he like? He's your father, isn't he?'

'That's none of your fucking business!' She glares at me.

'You sound really angry Rose.'

'Yer'd fuckin' be too.'

'Okay.'

'He was a *cunt*,' she spits it out.

'That's a strong word,' I reply.

She stares at me, her face a mask of hatred.

'Fucking bastard,' she mutters.

'Go on.'

I make a note *Pa... Nam... home... what happened?*

'What do ya think he was like?'

She leans forward, hugging her legs. She's wound up like a clock.

'I kept outa his bloody way, didn't I?'

'Okay. I can understand that, Rose. It sounds like he was a very hard man.'

She looks away.

'They fought. All the time. She always ended in tears. He kept drinking. He cursed her… and she still made his bloody supper,' she sniffs. 'I'd lay awake, stomach churning. Eventually I'd go to sleep. Pillow stuffed over my head.'

She wraps her cardigan around her chest holding it closed. Arms crossed.

'Nights were the worst. I couldn't escape them. When they went to bed… I could hear them. Together… you know…' Humiliation writes its own story on her face. 'She always sounded so distressed.' Rose shakes her head. Tears in the corners of her eyes, she swallows. Fights to control her memories.

'She used to argue back. Stand up to him. Sometimes she even tried to fight him off. God, I loved it when she did that. But… he flogged it outta her.'

She's silent. I watch.

'The beatings. They were bad. But it was the denial,' her voice rises. 'At breakfast. It terrified me. More than her bruised swollen face. It found its place… in here.' She holds her upper chest.

'She hid her shame from me. In make-up and rouge. She completely denied the revolting life she led.'

Rose stops. Rises. Paces up and down. Turns at the door. Swings back towards me. Hands fiercely rub her face.

'Do you need a break, Rose?' I stand. We meet eye to eye. She looks straight into me. Terror shades her face.

I hold her gaze.

Steady!

'Would you like a cup of tea?'

~

I return and find her sitting on the floor. I pass her the tea. She drinks, her self-soothing working this time. We breathe together. Moments pass. The soft ticking of my clock marks the seconds.

'You can read yer future in this them tea leaves ya know?' She swirls the cup.

I nod.

'Yer whole bloody life's in there. Can't hide from those little buggers,' she says, swirling them more vigorously.

For the first time in all her sessions, Rose's humour tickles the edge of our conversation.

'In the '60s, Brisbane was said to be the spiritual city of Australia,' I reply. 'When I first came here to teachers' college, there were tea cup readers in the Mall. Did you ever visit them?' I ask.

'Yeah. Lots.' She smiles.

I make a note. *Check it.*

We sit quietly. I relax my body into the beanbag in the corner of the room. She still sits on the floor, smoothing out her crumpled sketch. She reaches out and pulls two cushions into her, squeezing them under her buttocks.

'Do you want to stay there?' I ask.

'Yup.'

'You were talking about them, Rose. It's very hard. Do you want to continue?'

She looks up. Her face is a myriad of emotion. Her pain sits just beneath the surface.

I inhale… *Don't tip it.*

Then that nod.

'I was there. Remember?' she replies. 'Done it before. Can do it now.'

I am amazed at this strength.

'Okay then. When you're ready, Rose.' Soft, affirmative.

'He loved the pub. When he was in town, that's where he was… The only person that made him okay was our priest. He seemed able to talk to him. Calm him down. Make him better.'

'He even went to confession. Bowing and scraping to God and his witness,' she snorts. 'He vowed to give up the liquor. Go straight. Look after me and her.' Her head shakes, anger colours her cheeks.

I watch. Silent.

'My life felt almost normal then. When he could rein in his demons. Step out from his shit. Be there for me.'

'What was he like then, Rose, when he had been with your priest?'

'He'd call me his princess. His special one.' She stops abruptly. Wraps herself in her arms. Grips her body. Trying to disappear into herself. Her head is buried into the folds of her coiled tension. She rocks back and forth.

The room fills a suffocating sense of shame. I wait, alert.

Then.

There's a sudden warp in the air and a release. The counter motion of a pendulum swings her back to herself. She lets go of her body. Takes a breath. Rubs her face. Then the deep inhale. Pause and the explosive exhale. I'm riveted by the mechanism behind this change. She continues as if nothing has happened.

Her voice changes. It's stronger. Deeper. More assertive.

She turns to stare straight at me. Her eyes are blank. Hypnotic. She's the storyteller. The director. I'm the audience.

Her unpredictability is unnerving.

'He showered me with gifts, treats and excursions.' She pauses.

'He sat me on his lap.'

My eyebrows rise. She catches my look, her eyes unblinking. It's mesmerising. She speaks more slowly, commanding my attention.

'He told me fantastic tales. Of strange lands and jungles. People who lived in villages, high in the mountains. Who grew their own food and tended their livestock under their houses. He raved about the impenetrable forests carved with deep, clear rivers. And massive terrifying waterfalls that plummeted hundreds of metres, cascading over colossal rocky outcrops.' Her hands dance in the air. She takes a breath, then changes, firing off, like the stutter of machine guns.

'He filled my mind with fantasies. Beautiful, strange plants. Colour and scent of the jungle. Massive leaves. Miniature hand-hewn huts. Elephants that worked the arable land. Children that rode naked on their backs. People that loved him.' Another sharp inhale.

'A Buddha. In a forest. He prayed at its feet. Asked for the best life possible. To be a good man. A great lover. A faithful husband.'

'He said the war made him a man. That he fought hard. To help us live better lives. To save us. That he was a warrior and a hero.' Her body shakes uncontrollably.

'He was a fucking *liar!*' Her voice shrill, in a crescendo of confusion. Anguish envelops her. Her face contorts with anger and her body curls in on itself. She crosses her arms and legs and hunches into her own embrace. Pain swims around her.

She leaps to her feet and fiercely paces the room.

'Rose. You don't have to keep going.' I watch as brutality erupts through her.

She strides up and down, fighting to stay calm.

'Let's go outside, Rose.'

I open the door. She thrusts past me and is out on the veranda before I can shut the office door. I follow.

The mauve of the jacaranda flowers carpets the stained timber in a floral pattern of peace. The sweet melody of the butcher birds floats a refrain of serenity.

She paces.

Holding her head.

Rubbing her upper arms.

The traffic from the street hums loudly.

Then…

Rosanna doubles over as sobs erupt from her, wracking her emaciated frame. Her voice is the sound of a trapped, wounded animal, echoing through the long shady veranda with her lifetime of pain.

She collapses. Curls into a ball on the rough floorboards and fiercely rocks herself.

I kneel beside her. Reach out to hold her shoulder.

She convulses with torment as I watch her begin to unravel.

~

Nimbin, May 1973

The night air floated through my window as I sat looking out at the star-studded sky. Speckled light from far off galaxies shone down on my upturned face. Shadows from the trees danced with the moonlight. Dark silhouettes guarding my thoughts.

I cherished those moments of solitude and grace just before sleep.

That night, locked in my room, I felt safe. I could see forever, the star-light my only companion. The soft breeze a comforting refuge.

43

It was my fourteenth birthday.

Pa was out of town and Ma had allowed Sarah to visit. To share cupcakes and Coke.

We played 500. Laughing together. Laying bets. Spinning match sticks across the room and counting our millions. Gambling hard.

Later that afternoon, we had walked into town snuggled into the crook of each other's arms, singing and kicking stones that were strewn along the dirt road. We swung our basket of snacks, paints and flower shears to the rhythm of our pace. The closeness of her body pressed against me, a soft blanket enveloping my heart.

'Smile, Rosie-rose,' Sarah chirped. 'It's your special day.'

Why can't this be my happiness too? I thought as Sarah skipped around me.

That afternoon felt like forever. Her peals of laughter turned the corners of my mouth into a contented smile. Her energy wove a protective mantle around the inner recesses of my mind, wrapping the dark shadows with its brilliance and filling me with warmth and longing.

We turned off the small dirt track leading down to the swimming hole, where the river flowed sweet and full.

'You look beautiful, Rose.' She turned to pat my cheek before jumping off the small embankment onto the sandy water's edge. Her golden curls bounced freely down her back as her feet skipped over the sand, leaving small dainty imprints in its soft surface.

'Yer always gonna be my friend, Rosie-rose,' she called, her back turned to me.

She picked up a pebble and tossed it at the reflective surface, her petite figure spinning. Laughter rang out, tinkling melodies of loveliness. The pebble skimmed the surface of the cool clear water as she glanced up. In the shadows behind the trees a shape moved, catching my eye.

'Come on Rosie, smile,' she beamed, unperturbed by my sudden mood change. 'It's yer birthday. Yer day. Just for you!'

She clambered back up the embankment and hugged me.

'Got you a pressie,' she grinned. 'Cos it's yer birthday. The faeries helped me choose.' Her eyes twinkled with humour.

I looked away, embarrassed.

'Hey, you. None of that stuff today,' she clucked. 'Forget about him. He's not here. And anyways, he never needs to know. Okay?'

'Yeah, but…'

Sarah reached into her pocket. A small parcel, wrapped in delicately painted paper and tied with curled ribbon sat in her hand.

'Go on! It's for you silly!' she giggled, proffering the gift.

Inside lay a beautiful golden locket, embossed with stars.

'Got it in the op shop,' she grinned. 'The things some folk chuck out. You like it?'

Words caught in the lump in my throat as she reached up, circling my head with its chain and gently placing it under my threadbare shirt.

'There,' she murmured. 'It's hidden now. They won't see and if he ever harasses you again, just hang onto this and think of me and Dad,' she beamed. 'That'll scare him off, Rose Petal.' She kissed my cheek and hugged me to her.

'Come on you. I got us sumthin' else too. Dan's gonna kill me. Pinched it out of his undies drawer!' She winked, holding up a crushed packet half filled with cigarettes.

'I'm having a fag even if you're not.' She laughed, pulling one out, lighting it, drawing back hard as irregular rings of dancing smoke floated up into the trees.

~

Later that evening, as I sat in my darkened room, silvery beams glimmered on the gold of the locket, picking out small gemstones as they glinted. I bent to catch its light, the tip of my finger tracing the smooth edge of the heart.

I opened it carefully, holding it up to the moonlight, touching the twist of Sarah's golden hair entwined with my dark threads.

~

'Rosie-rose. We have to put sumthin' into your locket.'

I was half asleep under the arcing branches of the old oak tree, sheltered from the late afternoon sun. Sarah was lying on the riverbank sunbaking, legs crossed, hands behind her head, singing softly to herself. Melodies from The Beatles' last album. The sun turned her skin to a perfect caramel bronze.

45

'Reckon it sucks that they busted up.' Her voice broke through my daydreaming.

'Hey,' she called. 'You listening to me? We have to put sumthin' in it! In yer locket! Sumthin' to remind you of us.' She propped herself up on her elbow and grinned.

'Let's cut our hair,' she urged. 'Then we'll always be in there… you 'n me. Forever sistas!' Grabbing the flower shears, she hopped up beside me, bent over my head and clipped a strand of my black locks before twisting it with hers.

'Do you reckon John 'n Yoko will ever make art together?' Sarah asked, gently unclipping my locket and adding our entwined curls. I watched her, deep in thought. She gazed at me, a softness emanating from her.

'Yer don't talk much do yer, Rosie-rose. Not when yer in there.' Her hand brushed my chest as she reached up and kissed me gently on my cheek.

~

Sighing, I lightly snapped my birthday gift shut, carefully stowing it under my top against the soft cloth of my worn pyjamas. Her voice trailed into my thoughts like a lifeline to my heart as my mind traced memories of forests and rivers and fishing tackle.

~

Brisbane, December 1987

The phone rings at my desk. Three loud bells of warning. It's early Christmas eve in Brisbane and the city hums with activity. Coloured lights adorn the windows as dusk casts an apricot glow over Red Hill.

I pick up.

'Hallo?' Static buzzes my middle ear as the line clears.

'Hallo?'

'It's me.' Her voice is thick, heavy with emotion.

'Hi, Rose,' I answer. 'How are you feeling?'

Pause.

'Really shit-full.' Her words struggle with her breath. 'Really fuckin' bad.' Her pain travels through the phone. The inhale and exhale sit on top of each other. Words tumble. 'Can't remember the last time I lost it like that. I feel so fuckin' confused. Got a seriously bad headache.'

'That's understandable,' I reply. 'That was really hard for you.'

'But ya don't understand. I don't know if I can keep doing it,' she says.

'I do understand. I hear you.'

Her breath is audible, it feels like she is right beside me.

'What will happen if I don't?' Her voice is low.

'You'll lose them. They made that clear.'

Steady!

'Lose them…?'

'Yes.'

My heartbeat quickens and I breathe slowly. Controlling my rising emotion.

Settle yourself Anna! Her story.

Then, silence. Only her thick heavy breath.

'How can I do this? So that it doesn't hurt so much?' Her voice is full of tears.

'We'll take it gently and slowly. In your time. That's how we get there.'

'Oh fuck. Why? Why do I have to go through all this again? It fucking hurt so bad then. Why? Why talk about it all again? Why?'

I wait. Collecting my spinning thoughts. Her distress requires me to say exactly the right thing.

'Rose. I need to ask you to breathe. To calm down, so that I can talk to you. You can tell me as much of it as you wish. Or as little. You can come, have tea with me. Paint. Talk about the weather if you want. Then leave. Or we can let it unravel. Your story is your life and there's plenty of time.'

'But I want my life back.'

'That's why I am here. To help you do that, in whatever way possible.'

'Do you think I'm bad?'

First time. I make the note.

'No, not at all!'

She's silent.

'Don't you think you need to get well? That your children need that, Rose? Isn't that why you come?'

There's a hum at the end of the phone. The long distant crackle disguises her breath. Her anxiety breaks my heart open.

'Rose?'

'Do ya blame me?' Her self-loathing rasps across the wires.

'No. No I don't. And why would I? Things have been really tough for you, Rose. I really hear you. Your experiences have made you turn many corners. Towards places and people that really haven't served you well. I don't blame you. I would never do that.'

A muffled sound of her nose being blown.

'Yer don't?'

'No. Not at all. I'm here to help you. To find your way again.'

'I need to tell you something.'

She struggles to speak.

'Sure. I'm listening.'

Silence.

'Can I tell ya next time?'

~

Brisbane, January 1988

'How are you feeling, Rose?' She sits on the chair's edge, her hair a filthy mat of dreadlocks. Her breath reeks. Her clothes are torn, eyes bloodshot, face drawn. It's been three weeks with no connection.

'I dunno… confused.'

'Would you like to share with me where you were last night?' I ask.

'Where do you think I was?' she spits. 'Out earning a living. On the streets, of course!'

'Drugs?'

'Yep.'

'What sort?'

'Anything I could lay my hands on,' she mutters.

I pause, looking at her. 'Rose. I don't judge you, but your welfare is my business. I need to know what you do outside of our time together.'

She scowls and turns away. 'Well, what do ya think I'm gonna do with my damn life?' she grunts defensively.

'Last time you said there was something you wanted to tell me.'

She shakes her head and turns away from me.

'Okay, remember your breathing.' I watch her hands clench and unclench.

'Yer want me to talk about them… don't ya?' she mumbles.

'Them?'

'Yes. *Them!* She kicks the word at me.

'If you'd like to start there, that's fine with me.' I watch her carefully.

Them? Ma and Pa? Check it!

'Don't know why they stayed together,' she glowers, a fleeting glance at me.

'Go on.'

'Their relationship was that bad. When he was away, we got on okay… I guess… Her 'n me… It was peaceful. She fed me well enough… Was never affectionate. Always somewhere else in her head… Only looked after my basic needs.' Her voice trails across the room.

'She rarely talked to me. Never answered my questions. Never knew how I was inside. She never saw me, did she? She never spoke about that stuff…' Rose stops and holds her breath.

'What "stuff" are you talking about Rose?'

'About… him… and…' Rose stands abruptly and grabs her glass of water.

She gulps it down.

I make a note. *Stuff?*

'I'm so fucking tired… Ever been on the streets?' She turns and walks to the door. Her hands clench the glass.

'No, I haven't. But I had a friend and her teenage daughter who did.'

I watch her back. 'What's it like for you?'

Careful.

'It's kinda okay. There's some real nice folk out there. Better than ya think.' She turns slowly, facing me. Her eyes are different.

'Where do you like to stay?' I ask.

'By the river. It's cool there. Met a monk. From Tibet. He has a tarp. Like, yer know, they live in tents there.'

'Yes, the Tibetan people are nomadic,' I reply.

'He has a spot. Right there. Looking out over the river. The lights are real pretty. He told me come stay with him.' A smile flickers.

'Where's that?'

'Close to the bridge,' she pauses. 'We crawl in under the bushes. At night. When there's no one around. His camp is there. He always has food. Gives it to me. It's safe, with him. I like him. He's really smart, you know. Tells me heaps of stories. At night. Before we sleep,' she sighs.

I make a note. *Monk! Sleeping together?*

'Ya know, they stabbed him in the back. He's got these scars. Showed them to me. He fled across the Himalayas. In the snow. To get away from them. Then, got a flight to Australia. Can you believe that?' She looks overawed.

'They let him in?'

'Yep. And then they gave him fifty bucks. Left him to live on the streets. Didn't know any English. Had to make his own way. Use his wits to survive. He's a great scavenger.' She smiles at last.

'Finds stuff that rich cunts chuck out. In the bins. Parks. It's amazing what's out there. Ya just hafta look.' She turns in her chair stretching her body. Easing into sharing this part of her life with me.

'The Salvo's. They feed us and he finds food everywhere. Think it's because he used to do that stuff back in Tibet. You know, they eat so much meat. And drink animal blood there.' She pulls a face.

'Sounds interesting.' I smile.

'Apparently, they eat this yak curd. It tastes like yogurt. And make cheese too.'

'Did he study with the Dalai Lama?' I ask.

'Yeah. Before he fled to India.'

'Okay.'

'Yeah… and the monasteries. Yer know… he went there when he was four. Became a monk. Looked after folk. He's real pure. Like… clean… untouched by the world. He doesn't blame them. Reckons we have to have compassion for them. What they did to him makes me sick. They're fucking barbarians you know. Don't care about other people's religion. Or beliefs. Or country. Just went in there and fucked it all up. How he got over those mountains… I don't know…' Her voice trails off. An audible inhale. Then that explosive exhale.

'What's his name?'

'Rin. Short for Rinpoche. They all get called that.' She grins. 'All them monks. Think it's something to do with them being an incarnation of some sort of holy bloke… but he's just a really amazing friend. And he can see me.'

She pauses, rubs her hands together. Anxious again.

'See?'

'Yeah. Yer know… like… he just knows where I'm coming from. He's wise. And gentle.' An imperceptible shake of her head.

She looks at me. 'I've taught him heaps. He speaks English real well now.' Her eyes are pools of sadness.

'He doesn't like the drugs. Tells me to stop. Gets real quiet when I get home from work.' She looks down, her face colouring.

'Work?' I comment.

'Yup. But you know, he's so supportive. Even though I know he hates me doing it. When I'm finished, he waits for me. Makes me go and take a wash. Stands outside the dunnies, watching out for me.' Rose slides her hands between her legs, pressing her thighs together, hunching her shoulders.

She's silent. Withdrawn. Then that elusive shake of her head. I make a note.

I change the subject. 'You were telling me about life at home when you were a kid.'

'Huh? Oh yeah. Okay.' She speaks slowly, controlling her breathing. 'She was real religious. The only book I remember was the Bible. Most nights when he was away, we sat at the kitchen table, after supper. She'd read it to me.'

'I loved those fables. Jacob. Jesus. The Apostles. I always thought God would help me. That he'd guide me. That he was the one who looked after the earth. And us. She loved the archangels. Told me they await us.' She shakes her head again.

'Ya know, I knew every word of it by the time I was eight. Could recite all the commandments.'

'It sounds like she held strong spiritual beliefs.'

'Not spiritual. She was a Jesus freak. That's different.' Emphatic.

'How?' I ask.

'Spiritual means a shitload more than just praying to God! She was narrow. Too narrow. But… she loved to pray. And when she read and prayed… you know, she changed. She relaxed. Said God loved her. Loved me…'

A muscle in Rose's cheek twitches as she looks quickly at her feet, swallowing hard.

'I just wanted her to love *me*.'

I wait, watching the mood change.

'I always slept well after those evenings together. Just me and her. Sometimes I'd catch her, standing at my door, looking at me. I know she had a secret. About me. About Pa. About our family. Could see it in the shadows on her face. It stopped her from reaching me.' Rose's brow furrows. Her hand flicks upwards.

I make a note. *Secret?*

'I'd wave at her. That was the only time she ever smiled.'

She pauses and places her hands over her face, rubbing her eyes. She holds the back of her head.

'She's in a home now. Doesn't know who I am. She's lost her mind. She…' Rose's face fills with pain. 'She could never face it. Not ever.'

'Face what Rose?' I ask.

Rose's face is a mask of denial. Darkness plays under her eyes. She slowly stands, turning to face me.

'I can't do this today, Anna,' she whispers, and opens the door to leave.

~

Nimbin, 1972

Throughout my childhood, Ma was a silent shadow that played on the walls of my room. A figure of occasional presence and authority. She was the ache in my heart. The void where maternal warmth was meant to seed innocence with trust and safety.

Her marriage to Pa was a sham. A religious obligation. She spoke little of her past life, only sharing that her family had been wealthy.

Her parents were staunch churchgoers.

Pa's father was a drinker. His mother disappeared without a trace when he was ten, leaving Pa to bring himself up alone in the backwaters of coastal New South Wales.

Ma was a soldier's wife. She stayed for the meagre keep that arrived each month in her bank account. She denied Pa's reputation with the local ladies. His indulgence in the darker side of sexuality was a publicly debated ridicule in our village. I heard it in the streets.

The gossip.

Family meant nothing to Pa, and by the time the Vietnam War was in full swing, my presence in his life had become his deepest thorn.

Our community was profoundly religious, the relationship between Pa and the village Reverend his only saving grace. But any fleeting moment of sobriety made Pa a more feared man, his prayers and platitudes barely veiling his foul temper. He was trusted only to fix the electricity, dig the footings of a new house or entertain other drunkards in the village streets with wild tales of strange lands and heroism in Vietnam.

As I grew older, the war brought a deepening darkness into my besieged life. What was once early childhood shadows of my past, that called me to numbing flights of disassociation, became waking nightmares. Pa's mind was stalked by the memory of battles that had no boundaries. Most afternoons he slept on the couch in our tiny loungeroom. The television boomed through the thin walls out onto the street. The vapour of alcohol and the reek of cigarettes, a pungent reminder of the troubles that lay barely hidden beneath each snore.

The day the Anti-Vietnam war sentiment arrived in town Pa was home. The sound of breaking glass, and shouts of *child murderer* and *rapist* rang out. A small menacing group had gathered outside our home. Rocks pelted the walls, shattering windows, splaying shards of glass into the lounge. Pa leapt to his feet. Grabbed his rifle and charged outside, thundering and shooting over their heads. Ma cowered to the floor as I hid behind the couch.

Later that afternoon, as I worked in the kitchen, Pa arrived back from the pub swearing he would *kill them all*. Collapsing in front of the TV, he fell instantly into a drunken sonorous unconsciousness. Ma's couch bore the marks of his muddied boots and the imprints of his self-obsession. Ma's only joy was her clean home and in a moment of indecisiveness, her hand floated over his sleeping body.

Pa's foot twitched and he leapt from his sleep. He pinned her into the wall, his forearm across her neck. Horrified, I watched as his face contorted in front of hers. Snarling lips pulled back inches from her face. His other hand formed a fighter's fist. Ma hung there, feet suspended from the floor, a strange gurgling sound coming from her open mouth, her eyes popping. Her hands helplessly plucked at her husband, trying to push him away.

For an eternity, he crushed her before I threw myself at him, screaming.

'Stop Pa, *STOP!*' My tiny frame bounced off him as I hurtled into the coffee table, winding myself on its splintered timber edge. Pa bellowed at me, and just as quickly as he had Ma pinned to the wall, he let her go. Gasping for breath she slid to the floor. Howling vitriol, he staggered out the back door and smashed it shut behind him.

I crawled to Ma, inching in close, reaching out to take her hand. But she shrunk from me, turning her disavowal against my confusion. My heart clamped shut. And as my soul reached into a bottomless pit of rejection, I swore that I would find a way out of this life.

~

Brisbane, January 1988

Rosanna's hands trail the smooth sheen of the marble fireplace, her gemstone mobile casting flecks of rainbow light around my room. Her fingers dip into the round bowl of blessed water, a gift from her friend Rin. She touches the liquid to her lips.

Pausing before the carved teak bookshelves, she observes the uneven stacks. Her palm reaches forward, resting on the bound manuals, paper backs and spiral notebooks, as if to absorb their contents with her touch.

She pauses before the novel section, reaching high, head tilted, fingertips caressing each paperback. Her profile is one of puzzlement and awe.

'I love books,' she murmurs. 'You have so many. Have yer read them all?'

'I've read most of them. Some not front to back.'

'I'm the same.'

Her hand comes to rest on the worn spine of an old volume.

'*Bury Me in My Boots*,' she reads, 'by Sally Trench.'

Her fingers find the top of the bound cover as she draws it to her chest, returning to her seat.

Her legs cross as she opens it, absorbing its front cover.

'Why this book?' she queries.

'It's one of my oldest,' I reply. 'I bought it at fourteen. It changed my world.'

'How?' Head bent. Flicking protectively through the pages.

'It helped me believe that I could make a difference in others' lives. It's a true story.'

'Like mine?'

'Yes, like yours.'

'Looks like it's about street people.'

'Yes.' I watch her carefully.

'Like me!'

'Yes. Like you.' She looks up briefly then continues to scan.

'What happens?'

'She dedicates her young life to feeding folk on the streets. She was passionate about helping them. She fell in love with all the people living in the warehouses. The alcoholics.'

Rose looks up at me sharply.

I continue. 'She used to climb out of her bedroom window to take them food from her parent's kitchen. There's a fire. It's sad but beautiful.'

She looks at me. Her face neutral.

'And you've kept it all these years?'

'I keep all my books,' I reply.

She closes the book, resting it on her knees. She's quiet, pensive. Her breath easy. 'So, Sally helped you, huh? To find your way. That's pretty amazing. All these years. And you still do it?'

I nod.

'Why didn't you do something else?' she asks.

'I did for a while. In my younger adult life.'

'What did you do?' she asks.

'I taught kids in primary school.'

'Yeah. You said.' She's watching me thoughtfully. 'Okay.'

'But then things changed. I wasn't happy. I knew that I was meant to do something else, so I retrained. In art therapy.'

I watch her responses. She's interested. Focused.

'What weren't yer happy about?'

'Many things, Rose. My past. That calling that had nagged at me since I was a kid,' I reply.

'Calling?'

I nod.

'What, do yer mean since yer were a kid?'

I pause before speaking. Wondering how much to divulge.

'I grew up out west, Rose. On a cattle station. In those days we worked with the Indigenous folk. They were our farm hands, stockmen and house keepers. Our family had a great rapport with them. But this was not the case elsewhere. Town folk treated them really badly. Parents had no rights with their kids, and poverty was rife in their communities. They had less voting power and economic privileges than the minimal ones that have been recently granted. But they were family to us and we looked after each other.'

'Hmmm.' She watches me with keen interest. 'So how come ya had this calling?'

'It's something that came to me. Very early in my life. Watching this changing landscape of how we Australians operate with the underprivileged. I knew really early on that I wanted to work with people. Many have asked me your question. I love my work and I know I help.'

'But why folk like me?'

I quickly make a note. *First positive engagement.*

'I believe that dignity is a choice. It's not something you can weigh against your income or the size of your house or the school your kids go to. Some of the most spiritually evolved people I have ever met live on the streets. Some of my most revered teachers have been people with very little. Some of the wisest, the men and women whom society has rejected. This is where I get my inspiration from, Rose. From the lives people like you lead.'

'From the lives we lead? They're fucked. How can ya do that?'

'It's the changes in you I see that inspire me. The possibility. The courage it takes to step onto the path of healing. This is what I mean. It also helps me to deal with my own stuff.'

She looks at me puzzled. Then spins it back.

'So, facing my shit… how I move forward from it… is that it?'

'That's a part of it.'

Rose stops and looks at me. She wraps her hands around the book. Then hugs it to her breasts. 'I was fourteen too,' she whispers.

4

Nimbin, May 1973

NIGHT descended as I cuddled into my eiderdown, propped up on the window ledge in my room. The stars twinkled against a darkening sky and in the distance the full moon cast eerie shadows in the paddocks beyond our home. I could see the tall rocky outcrops scattered across the paddocks close to the forest, shining as if it were day. Their tree-tufted tops creating giant elks in my imagination. I wondered what would happen if they could lift their ancient rock roots up out of the ground and march across the landscape, rearranging the vista to their liking, rather than how they had landed there eons ago.

Cows close to our home stirred, occasional soft mooing reaching my ears. A still peace echoed into the valley, returning to fill my mind with effervescence and rumours of enchantment.

My room glowed as if the faeries from Dad's garden had paid a visit, placing small lanterns into the corners to show me the way and keep me safe. There was a strange softness in my stomach. An aliveness that made my chest swell and my thighs and belly ache. The carefreeness of my fourteenth birthday warmed me as distant melodies from a deeper source played softly within the corners of my mind.

I felt alive in that full moon, as if the hippy dancers from town had bewitched me. Drawing me from the safety of my normal wariness into a place of untroubled vulnerability. I wished that Sarah had been allowed to stay the night with me. To share this special moment. She would have felt this magic too. But even in my euphoria, I knew that I would never be allowed such leniency.

Harsh sounds, discordant and rough, distracted me.

I hesitated in my reverie, wondering how many men he had returned with that night. They were starting to gamble. Coarse laughter, foul language and the smack of cards on the kitchen table warped through the walls into my room. Ma's voice was mostly absent now, only intermittently rising above the deeper harsher masculine commands for attention. I could hear the clink of glass on glass as she moved bottles from the table into the sink and brought them biscuits and chips.

~

'I don't get why they had to bust up.' Sarah was on her back on the riverbank. Hands clasped under her head. A thin stalk of grass twirled between her teeth. 'I mean… they're brilliant, aren't they?' she mused.

I watched as the dusk light cast golden embers in her hair.

'Wouldn't it be amazing to see them in person. I love 'em on the trannie! Dan bought himself one for Chrissie. He spent all year saving up. All those clapped-out bombs he's helped Dad with.' She sat up, a mischievous glint in her eyes.

'He guards the bloody thing with his life. He never wants to share it. With anyone. The rotter,' she giggled, reaching into her bag and pulling out a small black box.

Flicking the lid, she tipped out the content. A red transistor radio lay in the circle of her palm, the wrist band dangling.

'National Panasonic,' she declared. 'Only the best for Dan.'

Sarah looked at the dial, her fingers slowly turning it.

'Let's see if it'll pick up anything,' she said, flicking the side switch.

Static buzzed briefly, then the soft barely recognisable strains of The Beatles' *Help!* travelled out into the air, filling the glade.

'C'mon,' she called turning to me. 'Let's dance!' Her eyes shone with fun.

~

I hesitated.

Furtive movements seemed to circle close to my door. The scrape of boots kicking against wooden floorboards, followed by a stealthy pause in the lounge next to my room. My heartbeat jumped as the heavy footfall receded into the kitchen, and rough tones joined in the drunken revelry. I could hear crude laughter and swearing as the men slapped each other on the back and cursed.

I released my breath; a soft explosion of air.

~

Sarah planted a warm good-bye kiss on my cheek. The day was done.

The dusk light backlit Nightcap Range, its tall peaks capped by fluffy golden clouds.

We had walked back home along the railway line. Sarah danced on the tracks, precariously balancing on their steel surface, laughing at herself when she slipped, urging me to join her.

'When I leave home I'm gonna be a singer, a song-writer,' she declared. 'Dan's gonna write my songs. Dad will be on the guitar and double bass. And you, Rosanna, will be our manager and organiser. And then… then you will *have* to talk and talk and talk and tell the world about me and you won't be able to shut up,' she giggled as I poked at her.

'You'll love it. And we will be famous and wealthy and we'll have tons of kids and… I know you. You can do it. I know you will.'

She fluffed herself up and warbled into the growing dark.

'We'll call ourselves *The Rosettas*,' she exclaimed. 'After you, but Rosetta instead of Rosanna. That'll be your num-da-plum,' she sang.

'Nom-de-plume,' I corrected, smiling.

'That's what I said, silly,' she giggled, tugging at my arm. 'Come on! Hang onto me. I want to walk all the way home without falling off again.'

~

An aura of rainbow-light playing with silver shadows seemed to whisper, *be careful, Rosanna*. Dark corners began to grow in my mind, sending cold shivers down my spine as an ominous foreboding wrapped around me.

The night had changed. Wariness stole into my heart. The joy that had lifted me just moments before retreated as a sinister darkness obscured the moonlight. Trembling, I crept into bed, covered my head with my pillow, said my prayers, burrowed under the blankets and drifted into sleep.

From deep in my slumber, I heard it.

Thud.

Scrape of metal on metal.

A door being forced open.

I struggled to awaken; a heavy hand of unconsciousness pinned me beneath a weight of steel. Talons of fire flowed in under my door, into my room. Darkness eclipsed the moonlight as my faeries fled. Terrifying shadows filled the space as a deadly ogre flexed its wings of destruction. The earth shivered and shook, rock and crystal breaking, devouring my spirit, consuming me.

I struggled to wake, to defend myself. But the monster did it for me as my sleeping body was smashed into consciousness.

I was crushed by a massive weight. My mouth was clamped shut. No breath made its way into my small frame as I struggled, my face pushed into the pillows. A wild vice held me trapped under it. Claws of steel tore into my flesh, smashing into the back of my head, ripping into my neck, pinning me helpless underneath. Foul carrion breath filled my nostrils as its bloodied carcass rammed into me. The moments of annihilation lasted forever as the predator took my life in its hands, ripping into my thighs, belly, face. Blood poured from every orifice in my body as knives twisted and turned inside me. I choked on vomit and bile, teeth grinding ivory shards into my mouth.

I died a million deaths in that eternity of madness and blind rage, as the beast consumed me. Over and over, I screamed a silence that filled the air.

Then, an animal instinct drove my body up and out as I writhed, twisted, kicked, bit.

As the claws of death struggled to hold me, my lungs filled the air, shrieking for survival.

And finally, the fire-eating demon released me.

I slipped out and up, reaching far into the ether, God's hand upon me. Fleeing and flying so high that all that I had ever known passed before me. Every shard of existence as I knew it morphed, warped – gone.

I plummeted. Tumbling a million miles into the forest below. I shuddered and turned in my death throes. Carried back to where I had been. Buried in the earth. Held within the bosom of the fern-laden forest. Breath opened into the freezing water that cascaded over rocky ledges. Cocooned in the succour of the faeries hearth I passed.

And then, nothing.

~

Auntie Mim found me, late that night, huddled in the corner of her kitchen, my night clothes shredded. Blood dried in my mouth and on my thighs. My face swollen beyond recognition. My hair matted with dirt and slime. My feet cut. Wrists bearing bruises and slashes.

Paralysed, I crouched, my back pressed into the kitchen wall. My feet positioned ready to kick, scream, defend. I rocked. Shivered. Gasped for air.

Mim frantically called for Dad. I cowered as he rushed into the kitchen. The looks of horror on their faces ripped through me as I pushed myself backwards into the kitchen cupboard.

Away from them.

Away from my life.

Away from whatever had happened to me.

And the scream froze in Sarah's mouth as she dropped in front of me. She touched me with the lightest butterfly's wings, her fingertips resting just above my swollen hands.

'What have they done to you?' she sobbed as I passed out.

~

The days that followed blurred into one. Pain filled my body as I lay in Sarah's bed, half alive. They washed and cleaned me, dressed my wounds, splinted and strapped my broken fingers. They held my head and spooned droplets of Auntie Mim's warm soup down my throat. Sarah lay next to me, stroking my arm, crooning, weeping and beseeching God to help. They called the doctor that morning, but I rolled away from him when he approached. Snarling and struggling, I fought my way clear, forcing my devastated body under Sarah's bed.

A wounded animal had overtaken me. But unlike my hurt animals, who went peacefully to die, this monster refused to release me. It had not carried me to the death I prayed for but left its foul mark on my soul where its memory spun away from me. The light of my survival snuffing it out, hiding it into the back recess of my mind, only years later to be remembered, realised, understood.

Auntie Mim led the doctor away, leaving Sarah to entice me out from under the bed and back into its healing cocoon.

Hushed conversations floated through the air as the doctor, Auntie Mim and Dad talked in whispers in the other room. Each word boomed in my head, an alarm pounding me into action. I struggled against Sarah's touch. She stroked my arms and whispered, 'It's okay Rosie-rose,' and gently pressed me back into the pillows.

The doctor reappeared, looked at me, shook his head, turned on his heel and marched out.

The policeman did the same.

He came to the front door and in the echo of his gruff voice, my mind spun into flight as I heard *filthy hippies*. I crawled out of Sarah's bed, pushing myself into her cupboard. Holding the doors shut, I stopped breathing, willing my body to disappear. Praying to die.

In those first weeks, Sarah sat with me day and night. She refused to eat or drink until I had taken something from Auntie Mim's pot. She sang lullabies and stroked my forehead. She applied cool moist towels to my face when my temperature rose and wiped away my silent hot tears. She changed my bandages, cleaned my wounds and helped me bathe, drying my back, holding my towel for me, helping me dress and return to her room. She softly massaged my body, loving strokes that eased my pain. She lit candles and closed the windows, drawing the curtains at night to stop the cold, piercing air from punishing me as she read to me, faltering over words too hard for her to pronounce.

She held my hand as I lay comatose, staring lifelessly out of her window. At night, she crept into bed next to me, warming me, her friendship easing my devastation.

Auntie Mim watched over us, her face a mask of concern as she tended my injuries. She consulted her nursing and herbal books and visited Dad's garden every day for comfrey and calendula. Soothing poultices made their way onto my body when I mumbled deliriously, soaked in sweat. She cooked delicious, lightly salted meat stews to build my strength. She kept the younger children quiet and lit Sarah's bedroom fireplace to keep us warm.

I remained mute. Sarah whispered to me at night that it would be okay and that the faeries were waiting for me in the garden. That when I was ready, they would help me get my voice back.

I heard her talking to Auntie Mim, asking her if I could stay with them and finally, Mim baked a loaf of bread and went to visit Ma.

~

Brisbane, January 1988

Silence fills the room in the aftermath of Rose's story. She hugs her knees to her chest as she huddles into the cushions on the floor. Night has made its way in through the windows. Honouring her release, time stands still. She is inert. Unresponsive. Silent. Defeat fills the room.

I am shaken to my core.

I slowly walk towards the sound system. I press the dials on the tape deck. The strains of Carol King and James Taylor's *You've got a Friend* fills the room. I light her favourite incense. The candles she brought with her, imbue the room with a muted glow. Her sketches and figures scatter the floor in front of her.

My hand rests on the dial as I breathe, controlling the feelings. The image in the small photo looks back at me.

'*...She knows your pain, Anna...*'

I turn back to her, pick up the book lying on my desk and open it at the marked page.

I start unsteadily.

'*This being human is a guest house. Every morning a new arrival. A joy, a depression, a meanness, some momentary awareness comes as an unexpected visitor. Welcome and entertain them all. Even if they are...*'

'*...a crowd of sorrows.*' Rose's voice is muffled as she joins in to recite the next line of the Rumi masterpiece, *The Guest House*.

'You know this one?' I lower the book. Rose stirs and looks up at me, her eyes filled with the numbness of trauma.

'Rumi,' she whispers.

'Yes.'

'Our favourite.'

'Sarah's?'

'Yes. I read it to her. When I was fifteen. She loved the way he put his words together.' She moves for the first time in the hour, unravels her body and painfully climbs to her feet.

'Why does he say that?'

'About the Guesthouse? I believe he's talking about the human experience. That we invite to us that which we need to learn from. That we need to welcome in all, no matter how hard it is. And in some way, all of it is guided by an unseen hand.'

'God?'

'Or spirit. Or a higher source.'

Rose stands still, looking at me.

Then.

'He's telling me to be open to my past, isn't he?' Unsure.

She looks down at the twilight suburbs aglow with the sparkle of streetlights. The hum of early evening traffic on Waterworks Road, a constant companion to our session.

She rubs her neck and massages her shoulders, turning to me, watching me with an intensity that draws me towards her. In our pain, at the edge of understanding, depth and knowing hide.

'That I need to welcome it? Learn from it? That all this stuff is *a crowd of sorrows*?'

'Do you think that's true, Rose?'

'I dunno.' She shakes her head. 'Ya know, I've never talked about this. Not ever.'

She changes. She is a trapped deer in the deeper forest of her mind. Her eyes reflect a turmoil I know well. The pain of her past cuts through my heart.

'Rose, what you have shared is massive. How are you feeling?'

Brief clarity sweeps past her darker depths and the grey in her eyes fires with a steely determination – the hallmark of her survival. She is like the changing currents of a wild ocean. Her moods reflective of its dark depths, and its brooding, stormy surface.

'But what about my shame?' she asks, her lips narrow.

'How do you see that, Rose?'

She circles the room, stretching her body, bending to pick up her backpack and art. 'You know?' Her eyes are awash with emotion. 'I knew what Sarah said was right. That it wasn't my fault. Deep down. I knew.'

Her eyes fill with tears. Her voice hushes as she continues, 'Is it an *arrival*? Is my shame another *guest*?'

'That's what comes up for me,' I reply.

'And the *dark thoughts*?'

'Those also.'

'So, all this was meant to happen. Is that it?' Her eyes track the crystal light across soft, thick carpet.

'What do you think, Rose?'

'I've never seen it like that before. Is Rumi saying that we have to learn from our experiences? That all of it is sent to sweep us clean?'

She stops.

'…*even if they are a crowd of sorrows, who violently…*' She looks up. A light, shining in her eyes. A glimmer of recognition.

'…*sweep your house empty of its furniture?*'

Pain and understanding dance shadows across her features.

'Oh wow!'

'What is it, Rose?'

'I think I get it!'

~

It is dark outside, except for the glow of the streetlights. Waterworks Road is silent.

Despite the progress I see in her, this part of Rose's story has affected me. I ease myself away from my notes and reports.

I wander out into the waiting room, straighten the cushions and magazines, and head into the kitchen. The teacups from our session sit unwashed on the bench. I gaze at the empty packet of chamomile tea, our favourite. As I fill the sink, my mind travels through the landscape of my past. Throughout the years of consultancy, no story has rocked me the way hers has today.

I open the pantry and reach for the Jim Beam. My only concession to stress management in this profoundly, disruptive influence that has arrived in my life. I pour a shot and return to my room.

Rose's paintings rest against the white marble of the old fireplace. I squat before them and reach out to her latest creation. There's an eerie familiarity in it. An indefinable, graphic image peers out at me, surrounded by nebulous spheres and dotted radiating lines. I look up at the art that adorns my wall. Picking up her *Circles,* I prop it close to my oldest work and sit down at my desk, my feet up. As the liquid warmth of the bourbon relaxes me, I study the marks and patterns.

Then I see it.

Picking up her notes, I search for a birth date.

~

Nimbin, July 1973

Eight weeks after Auntie Mim found me in her kitchen, she called on Ma again. Pa had disappeared, returning to the army for further duty. Ma had not visited nor attempted to contact me. She sat silent in her kitchen, eyes downcast, avoiding Auntie Mim's gentle enquiry. Wordlessly pouring cups of tea. Automatically cutting Mim's butterfly cake into bite-sized portions and layering them with our fresh cream.

Auntie Mim sat through several of these meetings, but Ma's numb taciturnity brought no further information. I too remained mute, communicating only with Sarah when necessary.

The doctor was unable to get near me. The police had washed their hands of me.

Auntie Mim turned the tables, sheltering me with the staunch protectiveness of a mother with a wounded child. The sacred beauty and wisdom of Celtic medicine, passed on by her mother, imbued in her a respect for life and a generational commitment to the healing vocation. She was the herbalist, midwife, and counsellor in our village. The one to whom others turned to assist in bringing forth life. To turn a baby in the womb or to help draw a protracted labour safely to an end. Or to simply administer to a cold or flu or the health needs of the local farming animals.

And it was her arms that comforted those who held the lifeless body of their stillborn child.

When I was able to walk again, Auntie Mim took one more of her freshly baked loaves down to my home. She asked Ma if she would allow me to stay with them until I was able to go back to school. Ma nodded her head, stood and showed Auntie Mim to the back door, the steaming hot bread untouched on the kitchen table.

Later that evening, I heard Dad and Auntie Mim by the fire, talking quietly. I lay in Sarah's bed, her warm body cuddled into mine, breathing deeply as she slept.

I was absorbed in the melody of their voices. The cadence of Dad's timbre drew me back to the forest and our secret place. In my mind, I saw his eyes twinkling as they had the first time we met. And as I listened, the memory of the cool spray of our waterfall soothed my nerves.

Auntie Mim's lilting tones spoke to me in lullaby. It was about me living with them. Before I knew, I had slipped into a deep slumber, cradled by their presence.

The next morning, Auntie Mim came into Sarah's room to awaken us. Sarah slipped out of our bed, disappearing into the garden as Mim sat down next to me. She took my hand in both of hers, her warmth seeping into me.

'Rosanna,' she said, 'yer Ma has told me that it is okay for yer to stay with us for a while. Would yer like that?' she asked. 'You can share Sarah's room. She'll take yer to school when yer ready.'

I watched her concerned face. Her beautiful full lips parted into a smile and her long black hair corkscrewed down her back, shining in the early morning light. Her face, a perfect oval. Her emerald-green eyes framed by high arched eyebrows, swept with a curve of jet-black lashes. She had the same piercing look that Sarah had when she was worried about me. Her skin, porcelain white; clear and unblemished. For a woman who had borne six children in ten years, she was still full of energy. Strong bodied and ample breasted, Maureen O'Reilly was a woman made for loving life in all its ways.

As we sat together, I wondered how it was that Ma was so absent in my life during this time. How it was that Auntie Mim could love me in ways for which I had yearned but had never experienced in my own home.

Overcome with confusion, I looked away.

'Rose, lassie,' she said, reaching out, stroking my cheek. 'I need yer help picking some herbs for dinner. How's about we go down to the garden and see what's there?' she asked, watching me carefully.

I nodded, pulling my hand from hers, trying to calm myself.

She sat still, so close I could smell the sweet yeast on her arms. I looked up and saw tears in her eyes.

'Rose Petal,' she murmured, 'yer can stay here as long as yer like, lassie. Yer safe here, with us.'

Her words loosened the knife embedded in my chest, releasing a flood of searing pain. Covering my face with my hands, I burst into tears.

Auntie Mim helped me to dress. Supporting me, we walked

together down the back steps and into the garden. The warmth of the winter sun heated my skin, transforming my darkness into rainbows of light.

I turned my face towards a clear blue sky. A breeze cooled me as I held on to Auntie Mim, savouring the life-blood seeping into my veins. As we walked out into the garden, she chatted to me about what we needed for her hearth.

Rosemary to flavour her roast lamb. Mint for the sauce. Snow peas and climbing beans to be tossed in butter. Mother Earth's potatoes for baking with garlic, onions and pumpkin. Zucchini to steam and round, red tomatoes to blend with the parsley and basil for our salad.

The fragrance in the garden filled my senses. Flowers perfumed the air. Aromatic sage and thyme rose up, calling me. Pungent wormwood and bitter tansy spoke to me, whispering medicinal stories from eons ago, as I brushed against their soft curled leaves.

Delicate lilac lavender reached out to me. Climbing jasmine smiled from the corners of the garden, their pretty white-pink petals humming a low refrain, gentling my jarred emotions. And a carpet of mint and chamomile massaged my naked feet.

For the first time in eight weeks, I felt the earth turn below me.

But everywhere I looked there were reminders of my former life. Memories of hours spent in that paradise with Dad. Planting, digging, harvesting a garden that grew a life for me, far from the nightmare of the one that I knew at the other end of town. A life where human dignity and respect were the hallmarks of every relationship. Where love overflowed like Auntie Mim's kitchen wicker basket as we gathered goodness in that fragrant, healing space.

A soft calling beckoned me to awaken from numbing terror. My frail body shook as faerie whispers and the nodding wisdom of the leprechauns reached out. I stood there, transfixed. My spirit floated up and above me, reaching into the heavens to fly with the scudding white clouds as my legs gave way underneath me.

I drifted to the ground, landing gently on soil, slowly toppling forward onto my face, conscious only of my breath and the caress of an angel's wings flying high above me.

Brisbane, February 1988

Rose pauses, her hands fold in her lap. Her face creases with intensity.

'That garden. It was so beautiful. Like a dream. From another world.' She speaks slowly as she presses her hands into her belly. 'I could feel those leprechauns. Feel them all around me.' Gently, she rocks.

'It was magic. We grew it like that. Dad and I. He knew all about them. Told me they were my warriors. Reckoned if I was patient enough, they'd come out. To help me. He had that magic. I just followed. But my hands?' She holds them up to her face.

'They itched for that soil. I wanted to bury myself in it. Not ever come out. Hide in there forever.' Her rocking intensifies.

'But good soil? It smells amazing ya know. Our soil was something else. Like the forest floor. That smell… like the plants have left something. Something for us. They don't take it all away. Like people do. Even when they die, they leave something there. Our plants. They were just like Jack and the Bean stalk.'

Rose's growing distress is palpable. As the hands of the clock turn past her finishing time, her session enters a flow that takes us deeper into her journey.

'Do you want to stop?' I ask.

She shakes her head, her forehead furrowing.

'And the faeries. They're different from the little green people. Do ya believe in them?' She looks at me, searching. 'They're there. Lots of folk reckon I'm mad, but they're there. They help me all the time.' Rosanna pauses. A deep inhale. Then silence.

'I'm listening, Rose.'

A shuddering exhale. 'Hmm?'

'You were talking about Auntie Mim and Sarah,' I say.

'Yeah?'

'And how it was in those early months with them'.

'Mm?'

'Rose. What's happening?'

Silence.

'It's hard,' she falters.

'I know.'

'Do yer?'

'Yes, I do.'

'What about you?' Her brow furrows.

'What would you like to know?' I ask.

'More about ya. All you professional people are so… I dunno.' She fades away, looks towards me, her eyes pooling confusion.

'So, what, Rose?'

'So different from me. Ya never share much about yourself. How can yer understand me?'

I wait.

Temper this curiosity Anna…

'I mean… *how?*' She persists.

'How do I know what it's like for you? Is that what you're asking?' I reply, assuaging.

'No! I just want to know more about *you*,' Rose despairs.

'What would you like to know?' I repeat.

She looks at me, her eyelids fluttering. Then abruptly turns away as the wheels begin to derail.

'Yer know, Sah was always there for me.' She folds her arms over her body, hugging herself. 'She was my only friend. A real sister to me.' Rosanna stops. Tears prick the corners of her closed eyes. The pendulum swings as her face screws into a ball of pain. In the still room, Rosanna begins to unwind.

'Has something ever happened to you? That totally changes everything?' The violent shake of her head. Her arms open and then cross in front of her, palms cradle her belly as she rocks herself. Then that all-encompassing distress.

'All or nothing?' she whispers.

'Yes.' I pause. 'It has…'

~

Nimbin, July 1973

I was in Sarah's bed, a cool flannel gently sponging me. Auntie Mim's worried face floated in and out of my vision. She spoke quietly to Sarah, who disappeared into the kitchen, returning carrying a tray with a steaming bowl of ox tail soup and hot peppermint tea. They assisted me to sit up, plumping pillows and tucking in the covers. Mim insisted that I eat and watched me with an unfamiliar expression as I attempted to sip her delicious brew.

But my stomach rebelled. I leaned sideways, heaving its contents onto the floor. Mim helped me out of the bed, half carrying me to the bathroom, holding my hair as I vomited. She cleaned my face and hands, and then supported me back into the bedroom.

Saying nothing, she tucked me back under the covers, stroked my hair and left the room. I heard her making a call later that morning, after the little ones had been walked to kindergarten.

When Sarah came home from school, Auntie Mim called her into the kitchen, speaking in low, firm tones. Soon after, Sarah skipped into our room and bounced up onto our bed. 'Rosie-rose,' she chirped, reaching down and kissing me on the cheek, looking intensely into my eyes. 'Mum just asked me if you need any pads for your monthly. She's off to The Store later.' Sarah jumped off the bed and spun in front of the mirror, admiring how her hair bobbed and floated with her movements.

'Yer can use mine if ye like,' she piped, humming as she brushed her hair. Then Sarah turned back to me, a puzzled look on her face.

'Come to think of it,' she said. 'We didn't bleed together last month, did we?'

Our periods had always come together and Auntie Mim insisted I stay with them at that time of the month. Her pungent herbal brew, imbibed at the beginning of each bleed, always relaxed us.

'Tis your time to stay at home a few days, lassies,' she would assert. We happily agreed, relishing the time off school, cuddling in bed as I read Sah's favourite books to her and she combed and brushed my hair.

I looked in confusion at Sarah. I had not noticed my lack of periods.

Sarah sat down. Sober now as she looked at me. 'Rosie-rose,' she said, 'did you bleed last month?'

I sat, mute, as her face clouded with concern. She stood and went out. I could hear her talking to Auntie Mim in the kitchen. Then both of them filed in. Auntie Mim sat down on the bed. 'Rose,' she said.

'Do you remember your last period?'

I shook my head, wondering why she was so insistent.

Auntie Mim turned to her daughter. 'Sarah?' she asked.

'Dunno, Mum,' Sarah answered, thinking. 'I reckon… it was…'

She looked up, trailing off, a frown forming on her face. Auntie Mim gazed at her daughter, then at me. Then leaning over, she took my hand and kissed me softly on the forehead.

'It's okay, Rose,' she murmured. 'Rest now.' And beckoning Sarah, they disappeared into the kitchen.

That night, Sarah cuddled me close, singing and stroking my face with her fingertips. A caress that transported me into the forest, filling me with hope.

'Rosie-rose,' she murmured as I began to drift off to sleep. 'In the morning, Mum wants you to pee into a bottle,' she giggled. The lilt in her voice softened the darkness, hushing anything else lurking in the shadows. 'Tink she wants to check to see if yer been eating too much of her stew.'

The following morning, I vomited again. Auntie Mim found me and insisted that I catch some of my urine in a wide-necked bottle. Then, I crawled back to bed, sleeping the morning away as Sarah left for school.

I had begun reading the many books that lined Dad's library shelves. Absorbing the syntax and rhyme of Keating and Shakespeare. The radical notions of Belkovsky spun me out beyond the stars and in his world of illusion, my mind slowly started to heal.

Sarah loved me reading to her at night. Her only lack of scholastic ability was that she was hopeless at English. Her heart-shaped face shone at the adventure books I read. She would jump off our bed, shouting with glee, declaring that we were going to conquer the world just as her heroines had.

But that afternoon, after school, Sarah didn't come straight into our room. I heard her speaking with her mother in the kitchen. Then crying and pleading. Auntie Mim's voice reached through the walls of that beautiful old house as she calmed her favourite daughter. It was raining gently, soft on Sarah's windowpanes, forming cool rivulets down the glass, when they appeared at the bedroom door, their eyes red-rimmed and swollen.

Sitting down on our bed, Auntie Mim took my hand in hers. Her soft heartbeat pulsed through her fingertips. 'Rosanna. I need to talk to you about something very important.'

My breath quickened.

'I took your urine to the doctor for a pregnancy test. It has come back positive.' Her firm touch held me still.

I stared at her, my belly convulsing with denial. Auntie Mim's eyes filled with tears as Sarah took my shoulders in her hands, pulling me towards her.

'Rose,' she said. 'We're gonna have a baby. Your baby.' Sarah spoke with unquestioning authority. 'I'm gonna help you,' she continued. 'Yer baby will be ours. You'll have him here. In this house. At home. Right, Ma?'

She held her mother's gaze.

~

That night, Sarah slipped into bed, pulling the covers over us and cuddling down next to me. Facing me, our bodies were so close in the half-dark that I could see her pupils dilating in the deep green of her eyes.

A whirlpool of images and questions swirled as I looked into her. Darker visions gripped me.

'I'm worried about yer, Rosie,' she whispered. 'Yer must eat and drink now yer gonna have a baby.' Her eyes filled with pain.

I tried to collect my thoughts.

I had heard the low murmur of Auntie Mim and Dad talking by the fire that night, prior to Sarah coming to bed. They were in earnest conversation with her. Her high sweet musical notations rose in protest and assertion, responding to them. They were clearly talking about me. I could hear many things being said. Many things that I didn't understand.

I pressed my hands into my ears and buried my head under the pillows.

Sarah eventually took over and for a long time she spoke, as her parents fell quiet. I heard Dad reassuring her as she tearfully responded. The fire crackled and the couch squeaked as he stood, murmuring to his eldest daughter, telling her to go and talk to me. Then they embraced her goodnight.

She lay looking at me now. Sweetness and concern flowing from her, like a rising spring from her depths. The heat in her body warmed me.

'But I don't understand, Sah,' I whispered.

Sarah folded me in her arms, her hot tears falling on my head.

'Rose, sweet Rose,' she murmured finally. 'Ye've never done anything bad.' Her voice choked. 'There's evil in this world, Rose. Not you. Ye've done nothing!' She eased me upright.

'Then why?' I asked, looking into her, trying to read her mind. She paused.

'Because they left a seed in your body. That's why yer having a baby,' she managed.

Her words plunged a knife into my belly. I bent over double, shaking violently. I fluttered like a leaf being ripped from its secure attachment to its mother tree. Tossing helplessly into a violent storm, I fell to earth, crushed under the weight of my violation.

I dry retched as Sarah held my shoulders.

'Rose, it wasn't yer fault, they're the ones that did the bad. Not you.'

She wiped the tears from my face.

'What am I going to do?' I sobbed. 'What's going to happen to me?'

Sarah looked earnestly at me.

'We're gonna have a baby. Our own forever baby. There's life in yer belly. That's the important thing. Yer gonna stay here, Rose. With us. Mum and Dad have said its okay. Mum will help yer have yer littlun.'

My mind swam with images. Girls from our town who disappeared to the big city with round bellies and red-rimmed eyes. Their return to our village a travesty. Flat stomachs and no babies. Broken hearts and lost children and prayers fused in my memory as Sarah's fingers pressed into mine, calling me back.

'Yer to stay here as long as you need. Dad will look after everything. Yer safe with us,' she added. 'I talked to them. Yer must keep yer baby Rosie. I'll help yer with him. It's going to be alright.'

~

Auntie Mim found me in the kitchen early the next morning, making a hot chocolate, my emaciated frame bent against the bench. Silently, she helped me warm the milk, added the cocoa, stirred it slowly to make it smooth. She went to the fridge and took out a bowl of clotted cream and, spooning a large golden lump into my mug, picked it up and coaxed me into the lounge room. Guiding me to the couch, she tucked an eiderdown around me. She went to the fireplace, blew on its red embers, adding dry leaves and logs of hard wood. Then she sat with me as I sipped the chocolate.

The fire's growing heat felt as radiant as her body next to mine. Her eyes were deep but tender. Her warmth reached out to me. I was spellbound.

'Auntie Mim,' I whispered, 'thank you.'

She stroked my face and drew me to her, holding me as close as one of her own. And in that moment, the wheels of my fate turned to face the only path possible.

~

Brisbane, February 1988

Rosanna sits quietly, looking out my window. Her charcoal and water colour sketch of a child lies unfinished in her lap. The day has lengthened and her obsession with the hues of the sunset captivates and holds her attention.

'There was so much I wanted to ask. Auntie Mim helped me understand. About birth. She looked after me. But the shock. It was… was hard.' Rose takes a breath and slowly releases it. 'Yer know what got to me most?' Rose screws up her face. 'It was her! What would you have done if that happened?' She peers at me.

'I would be there. In whatever way needed,' I answer.

'Yeah?'

I nod.

'*She* never was.' She looks at me. 'So, I guess that's one of my problems, huh?'

'How do you feel about it?' I ask.

She pauses, her chest rising and falling.

'Back then?' She glances at me. 'I dunno. It was so confusing. I was blown away being pregnant. I felt different. Alive. Whole. First time ever, it was so weird.'

'What about Ma?'

She looks down, her lips barely moving.

'Sorry Rose. What did you say?'

'She *never* cared,' she mutters.

'What do you mean?'

'I never saw her. She never came near me.' Rose's body shudders and she turns away from me. Her voice is thin. Cold.

'Fuckin *bitch*!' She flings a look at me. Her eyes dark, pained.

'Ya know, I didn't *ever* wanna see her. Never. She's a betrayer. A *loser*. She woulda told me to abort. I know *she* would have. Like all those other girls. She wanted me to be like her. To have the same fucked-up life she had.'

'In what way?'

'She said she wanted me. He didn't.'

'Okay. What does that mean Rose?' I watch her carefully.

'He said I was *bought* trouble.' Her lips clamp shut as she sits on her hands.

'I'm not sure I understand what you mean, Rose.' I breathe, trying to focus on her words. My heartbeat accelerates.

'It was like I didn't belong to them. Fucked up family!'

I make a note. *Bought trouble? What!*

Silence. Then, the wheels turn again.

'What was really screwed was… when I saw her… in the streets. She avoided me.' Her voice chokes up. She stops and tips her head back. Looking at the ceiling.

'They were both liars. Fuckin' idiots. A total non-family.'

'Non-family?'

'That's what Dan called it,' she mutters.

'I hear you. It must have been very hard,' I reflect.

Rosanna shrugs a shoulder and snorts.

'But how she behaved was bullshit, wasn't it? I mean, she was the same as when I was at home. She never understood me. She always pretended stuff didn't happen. Made believe that I was okay, didn't she? That our family was normal. But it wasn't, was it? It was fucked up big time. So, it was the same crap.'

She squeezes her nose and rubs her eyes.

'But, in some weird way… what happened… being pregnant… it allowed me to escape from them. She never protected me. Not ever. What do you therapists call that?' she challenges.

'It's abuse,' I reply.

'Abuse? Pigs arse! He was a monster. And *her…*' Rose spits the word. 'She just could never take responsibility. For anything!' Her hands flick outwards as her upper lip curls. 'And now she's rooted. Gone mad. Just so she doesn't have to face it all.' Her face discolours with high emotion.

The energy in the room is oppressive.

'Go on. I'm listening,' I say steadily.

She's silent. Her head bowed. Her heels drum the floor in a rhythm of anxiety.

'What do you think about all this crap?' she hisses it out.

I choose my words carefully.

'In my experience, when a daughter loses her family during puberty, especially the significant maternal carer, it is often never resolved. Particularly if there is a betrayal. A woman's role in a teenage girl's life is pivotal to how girls see the world. From what you've shared, Ma was an absent mother. This would have made things very hard for you and it is totally understandable that you are still very angry with her.'

She looks up at me. Her eyes flare with hatred. She ducks her head. Holds her breath.

'Remember your breathing, Rose,' I say quietly.

There's an explosive out breath.

Then.

'Yeah. But my issue is that if I get angry, you'll tell the psych, and she will stop them coming home. Then I won't get them back.' Her voice shakes as she attempts to control her feelings.

'No, that's not accurate. Your anger will not affect that decision. It is how you learn to deal with it and what you're able to release constructively that will make the change.'

She looks at me. 'Jesus, Anna. If you had been through half of what I've been through, ya would be as mad as me.'

'I really see that, Rose. I truly don't blame you.'

She holds my gaze, then flicks her head and jiggles her feet up and down.

I make a note. Then wait. Calm my breath. Watch her change.

Her body shakes imperceptibly as she tries to control her feelings. On the shuddering outbreath, tears drop to the floor, forming a little pool of grief at her feet.

'What's happening, Rose?' I ask gently.

'It's just that… Auntie Mim. I made her my Mum. If it wasn't for her, I would never have kept him.' Now the tears fall fully.

'I feel like such a bloody drongo, crackin' the shits all the time. Then howling, feeling like I'm gonna top someone. Then feeling like I'm dead.' She looks up at me, her eyes pleading. 'I'm really scared yer gonna say I'm totally unstable. Can't be a mother again.'

I watch her carefully. My heart aching.

'I do understand how you feel, Rose. It's a real roller coaster getting through your life. Many years ago, I had to face myself too. And it was really hard. I shed an ocean of tears back then. I think that crying is good. A way of releasing your feelings. That's why I have tissues.'

Rose manages to return me a lopsided smile.

I continue. 'Don't you think we need to keep going? Ride these waves? Understand more of this?' I add, gently. 'You're doing really well today. Would you like to continue talking about them?'

Rose's face clouds over. Her eyes dull. Imperceptibly, she shakes her head and looks away.

'Would you like to draw for a while?' I ask.

Rose nods and reaches down to pick up her charcoal. I click on the cassette player, then resting back, observe her as she sketches, my mind racing as I search for answers.

~

'What about your life during your pregnancy?'

It's a little later. Rose has filled her page with sinuous circles and minute figurines. Her face is calmer. She folds her hands in her lap and studies her work.

'Sah was amazing. She got that excited. Kept reassuring me that it was going to be incredible. That she would help me with…' Rose's tears spill over as she quickly looks away.

'She was your best friend, wasn't she?'

'Yep.' Her voice cracks with pain. 'She sure was.' Rose hunches over and goes quiet.

'What about your education?'

She glances up, her eyes still flowing with tears. She continues haltingly.

'I wanted to study. Go to school. Try to forget about it all. But my belly got that big. A real whopper. And the folk in the village, well, they didn't give two hoots about me.' She swipes at her face.

'They didn't understand?' I ask.

'Yeah. But. I was already shunned in the village, so I guess it didn't make much difference.' Her voice is resigned.

'Shunned?'

'Yeah… cos… he was such a dickhead…' Her voice trails off.

'Did you ever go back to school?'

'Not until Chris came.'

'Did you miss it?'

'Hell, yeah. Heaps. I always loved it. When I was at home, it was my escape. I love learning. Can't ever get enough of it.'

'It sounds like you learnt a lot at home with Sarah. How did that happen?'

'Dad's books. He's really brainy. Taught it all to me.' She looks up at my bookshelf. 'Like you. Had rooms full.' She smiles through her tears.

'He liked the ancient philosophers. Like Socrates and Aristotle. And books on gardening. And religion. Rumi and the mystics. And politics. Holdens. He still loves those cars. And I read. All the time.'

She holds her belly. 'Those books. Dad. They… he gave me back my life.' She stands and moves to my bookshelves. 'Can I have a cuppa?' she asks, blowing her nose.

When I return, her back is towards me as she studies the bookshelf. She's gained some composure.

'Why so many books on home birth, Anna?' she asks. 'What do you think about it?' She looks at me. 'I mean, it's the best, innit?'

'Yes. It was my choice.'

'So. Yer do have a kid, ey?'

'Yes.'

She pauses, then turns and reaches up, drawing Gaskin's *Spiritual Midwifery* from the shelves. I pass her the tea and return to my desk.

'I read this when I was preggas. It was Auntie Mim's bible.' She sits on her chair, crossing her legs neatly. Her fingers trace the heart-shaped locket that rests on her chest.

She sips her tea slowly, silently thumbing through the book's worn pages. I make a note as her body language signals another step forward.

'Dad and I used to read together. In the morning. Before he went out to make a quid. Auntie Mim loved hanging around us. Looking after everything. They had such an amazing relationship. Adored each other. Couldn't get enough lovin' between them. When I was a bit better, they took me to The Store. Gave me the books to do. That's where I got to be good at maths. Could add up a row of figures no problems. And Dad? He loved his guitar. He and Danny used to play together at night.'

She turns away. Stops talking.

'What's happening, Rose?' I ask.

She shakes her head and reaches for the tissues.

We sit, waiting for the words.

'Mim's kitchen…' Her voice is filled with emotion.

'Do you want to talk about Dan?' I ask.

Her silence is my answer.

'You were telling me about Auntie Mim and Dad. Would you like to keep going?'

She nods her head.

'Auntie Mim loved her kitchen, didn't she?' I encourage.

Rose collects herself.

'Yeah.' She blows her nose, shakily continuing. 'She was magic in that kitchen. Could turn an empty cupboard into a feast. Maybe it *was* her faeries. She always reckoned so.'

Rose stands and returns the book, beginning to move around the room.

'She taught me to cook. And bake. And how to put it all together. Being with her, in her kitchen. It was a bit like this.'

'This?'

'Yeah. Like therapy. Healing. And the littluns. They helped me understand. About kids.' She watches the traffic in the streets below.

'Yer know, I didn't know anything about sex. Or babies. Or how they were made. Or how to look after them. I'd seen my animals. In the fields. I used to watch them. Doing it. It fascinated me. Ma said it was disgusting. But I loved it. It was like they were doing something really important.'

'How were Sarah's family about sex?' I ask.

Rose's face lights up.

'They were different. They talked about it. It was natural. It was about life. About relationships.'

'What about your birth, Rose? How did that all go?'

The pendulum swings as Rose turns to face me. Her eyes sparkle and small patches of pink begin to glow in her cheeks.

'That?' she speaks softly. 'That was amazing.'

~

Nimbin, Winter 1973

Winter air left lacy patterns on the glass. I loved to watch them melt as the fire heated Sarah's room. When she was at school, the laughter and play of her younger sisters and brothers were my companion. I wondered what it was going to be like to have a baby of my own. Most of the time I lay in our bed, reading; mutely accepting Auntie Mim's care and waiting for Sarah to come home.

Then, one afternoon, my teacher visited us. She arrived unannounced on the doorstep and Auntie Mim invited her in. I heard them talking in the kitchen, then the scrape of chairs as they sat. Mim served hot scones, jam and cream.

Their voices reached through the walls as I lay propped up in bed, listening. My teacher was asking questions. It was clear that she was urging Auntie Mim to keep me away from school.

Except for Auntie Mim's kitchen, I was terrified of going

anywhere. As she went about her work she explained how to combine and blend flavours. How to grind spices and crush herbs. How to mix in the secret ingredient of '*love*' into our preparation.

I watched her pound flour and roll it into long, cylindrical loaves for the oven.

'Do yer wanna help, Rose lassie?' she would ask, handing me a mixing bowl. Fresh ground flour and soured yeast frothed from the cup as I fetched the water, salt and cream for her delicious milk loaf.

'Mix it slow, lass,' she would say. 'Take yer time,' she added as I leaned against the bench stirring the bowl, watching the bubbles mix in with the flour, squashing the doughy lumps against the edges and trickling the water into the mix.

Sarah cuddled me in the evenings, chatting and chirping and laying out beautiful plans for our lives together with the baby.

Dad was a keen jazz guitarist and Danny his budding accomplice. Most nights they sat in the garden as the cold dusk air dropped around us. Danny loved to light the fire in the outdoor pit. Stoking it with logs, fanning with a folded newspaper. Early evenings were a time of family gathering. Hot chocolate, the laughter and play of children; music and the warmth of the fire began to light the embers of my frozen shattered spirit.

As the seasons changed, the cool of winter turned into the flourish of spring. Summer ripened our crops and heated the embers of my young life as I took my first tentative steps towards becoming a mother.

~

Brisbane, March 1988

'You're looking nice today,' I comment. We're in the kitchen, waiting for the kettle to boil. She holds my porcelain teapot in her hands, turning it around to admire the delicate pink and mauve flowers hand painted on its surface.

'Where did ya get this, Anna?' she asks.

'I found it in the antique shop. Around the corner from here. It's from England. I believe it's porcelain from last century. Once I saw it, I just fell in love with it.'

'It's exquisite,' Rose says, carefully placing it onto the heat pad.

'Chamomile?' I ask. It's her favourite. I'm ready to start our session.

Rose has come into her appointment, showered and dressed neatly. She is calmer than usual. A soft glow emanates from her. 'Yes, please.' She smiles.

'I also have some news too,' she continues. 'We've got a permanent place to live.'

'Rinpoche and you?'

'Yep. He found us a flat. In West End. Above the pub.' She looks suitably chuffed.

'That's great news,' I reply.

'Yeah. I'm stoked. The government gave it to him. Well, he has to pay. But it's cool. It's got a shower. And a dunny. And a double bed. He reckons I have to stay with him.' She smiles a little.

'I'm really pleased to hear this,' I say.

She is watching the kettle boil. She picks it up and pours the water into the pot, carefully replacing the lid and picking up the cups in her free hand.

'Can we sit outside this time?' she asks.

We settle into the wicker chairs on the veranda, placing the tea pot and cups onto the small coffee table. A warm early autumn wind blows around us. The noise on the road is loud, a blanket of privacy around her as she settles. Filtered sun shines at our feet.

For once, Rose booked a midday appointment today, saying she has chores to do.

'Rinpoche says he doesn't want me to pay. But yer know, I have money.'

I can see the subtle changes in her skin colour and moisture. A small movement forward.

'That's excellent,' I reply.

'He's hung all his stuff up. That he scrounges from the bins. He's got enough furniture. And the bed? Well, he carried it with some mates. All the way along Boundary Road,' she laughs. 'If he was an Aussie, he'd be filthy rich. He's brill at scavenging and bartering.'

I smile with her. I have still yet to meet Rinpoche. A part of me is wary. The haze of delusion still rests lightly on her.

'There's a little kitchen there too. We can make our own tucker. I'm gonna give him dosh for it all.' She tucks her feet up under her as she sips her tea and gazes into the leafless branches hanging over the veranda.

'He wants to share the bed with me,' she says, crinkling up her nose.

'How's that for you?' I ask.

'Weird, I guess,' she answers. 'He's been a monk and all, ya know. But…' Her eyes sparkle, 'It's a home, Anna. A home!' she enthuses.

'That's really great,' I reply.

'It's the first one. Since they took them.' Her eyes cloud briefly.

We sit for a while in silence as swallows dip and glide into the rafters.

'Ya know, I love these birds. They build beautiful nests. Even in the middle of the city.' A female flutters close to the edge of the spherical nest, feeding her young.

'You mentioned Danny last week, Rose. That you liked him being around you in those early days of your pregnancy. Would this be a good time?' I ask.

A veil glides over her eyes.

'Yeah. Okay… I guess that's okay,' she says, putting her cup down. There's that characteristic hunching of her shoulders, heralding a new change.

'It was weird having a boy there. But I really dug him. Was too shy to talk to him much. He was a real dag. Funny. Silly. Made me laugh. He loved to do stuff. Ya know, boy stuff. Cars. Building with Dad… was always nosing around him… helping him.'

She unravels her tucked-up feet and walks over to the veranda rails.

'They made this incredible chook house. Out the back.' She turns to face me. 'I watched them. From our window. It was shaped like a dome. The chooks loved it. Scratching around. Turning the soil for us. Dad said they would move it after a bit. To make a round mandala garden. But the chooks hung out in it 'til then. It kept them out of other parts of the garden.' She smiles.

Then more softly, 'I love chooks.' She's pensive. I wait as she returns to her chair. Then the inhale. The hold. And the sharp exhale.

'Are you okay, Rose?' I ask gently.

'Yeah. I'm fine. It was a really great time. Him. Dad. Auntie Mim. Sarah. The kids. Pregnant. I was so young then. So young.' She pauses and picks up her cup, sipping the tea slowly.

'And then Chris came.' She looks at me, her eyes clear and strong. 'Now *that* was something else!'

~

Nimbin, February 1974

The heat on that evening heralded the coming of another profound change in my life. Auntie Mim watched me carefully as unbeknownst to me, my body ripened for birth.

She sent Sarah out to the garden to pick fresh raspberry sprigs and the biggest leaves off the aloe plant. She dug up the comfrey root and brewed their greeneries in her glass herbal decoction pot. She pulled the largest tea tree oil bottle from the high shelf in the laundry and set aside spare towels and sheets. The calendula and eyebright infused oil sat on our bedroom vanity as she boiled the water to sterilise her surgical scissors. She climbed up into the attic to bring down her stethoscope and foetal heart monitor, and hired an oxygen tank from the local surgery.

And then she knelt in front of her cross and prayed silently; her eyes squeezed shut with concentration.

I slept fitfully into the early hours of the morning, waking occasionally to sit up as sharp pains ran through my belly. Mim watched me carefully, reassuring me.

Then Christian decided it was time.

My labour filled the night. Like the lullaby of the gentle cows labouring in our fields, I sang and crooned and screamed my way through the pain. At times, the contractions made me feel as though I would die right there on the floor of Mim's and Dad's loungeroom. And then, at each moment that he rested in my belly and held still against my fear, I drifted out into the garden and up into the heavens, to connect with the child that lay within me, waiting to be born.

I was smitten by strange visions that night. Green fields of rolling hills and mists that billowed around me. I could feel the bite of freezing mountain air in my nostrils and hear the lullabies of gypsies singing in the woods. Tall trees surrounded me, and small green folk danced at my feet. The footprints of furred animals across the whitest frost filled my senses with a euphoria that lifted me out of my body and danced me into the clouds above. I could feel the soft touch of a heavy bosom against my back, as skilled hands massaged my belly and the lyrical notes of Irish voices drowned out my moans.

My body felt as though it were to split asunder as the pain between my legs and deep up into me crashed around. I surfed the waves as white cliffs rose above and the ocean of birth tossed me like a cork from one end of the Celtic kingdom to the other.

Dad's baritone voice roused me in the morning, as his coarse but gentle hands took mine, his strength flowing through me like the currents of our river. Through the fog, I felt his smile. His words spun inside my brain, guiding me back on course like a father ship in a massive storm.

Soon after, Christian's head appeared and, with a final push, his small body slid out. His voice chirped its imprint into my brain, forever to lay there as the singular most magical sound I had ever heard.

Tears flooded my face as I reached down to my son, and as Mim's warm hands steadied me, I drew him up and onto my belly. She skilfully assisted the afterbirth from my womb and packed cooling, sterile towels drenched in aloes against my lower body.

Sah's tears of joy held me still to my newborn's needs. She stroked my hair lightly and with the gentlest of touches, caressed my son's face. He squeaked like a small mouse and looked up at her, dark pools of light shining from his eyes.

And within that warp in time, my heart opened like a ripening flower and my soul took in the undeniable grace of two lives to be lived as one.

5

Nimbin, 1975

CHRISTIAN was a happy, chubby, little baby whose presence filled our lives with delight. Sarah fully embraced him, carrying him on her hip and showing him her world.

'Yer so lucky, Rosie-rose. He's such a bonnie wee laddie,' she chirped, tickling him under the chin. His laughter filled our home with sounds akin to the burbling river waters in my forest.

To say I was in love was one thing, but to understand that I was in awe of motherhood was another. My young body ached for my son. When he lay in my arms, my breath quickened, his angelic face peeping out from under his blanket.

When Chris was six months old, I returned to school. Sarah kept an eye on things, fiercely protecting me from any comments or barbs from other teenagers. During the day, my grades topped the class and at night my life was filled with the warmth of family and the joy of my small son in my arms.

During my fifteenth year, the level railway crossing on the outskirts of town became the meeting place for me and Sarah. There was little to do in our village, so when our duties at home were finished, more forbidden places drew us to the call of adventure.

Auntie Mim turned a blind eye to our foray into teen freedom, insisting that she care for Christian most afternoons. Taking him from me, she would disappear into her kitchen, clucking and holding him close as he burbled and bounced his little legs against her hip.

One day, Sarah and I set off down the dusty road towards the tracks. To wait for the roar of the old locomotive to subside as it drew into the station. The sound of it bringing passengers to town. The prospect of meeting visitors filled Sarah's imagination with glee. I tagged along, filled with dread of encountering strangers.

Sarah was a veteran storyteller and gossipmonger. She

enthusiastically greeted every passenger with anecdotes and advice. I tried to disappear into the walls as I watched her charm melt the wariness of the visitors to our village. I was a perpetual shadow in the presence of her effervescence.

'Let's go up the line,' she said one day. 'Dan reckons there's an old shed up there.' Her eyes sparkled with the anticipation of adventure. 'We've got time before dinner. Mum's got Chris,' she reassured me.

We hopped and jumped rail to rail, singing and laughing. Sharing our dreams. Dancing with the innocence of youth.

Tucked into the bend of the tracks, the shed awaited us. Ferns and wild sweet-smelling lantana grew all around, partially hiding it from view. We stood entranced on the rails. Its blackened walls and rusty roof poked out of the bushes, revealing a mystery in its abandoned, corrugated shell.

Sarah crept up to it, gently pushing the broken wooden door open. It banged behind us in the breeze, revealing a dingy, dusty interior. Against one wall was a chimney, filled with cobwebs. On the other, an old sink hung from a single hinge. The blackened wooden beams which held the roof were solid and the roofing iron clear of any holes. The only window was broken, cracked edge to edge, the rays of light from outside casting shards of rainbows into its interior, illuminating split and worn floorboards.

There were no signs of human habitation.

This was exactly the kind of place we had dreamed of making our own. We explored the outside, checking if there were holes through which snakes could enter. It'd be our *Sista-Shed*, Sarah enthused. A space in which to dream our lives away.

Our walk back along the tracks to the railway crossing was filled by Sarah's contagiously good humour. She bubbled and chirped, dancing along the rails, enticing me with magical plans and ideas. We returned the following afternoon, after the milk train had shaken the tracks and disappeared around the bend.

We scrubbed and cleaned out years of dust and dirt. Danny pulled the lantana away from the outside, leaving just enough so that our secret hideaway remained mostly hidden from view. He banged and hammered at the old sink, securing it under the window, and filled a large plastic container with water, stowing it against the far wall. We salvaged old wooden crates from the tip to use as chairs.

My artwork adorned the walls and Sarah brought potted plants from home to decorate the floor. We found old Milo tins in which to place candles and keep matches. We hung curtains across the cracked panes of glass and snuck out broken cups and saucers from Mim's kitchen. Sah's family had an old kerosene light and stove that made a fine kitchen for us and slowly, as our place took shape, the essential sugar, tea and flour arrived in rescued jars.

We cooked damper on the fire and slathered it with strawberry jam, which Auntie Mim's pantry didn't miss. Danny brought over chopped wood, stacking it outside and covering it with a sheet of old corrugated iron.

A worn, decrepit couch from the local tip arrived one afternoon after school. Dropped off for us at the side as Danny reversed back up the road, grinning at the wheel of the family ute.

We dragged it along the tracks, pushing it inside and positioning it against the back wall so that we could see out the broken window. Its fabric was torn from rusty springs, so Sarah secreted an old rug from Mim's collection and tossed our brightly coloured home-made cushions onto it.

It was a lounge 'fit for a queen', she proudly announced.

Danny scavenged the local countryside for anything he could mend or tinker with. We often found useful bits and pieces waiting for us at the rail siding. His characteristic signature: the old paint tin resting upside down on them. We covered the floor with newspaper and the tip furnished us with pieces of carpet, carefully cleaned and laid out in colourful patterns. It was warm, dry and cosy in our *Sista-Shed*.

It was our secret haven, somewhere for ritual immersion into teen culture. Sarah was by now an enthusiastic smoker. I hated cigarettes. But the initiation into sisterhood required my compliant attempt.

'Here.' Sarah thrust her rollie into my hands. 'Hold it between yer two fingers and breathe in,' she exclaimed, her eyes sparkling as I pawed the cigarette and placed it between my lips.

'Go on,' she grinned. 'I dare ya!' She watched me as I inhaled. My face turned the colour of puke as I coughed and spluttered like I was about to die. Sarah rolled on the floor, holding her sides with laughter that tinkled up, mingling with the smoke plumes from my open mouth.

'You've gone green,' she giggled. 'Ya just have to try again.' She patted my back and took the butt from me, stubbing it out in the fireplace.

'Sorry, Rosie-rose,' she grinned, ruffling my hair. 'Ya don't hafta if yer don't wanna.' Smiling. 'Let's go for a burn instead?'

Sarah had just passed her learner's test and Dan had sweet-talked Auntie Mim into lending her the beat-up Holden Ute.

'Just on the back road, Mum,' she'd said with a grin.

We had driven to the dusty road just out of town, down its unsealed surface, screeching to a halt at our crossing. I treasured those moments of liberty, feeling the freedom as my long, dark hair blew from the open car window. Sarah screeched with delight as I held firm the door handle, praying that it wouldn't bust open and splay me onto the roadside. These were the instants in time where the pacts for our "forever-friendships" were made.

~

Nimbin, 1976

On the morning of my mid-year English exam, Sarah was home. All her assignments were over, and she was delighted to help with Christian. By the time I was ready to leave, Auntie Mim had already left for a quick errand at The Store. Dad was tending to his broadies at the back fence, before heading off to the garage to tinker with his latest antique model Holden.

Hugging me goodbye, Sarah pulled back, looking quizzically into my face.

'Now, Rose Petal, have you studied enough for this test?' she teased.

Warmed by her affection, I smiled as she reached up and stroked my face. I had studied late into that night, waking at dawn to find my head on my books and her gentle hand shaking me awake.

'Good luck, Rosie-rose. You're the best,' she enthused, her green eyes holding onto mine.

We hugged each other, shook our secret handshake, and I was off, down the garden path and onto the street. At the last moment, Sarah called out and, putting Christian on the large shady veranda, came running down the steps towards me.

Reaching out and taking my hand, she placed a tiny parcel into it.

'Don't open this until after yer exam,' she commanded. 'It's a good luck charm from da faeries, yer know.' She grinned, placing a soft kiss on my cheek.

'Luv yer forever!' she cried as she dashed back up the stairs, scooping Christian up and disappearing into the house, babbling happily to him. I carefully stowed her gift into the pocket of my jeans and walked to school. In the face of my toughest exam yet, I was more immersed in the feeling of her love than in any fear of failure.

~

The old ute screeched as Danny spun the wheel around and around the back paddock. Sarah rocked from side to side in the narrow confines of the cabin, jammed between the passenger door and Danny. Her mane of blonde curls streaked out of the open window as she threw back her head, peals of laughter filling the air. A giant cloud of dust followed them as Dan revved the beat-up ute to its capacity.

Danny skidded to a halt, then opened the throttle and thundered around the paddock, the steering wheel gripped tightly in his hands, triumphantly grinning.

He knew and loved that old car. He'd been driving it since he was eleven years old. Dad had taught him as he sat on his father's lap holding onto the steering wheel. Danny had a legal license so Auntie Mim allowed him free reign over the old ute.

Sarah and Dan were on their way to the local dairy, where the townsfolk bought their milk by the billy-full. The delicious fresh cream straight from the cow's udder was a much sought-after delight and an essential ingredient for Mim.

Dan and Sah had raced each other across the back paddock towards the ute, Danny winning by a foot. He had leaped into the driver's seat, teasing Sarah mercilessly about how slow she was. Sah punched Dan in the ribs. Then, admitting defeat, she clambered into the passenger seat side, slamming the door shut and turning to Dan, her eyes pools of mischief.

'I dare you to stop on the railway line, chicken breath,' she gasped, grinning at her older brother.

'Ah, lassie,' Dan snorted, 'yer doesn't have a clue what a dare is.'

Starting the motor and dropping the clutch, Dan spun the bald tyres as the engine roared and the ute was flung around the back paddock, Sarah shrieking with delight.

~

That day, as I stepped into the hall for my last exam, Auntie Mim returned from The Store. Sah and Chris had been racing along the veranda, chasing each other.

A game of tag. Their favourite.

Ducking toys and furniture, their voices had filled the house with hysterical laughter. Finally wrestling her to the floor, Chris had leapt on top of her, triumphantly announcing that he had 'got 'er'.

Sah threw herself onto the lounge, puffing, happily flicking through the latest Woman's Day when Auntie Mim walked in.

Swinging Chris up onto her hip, she clucked and scolded before disappearing into her kitchen to make soup for our lunch. Ruffling his hair as he squirmed, she put him down on the floor and bent over to open the fridge, inspecting what was needed for a hearty lunch for us all. Happily opening pantry doors, Chris hauled pots and pans out onto the floor to build castles, banging loudly as he jubilantly stacked them.

'Think I'll be needin' some milk,' she called to Sarah, her voice muffled in the fridge.

'Can yer go down to Mrs Flan's, Missee and get the billy filled?'

Sarah popped her head around the corner of the kitchen, smiling cheekily.

'Aw, Mum,' she exclaimed, 'that's a long way down. Do I hafta?'

Auntie Mim straightened, turning to face her. Sighing, she put one hand on her hip, looking down at Sarah's tight blonde curls and flushed happy cheeks.

'Well… I guess if those wee legs of yours just ain't up to it, I'll have to ask Danny-boy to go,' Auntie Mim announced, her eyes twinkling, teasing her favourite daughter.

'Danny?' she called, dangling the old ute's keys from her forefinger.

Mim knew how much Sarah loved a practice drive in that old beat-up car and smiled inwardly as her daughter grabbed the keys. Sarah spun around and flew out the door, calling for Danny at the top of her voice. Mim sighed as she turned back to the kitchen sink, shaking her head, smiling before Sarah raced back in squealing.

'Mum. Where's yer purse? I need 20c.'

Mim reached into her embroidered apron pocket, taking out a coin and holding it out to Sarah who was hopping impatiently from one foot to another, humming loudly.

'Now, Missee,' Mim cautioned. 'That old bomb needs its engine tuned. It stalls all the time. Yer tell that Danny-boy to be careful.'

'And don't yer go drinking any of that milk until I've had it on the boil, yer hear?' she scolded as Sah took the money, reaching up to throw her arms around her mother's shoulders, hugging her impetuously.

'Don't yer worry, Ma,' she clucked. 'Not a drop shall pass our lips.' Kissing her mother noisily on the cheek, she spun out the door calling, 'Catch ya lata alligata.' Mim paused. The sunny day suddenly felt cold. A whisper of spirit floated around her. The faeries playing in her hearth stopped to watch her curiously. A peculiar sense of foreboding stilled her as she listened to her footfall, fading.

Shrugging her shoulders, smiling inwardly at her superstition, Mim quickly crossed herself and touched the wooden bench in their kitchen.

For luck.

'Teenagers,' she mused.

The sun came out, warming the cooled air as Christian's racket on the floor distracted Mim from her inward reverie.

Sighing, she returned to her tasks, chucking Christian under the chin, singing sweetly to him as she began to cut potatoes and leeks, mixing them by hand with roughly chopped parsley and rosemary. Tossing it all into the frying pan, Mim hummed and sang as she fried and stirred, adding beef-bone broth and seasoned salt to her soup and including, a sprinkle of extra love.

…Just in case… she caught herself thinking.

~

I was finishing my final essay when I heard the sound of a locomotive loud in the far distance. It always sounded its whistle three times on the approach to the station. Not wanting to lose concentration, I continued to write.

My exam over, I left school and began to walk home to the other end of town. I was puzzled by the last question on my paper and distracted by the incongruities of my exam. I didn't notice that our normally busy street was almost deserted. The Store's doors were shut.

I turned the corner to home.

'Oh good. Dad will be back for lunch. I can ask him,' I thought.

~

The tyres bit into the gravel at the side of the road as Danny steered the car onto the broken-up bitumen and headed out of town. The dairy was about a kilometre down the road, over the railway crossing and around the curved back road. It was the local pick-up destination for fresh milk; our town undeniably produced the best in the district. Rich deep-green grass, grown on volcanic soil, fed Mrs Flannigan's Jersey and Guernsey cows with a fresh source of nutrient that made their milk froth with delicious golden cream. We all loved to take a secret quaff of the nectar before getting it home to Auntie Mim's.

The mission to collect the daily milk was an enviable one. All Auntie Mim's family would argue over whose turn it was. Danny, being the oldest boy, would usually ferry his younger siblings to the dairy, all piled into the back of the ute half under the cover, their hair blowing free as he spun them down the road towards the farm.

That day, the little ones were at primary school and weren't due home until lunch time. Sarah sat in the front, bubbling about her latest project at school and the grades she wanted to get in her exams. Danny teased her about her lack of English literacy as the ute swung around the bend, heading towards the dairy.

As they approached the railway crossing, Danny slowed the car, looking up and down the tracks for trains. The late morning milk run was due.

'Garn!' Sarah called. 'I bet yer too chicken breath to stop.' She laughed delightedly as Dan shrugged his shoulders.

'Yer know, Mum's not gonna like it,' he said, slowing down and stopping in the middle of the crossing.

'Too chicken to stop the engine?' Sarah teased. She reached across Dan, turned the key off in the ignition, pulling it out as the engine coughed and died. Danny looked sideways, snorting at her, as she grinned back defiantly at him, dangling the keys from her forefinger.

The day was still and sunny. The air sweetly scented with flowering tea-tree. With the engine off, Danny's senses relaxed into the peace and quiet surrounding them. In the distance he could hear the soft 'moo' of Mrs Flan's cows. Sarah babbled away next to him, joshing him and spinning the keys round and round. He caught himself thinking how joyful his sister was. How contagious her mirth and how much his heart sung in her presence. He smiled inwardly as she laughed and jabbed at his ribs, digging for a reaction from him.

~

Auntie Mim pummelled the dough for the morning's bread, skilfully folding and squeezing it with her strong flour-dusted arms, massaging its gluten into supplication. Christian sat in his highchair, noisily chewing on toasted milk bread, raspberry jam, cream and cottage cheese.

She smiled at him as he burbled, tunefully singing melodies that Danny and Dad had taught him. She sang back, musically perfect notes that harmonised with his.

'Let's go to the garden, Chris.' She smiled. 'We need more tatees.'

'Umma's gone school,' he announced, waving his jam covered hands at her.

'Yes, littlun,' she smiled. 'Last day. Then yer can play with her all the time.'

'My!' she exclaimed as she wiped his face. 'You like that jam?'

'Yummy!' he beamed, licking his fingers.

The back door banged as Auntie Mim set off for the garden. The bees that time of year were prolific, and Christian smiled with delight at them as she carried him under the arbour of jasmine that climbed over the back steps. He reached up to touch the sweet-scented flowers, disturbing a nectar-filled cup. Small, yellow-bellied inhabitants buzzed around them.

Auntie Mim lifted a protective hand to Christian's face and, as she stood on those back steps, the first siren of the milk train sounded in the distance.

'Good,' she thought. 'It's on time.'

As a small honeybee alighted lightly on her forefinger, she heard the second screech.

Turning to Chris she started to speak.

'See. They have so much love for us.' She smiled. 'Do yer think they are wise, lill'un or foolish not to sting? What do yer…' She paused.

And the swarm rose as one. A cloud of gold, yellow wings beat the air as the third siren reached out across that valley into Mim's heart. Danny and Sah's mother paused, and the scent of honey flowed over her as her mind lifted above the clouds into the distance.

~

I kicked rocks down the rough bitumen as I turned the corner home. My belly grumbled, released from the apprehension of my final exam and eager for a nourishing broth from Auntie Mim's kitchen. My mind was still contemplating what the examiners were looking for when I saw a strange light glowing at the end of the road.

'What's Dad up to now?' I thought as I proceeded past the last houses at the top of the street, before the paddocks next to home.

A flashing blue light at the end of the road caught my attention. Curious, I picked up my pace. The noon haze outlined more vehicles than usual.

'Must be Dad's new FJ Holden,' I thought, moving faster.

In the distance, a figure crouched in the gutter, surrounded by uniform-clad figures. Police cars filled the end of the road, their vehicles parked outside our home.

'That's weird,' I thought. 'Dan can't be in trouble. He's stopped taking pot.'

Then, from deep within me, that familiar churning in the pit of my belly. That all-knowing prescience of my life colliding into an unsolicited crossroad. A vortex of fear as cold icicles ran their tendrils through me.

My feet bit into the dirt road as I started to run.

Hugging knees to chest, Danny cowered against the bitumen. Gigantic sobs wracked his body. Two policemen squatted next to him, their hands firmly on his shoulders. Their faces expressionless.

I sprinted past them as my feet guided me towards the front steps. Then I heard it.

That sound.

My heart stopped as the shrill wailing reached my ears. A piercing eagle's cry sent a thousand shards of glass, shattering my heart into a million pieces.

Flying up the stairs, I threw the front door open.

Auntie Mim was collapsed on the floor, violently rocking herself. Her sobs wracked the room. Dad held her, his arms a vice of anguish. His massive chest heaved as devastation poured from him. Sarah's family surrounded them, frozen in shock. The youngest ones looked with bewilderment at their parents, the oldest wept with an intensity that filled the house.

Christian sat on the floor, his little face an impenetrable barrier.

A whisper flew around me, butterfly caresses of soft lips on my cheek.

Sarah was everywhere. Her laughter, an echo in the room. Her arms around me, hugging me to her. Her sweet babbling voice filled the air with the beauty of her song. Her understanding, fun, wisdom flowed over me. Wave after wave of love. Her sweet face filled with ethereal golden light smiled down at me.

Whatever happens, Rose Petal, remember I love you.

Then the tangible blanket of spirit wrapped around me for a moment that lasted forever. My senses reached out over time and space. Every sound slowed, amplified in my brain. Each grieving note hung in the air. In that room once filled with her life.

The physical lack of her presence crushed me as I began to shake.

Dad looked up at me. His face, ancient craggy features torn asunder with searing pain. His gaze, an express train thundering into me, shrill screaming freezing me to the spot.

'Where is she?' I managed, my voice laced with fear. My heart pounded, each beat an explosion in my chest. I waited a millennium for his answer.

He shook his head.

'Where *IS* she?' I screamed.

He held out his hand.

'Rose,' he sobbed. 'Rose Petal…'

Sarah's smile floated in front of me as my knees gave way beneath me. Leaning out to hold the door for support, my gaze took in that terrible moment. Then, I turned, staggering out from my home, past Danny sobbing in the gutter, past the police looking at me with stony, unreachable faces and onto the long, empty street.

Christian's cry echoed my flight.

~

In the moments between the pulse of life and laughter, he felt it. An almost imperceptible vibration ran along the tracks and up into the old ute. Danny froze, listening intently as Sarah grinned and shook the keys, oblivious to his change in mood.

Over Sarah's shoulder he saw it. A silver streak heading through the forest south of the railway crossing, flying towards them. Paralysed for a timeless second, Danny's mind tried to grasp what was happening.

Then, he moved with a speed that stopped Sarah's laughter short, the corners of her mouth twisted into a half grin.

Grabbing the key out of her hand, Danny jammed it back into the ignition, frantically turning it. The engine sputtered once and died. Danny twisted it again. The engine jumped into life as he rammed the gears into first. The throttle pulled, coughed and stopped cold. The car seated right in the middle of the railway crossing.

The locomotive turned the corner. Clearly visible now, it thundered straight towards the powerless vehicle. Bearing down on them. Brother and sister sitting rooted to their seats in an eternal moment of awakening realisation.

Then Danny catapulted into action.

'Get *out*,' he screamed as Sarah looked up towards the monster.

'*Get out!*' he roared, throwing his door open, frantically stumbling as he fell onto the rails, rolling clear of the car and into the grass at the side of the tracks.

Jumping up, Dan shrieked again, '*SarAHHH!*

As if in slow motion, Sarah turned to open her door. But the rust and the wear in that old ute held it tightly shut, trapping her inside as she pushed with all her weight against it. Unyielding, she pounded it with her hands. She was a prisoner in that cabin for a split second of truth.

The shrill scream of the train's warning whistle split the air, drowning Danny's voice.

'My side, Sarah. Get out *my side!*

Once.

The warning screeched.

Sarah looked up.

Twice.

The air ruptured with the ear-splitting siren.

Sarah threw herself across the cabin towards the open driver's door. Time stood still as she scrabbled, grabbing the driving wheel, hauling her body towards the outside. Her breath came in hot gasps as her legs kicked against the seat, propelling her sideways and forwards. Her face was a mask of concentration as she flung herself towards the freedom outside the car. Her blonde hair flew out before her, as if it too, could draw her more quickly to safety and away from the monster eating at her feet.

Her hands clawed at the sides of the door as she pushed herself half out of her death trap and for a split second, a look of absolute triumph flashed across her face as the third scream of annihilation was cut short.

A thousand tonnes of steel and metal filled the air; a crescendo of horrific sound warping out into that clear morning. Then the engine ploughed into Danny's old ute, ramming it along the tracks.

Silence filled the ether as Sarah's body catapulted up towards the sky. She seemed to reach into the heavens as she twisted and turned, angel's wings lifting her higher and higher, melting her physical form into a thousand butterfly tips that shone through her pure flaxen hair.

Above the wrecked car.

Above her brother as he screamed her name, over and over.

Then.

Sarah crashed to the ground, crumpling into a small, soft heap beside the railway track. Beside the crushed, twisted, burning metal of that dreadful fatal moment.

Danny knelt beside her on the ground, his body shaking violently, his hand reaching out to her, his face filled with terror and disbelief. Sarah lay motionless for a brief moment, a sweet golden light floating within her as her spirit hovered and pulsed. Her breath came in short, laboured gasps as her body tremored in her last moment.

Danny reached out, stroking her broken, twisted body. Convulsing and sobbing.

Then, gently, Sarah opened her eyes, smiled and whispered, 'Yer chicken breath, Danny-boy.'

~

My feet flew towards the forest, breath gasps of fire.

I staggered, spinning, falling. Picking myself up, my heart pounded like a huge drum, slamming against my chest, the bitumen grinding through my worn shoes. Angel's breath touched my cheek. Voices echoed within me. Shadows played at the edge of my mind.

Sarah was everywhere. Around. Within me. Holding me; pinpointing my focus on the trees in the distance. Branches reached out to me, pulling me into the thicket.

Somewhere, the forest took my shoes. My feet naked, I struggled towards the sound of water. Faerie laughter screamed in my ears as my toes met rock. Tripping, I fell, and for the second time in my life landed on the forest floor. Next to me a great torrent of water roared over the cliff's edge, the current snarling as I crawled towards it.

I reached out to God as I prayed for the water to carry me over its edge. My immortal spirit soared above its freezing spray as I fell upwards, a million times, willing my body to smash against the rock below, liberating my soul for a suspended moment to fly free. But I thudded to the earth, my body doubled over, gasping for air at the river's edge.

I clawed at myself, wanting to rip flesh from my body. To stop the pain. Snot, mud and tears smeared my face. My body writhed and thrashed as the air filled with the sound of my voice.

For every moment I had been raped and abused, cursed and tormented, my voice shrieked. For all the men that had looked at me with an intent that froze me, I screamed. For all my loneliness and abandonment, my voice pounded on the cliffs around me.

Not her.

Over and over.

NOT HER.

The shards of my life smashed against the escarpment surrounding me as I writhed on the forest floor, pleading with God to take me too. Death hovered around me, suffocating my breath, wrapping me in numbness. Slowly, the thundering in my ears faded to a soft hum that lifted me gently from my body.

Faeries danced around me. Sarah's face suffused my mind as she reached into me, caressing me with a touch that was filled with the sweetest, purest love. Heavenly music surrounded me as her angels wrapped me in a veil of protection.

Love you forever, Rosie-rose.

The sounds of the forest receded, and I blacked out.

~

I don't remember much of that terrible afternoon. My body huddled on the ground. I slipped in and out of awareness. Towards nightfall, I felt the touch of a familiar hand on my arm and the murmured tones of Sarah's father.

Half-conscious, I felt a warm flannel washing my face. Gentle, strong hands carefully cleaned my arms and legs. A rough rug was wrapped around me and a folded jumper placed under my head.

A mug of sweet black tea was pressed into my tightly clenched hands and my head held as the hot, sweet liquid ran down my throat and chin. I felt him sitting next to me, his strong arm around my shoulders, his body shaking in grief as he held me close. Firelight warmed my face as twilight dropped cooler air around us.

Slowly the warmth of the tea and the security of Dad's embrace brought me back to a numbed consciousness. I looked up at him as his face reflected the craggy rocks around us.

He had aged beyond description. Every line in his face carving massive gorges into wet cheeks. His eyes were swollen, tears poured from them. He had come to find me, knowing that this would have been the only place I could have fled to, to seek refuge. Where he knew that the faeries danced and played, and the angels of the forest would look after me.

He turned to me, wiping his cheeks with the back of his hand. His head bowed.

'Was an accident, lassie,' he whispered. 'Danny…' Giant sobs wracked his massive frame as shock rebounded within him.

Darkness filled the forest as small creatures scurried around us. Fireflies flitted, illuminating shadows against the cliff walls. The fire slowly dimmed into warming coals that cast unearthly light onto the trunks of the massive trees surrounding us. I could feel angel's wings whispering caresses as Sarah's faeries sat guarding our grief.

Dad finally stood up.

'Lassie,' he managed, 'we have to go now. Mim will be wanting to know yer safe,' he whispered. Reaching down, he helped me to my feet.

6

Brisbane, March 1988

ROSANNA sits, hunched forward, her face bathed in tears. Holding herself tightly. Arms circling her waist. Rocking back and forward. Soft moaning noises blend with her sobbing. Strands of her hair catch as she wipes her cheeks with the back of her hand.

I watch.

'And they say Jesus is a saviour,' she whispers.

Fate has dealt its cards. Paths that cross and separate, where those who are done leave, and those that need more time, stay. Her wound is profound, her grieving palpable. A tangible release of the anguish that has held tight her loss.

I sit immobilised as she weeps. My own tears sting as Rose's heart breaks mine open. Reaching forward, I lay her incomplete canvas at her feet and gently touch her arm. She looks up, startled, her eyes roaming my face. The fragile threads in the fabric of her psyche have met the rawness in her reality.

Her eyes are veiled in pain. I hold her arm more firmly.

'Rose. Can you see me?'

Rose blinks, sits up abruptly, pulls her arm from my touch.

'Rose. Do you know where you are?'

She looks at me, then slowly shakes her head.

'Rose?' I search. Her eyes are glazed.

'Yes,' she whispers. 'Yes?'

'Breathe, and look around.'

Rosanna's eyes roam my office, resting on the crystals and the books, traversing the terrain in this room that she has come to know so well.

'This is just so painful,' she whispers.

'I hear you,' I reply.

'I wanted to die. To take my life. Christian kept me going. It was like he had never lost her. Like she was still there to play with. He never let go of her. He still talks to her.' She holds her head. 'Like I do. She's still there. After all these years.'

She falters, wrapping her arms around herself again.

'Without him, I would have jumped. I just know I would have.'

'Rose,' I urge.

She reluctantly meets me, as she struggles to blink her illusion away.

'I just don't get why she had to go.' Her words catch in her throat. 'She was my only friend. The only person that really understood me. I look for her in so many people. In so many ways. I still see her every day. At night. In the shadows. With Chris. When he laughs. I can hear her voice in the sound of the wind. She's everywhere. I never understood why she died.'

She looks down at her art, confusion flitting across her features.

'Look at this. This is her, isn't it?' She draws the canvas to her. Diaphanous shapes with a luminescent atmosphere emanate from the abstruse marks and lines that cover the surface. Her finger hovers above a golden orb from which a linear arm and hand emerge.

'See. See! She's here. Here!'

She turns towards me, pleading.

'Anna. Do you think I needed her to die? Do you? Is that why I always paint her. To get over my guilt? Is it?'

~

Nimbin, 1976

In the days following Sarah's death, she was everywhere. Her laughter echoed in the babbling of the creek. At night, her voice whispered in the breeze. I felt her, holding me tightly as I sobbed, murmuring to me that it would eventually stop hurting.

She sat on the steps at The Store, grinning as I walked past. She danced and played with Christian in the garden as they giggled, chasing each other around my herb patch. She held Dad as he pleaded with God and she stroked Auntie Mims hair, brushing her eyes with her lips as she wept in the kitchen. She sat with Danny as he remained curled up on the couch, head in hands, mute to all, dry-eyed.

She danced up the stairs, singing at the top of her voice, and her golden hair streamed behind her as she sped across the bottom paddock towards the forest. She cuddled the little ones as they sat subdued on the veranda not touching their toys. And she leaned against the back of the couch, watching us all as we huddled there, together at night.

Over and over, she reassured us of her love. Whispering that she was okay. That we would get through it. She was a shimmering light in the ether, the softest butterfly beat in our hearts, the sweetest song in our thoughts and the gentlest caress in our souls.

I couldn't believe that she was gone. A forever lit candle that was my forever sister, extinguished in a horrific nightmare of error.

At night when I wasn't raging against God, I soaked my pillow with tears. Christian's small body climbed into our bed, stroking my face, his little boy kisses wetly placed on my pale drawn cheeks.

I tried to explain to Christian that his favourite Auntie had gone to heaven. But he knew Sarah was with the faeries in the bottom of Dad's garden. That the leprechauns were looking after her. After dinner, Dad and Auntie Mim insisted that we sit on the large couch beside the fire to read poetry, stories, and the Bible together.

Dan remained a silent ghost who followed his father everywhere. Dad said nothing, but his eyes welled as he looked at Dan, a pain I could not bear to watch. He reached out to him, patting the couch next to him and Dan would settle on the floor at his father's feet, arms hugging knees to chest, his head bowed. Dad's huge hands rested on his son's shoulders, not a word passing between them.

Sometimes I found Dad talking to himself as he tended his vegetables. Unaware of my presence, he called to God to give him strength, to forgive him for not tuning the old ute and for his inability to bring Sarah back to life. He dried his eyes and squared his shoulders before returning to his family. But the tell-tale greying in his beard spoke of his inner torment.

Auntie Mim's kitchen continued to nurture us with her loving meals, her tears mixed with the baked bread and casseroles. Sometimes the milk turned sour, for no other reason than her grief. Our garden continued to produce zucchinis, pumpkins and potatoes for our table and, at night, the glow in the corner of the herb patch told us that the leprechauns and Sarah's faeries had set up watch over us.

~

I hadn't visited the *Sista-Shed* since Sarah's death. But late one afternoon about a month after the accident, my feet were drawn to the railway siding.

It was early evening as I walked down the deserted path. Silvery tracks guided me in the twilight as they had before when we had crept out for late night feasts. The darkening forest cast long shadows over the railway line. As I approached, the smell of smoke scented the air. A flickering light from inside the shed warned me that someone was there.

Peeking through the window, I saw a huddled shape. Danny was hunched on our lounge. Through the streaks of dirt on the window, I could see tears coursing down his cheeks. Gently pushing the wooden door open, I watched him.

He didn't look up as I stood there, waiting for a sign.

Closing the door and securing it with the brick, I crept over and lowered myself onto the couch next to him.

The dancing light of the fire cast eerie shadows on the walls. Warmth and silence surrounded me, except for the crackle of the fire and the soft hissing of wood burning. The billy boiled gently on the side of the hearth. Danny's eyes were closed for such a long time, I thought he was asleep. The couch creaked as I got up to prepare tea for us. Cracked cups and saucers with faded patterns of yellow and green daisies sat neatly on a makeshift shelf. I popped the lid of the tea caddy open and measured grainy black leaves into the billy.

'I like mine weak and black, Rose,' Danny whispered.

He was looking straight at me, his dishevelled hair hanging in tight copper ringlets to his shoulders. He looked so much like Dad.

'Sarah always put too much tea in my cup,' he murmured. 'Brewed it too strong.'

I quickly made the tea, handing it to him without speaking and sat down next to him, struck with shyness.

It was then I noticed his hands on a small doll. An exquisite hand-crocheted lace shawl encircled her shoulders. She had a chequered apron, cross-stitched in the finest silk pattern. Her teal dress was embroidered cream and pink roses. She wore tiny felt shoes, buckles fashioned from the lightest wood and heels made of cork. Fine hand-knitted woollen stockings adorned her legs. Her hair was a mass of blonde curls, tied back with a woollen scarf. Her eyes were emerald green and her soft stitched smile lit up her face. Her cheeks were worn and rouged with pastel pink. She carried the smallest woven cane basket with crimson stitched berries in it.

I had never seen such a beautiful figurine in my life. Danny's fingers traced her hair and face as if she were a real woman, young and beautiful.

'She couldn't get out, Rose.'

Words lodged in his throat, sounded like the rasping notes of death. My heart pounded as the nightmare within me sounded its warning to flee. I began to shake, spilling my tea.

Danny placed his hand on my arm for the first time in the six years I had known him. His energy flooded me as I looked at him. His face was a mask of anguish. His deep-set blue eyes, infinite pools into which I fell, tumbling over. Time stood still in that awakening moment of unity.

'It was a dare, Rose,' he whispered. 'She dared me.'

He wept, softly at first, then with a desperation that shook me. As the fire crackled and the kettle hummed, our tears merged. Danny drew me to him, holding me against his slender muscular frame, entwining his body with mine. We held onto each other on our Sista couch.

I must have dozed off as it was dark when I realised that he was not next to me. Sitting up, I watched as he stoked the fire. Bright hot sparks leapt as he poured the tea and brought it to the couch.

He sat next to me, taking my hand, reaching out to lightly stroke my face. His touch was gentle. Filled with his family's love.

The soft hue of Sarah's smile shimmered before me.

...It's okay, Rose Petal...

Finally, Danny spoke.

'Can I tell yer, Rose? What happened?' he murmured.

I nodded, silently taking my tea from his hands.

~

The fire warmed us as the night settled around the *Sista-Shed*, chilled air seeping under the door. The candle flickered as the moon rose outside, casting a silvery glow through the dusty window.

Danny spoke softly, his voice cracking, his shoulders stooped.

Why did he stop the ute?

Why did she dare him?

He pleaded with me to forgive him as he paced the floor, berating himself. I sat still, listening to the sorrow pouring from him. Sarah waited within me, crooning her favourite lullaby. Telling me it was time for Dan to speak.

We slept on and off, curled into each other, finding strength in our closeness. In the middle of the night, I became aware of the soft fall of thick blankets across our bodies and the gentle fleeting touch of Auntie Mim's hand on my shoulder. Murmuring 'sweet lassie,' she quietly slipped out of the door, closing it behind her. Later she told me that she knew we would be there together. She had stood outside, listening to Danny's muffled voice. Then returned home for the blankets to keep us warm, some supplies to keep us fed, her eyes filled with tears of relief that her son had finally found his voice.

I awoke in the grey light of dawn, alone under the blankets. Danny squatted by the fire, stoking it back to life as the billy began to simmer.

He stood with his back to me, opening the flour tin and taking a cracked bowl from the shelf. I watched silently as he mixed flour with water to make dough, kneading and pounding it on the wooden bench. Then taking our cooking stick from its place beside the fire, he wrapped the dough around it in a long sausage shape, covering the end of the thick twig with a thin layer of damper.

Leaning back towards the fire, he began to toast it, slowly rotating it to an even brown. Only when the sweet smell of cooking bread filled the shed did I realise how hungry I was. When the damper was baked golden, Danny pulled it off the stick and filled the centre of the cylinder with jam and cream. Auntie Mim's visit the night before had also supplied these ingredients for our breakfast.

Placing it on a clean but stained floral plate Danny turned to me. His face was completely different from the night before. His eyes were steeped with sadness, replacing the impenetrable mask of before. His brow was furrowed in the middle, his cheeks pale against his tan. He watched me tenderly, the corners of his beautiful mouth turned slightly downwards.

'Mum must have come in last night,' he said. 'Or the faeries have been busy.' He managed a smile. 'Here lassie, this'll warm yer belly,' he said, handing me the plate.

As I bit into the crisp hot bread, the warmed cream mixed with Auntie Mim's sweet home-made strawberry jam and trickled down my throat. Danny turned back to his task, silently preparing another for himself. I ate slowly, not wanting to disturb the tenuous feeling of hope hanging in the air. Fixing a pot of tea and filling his plate with hot damper, Dan sat on the couch.

Finally, he put down his plate, wiping his face on an old tea-towel. Reaching into his pocket, he turned to me. In his palm was the beautiful doll I had seen him holding the night before. He looked at it, his hands motionless now as he held it.

'This was to be for Sarah,' he murmured. 'Great Aunt Elsie made it for her. To be a gift on her eighteenth.' He trailed off, gathering courage to go on. 'She had no daughters. So, when we was little, Sah was like her own,' he went on.

'Aunt Elsie made dolls. Just like this one. Sold them in the local shop back home. She sent this one out when we were kids. Mum kept it 'til...' His voice trailed away to a whisper as his fingertip traced the doll's cloth cheek. Looking up at me, pain etching his blue eyes, he held it out to me.

'Tis for you now, lassie,' he whispered. 'It's you who's the closest thing to her.' Taking my hand, he laid the exquisite doll in my palm. Speechless, I looked at him as he closed my fingers around the doll's waist.

'She loved yer like a sister, Rose. She'd want it this way,' he said, reaching out to stroke my cheek.

'I have to go away now,' he continued. 'To the city. To find work like. I can't stay here. She's everywhere, lassie.' He bowed his head. 'I'll never forgive myself.'

I watched him as he set his shoulders and stood. Taking my hand, he helped me to my feet. Drawing me close, he hugged me.

'I love yer, Rose,' he said. Placing his hands on my shoulders, he kissed my cheek.

And then, Sarah's gentle whisper filled my mind.

Forever sista, breathed a soft melody into my heart as words began to fall from me, tripping over each other.

'Danny, don't blame yourself. There was nothing you could have done. It wasn't your fault. Sah was like that. You know that she always loved to live at the edge. It was her way. If she had to go…' My voice choked. 'It's how she would have wanted to die. She gave me this, Danny. When I was going to my last exam. Just hours before…'

I took out the small stone wrapped in hand-embroidered, pale pink silk. On it were Sarah's and my initials and the words *Forever Sistas* stitched across its shiny surface. I unravelled the cloth to reveal a perfect round rose-quartz crystal, with two tiny flecks of purple in it. It was warm from being so close to my body.

'You know that she had the gift. She told me two days before she died that she had seen angels hovering. Over our bed. At night. Said she could hear heavenly music playing. She told me she felt so happy. She knew she was going to die, Danny. You couldn't have stopped her,' I whispered.

He paused. Then, he reached out and took my hands. His gaze flew into me as the yearning in my heart met his, entwining us together.

You'll always be a part of me, Rose… His voice echoed as my tears blurred the clarity of his face.

'I'm scared, Dan. Of him. Of what to do…' I stopped, not able to go on.

Danny wrapped me in his arms as I hugged him with a fierceness. I rested my head on his chest; his heartbeat a great drum that repeated its cadence of love, reassuring me with each beat.

'When yer finished school, Rose lassie, come to the city. I will look after yer. I'll wait for yer,' he murmured. 'And if your Pa does anything, go upstream. Tell Dad. I'll find you.'

He kissed me on the mouth with a softness that held my heart still. Placing Auntie Elsie's figurine back into my hand, next to Sarah's last gift, he caressed my cheek once more and disappeared out the door.

~

We took Dan to the local bus stop. Dad shook his hand and hugged him tightly, whispering in his ear, then stood back as he made him promise to call every Sunday. Auntie Mim bustled around, handing him a bag full of her home-made baking, fresh jam and boysenberries. She clung to him, kissing him and gazing into his face.

'Tell me, Danny-boy, that yer gonna be okay,' she said. 'Yer sure 'tis what yer want?' she asked, her face wet with tears.

'Yeah, Mum,' he said. 'I need to go away for a while. On my own, like. Can make a quid up there in the big smoke. I'll send ya back some dosh. And I'll call yer every week. Promise.'

Auntie Mim held his hands.

'I'll be back at Christmas for sure,' he said, kissing her.

Then he turned to me as they fussed over his bags. Taking me gently in his arms, holding me close, he murmured, 'Remember, Rose Petal, Sah and I will look out for yer.'

His lips grazed my cheek as he picked up his backpack and clambered onto the bus. I could see him in the back seat as he held up a hand to wave goodbye.

Over the ensuing weeks, I concentrated on my last assignments for the year, Sarah's absence a lead weight in my heart. Danny's confession had shaken me to the core. My mind was filled with her death.

Her shadow followed me everywhere.

The *Sista-Shed* remained locked and empty. A relic of my past. In the aftermath of that night with Dan and in his absence, my voice became silent. Not even the phone ringing to announce his Sunday calls could entice me.

~

As December ripened into the festive season of '76, Dad insisted we get on with life, continuing as Sarah would have wished. With Christian's explanation that *Auntie Tha* lived in the bottom of our garden, our lives began to return to a new kind of normal.

Dad started another vegetable garden to help the faeries look after our hearth. He needed my assistance to gather manure and mulch and to plant out his seedlings. Despite the heartache that wrapped our home, filtering out the sunlight and turning down the temperature, our garden flourished.

Our home was festooned with the love and creativity of Sarah's family as Auntie Mim baked. Rich, moist Christmas cakes appeared overnight, filled with nuts and glazed fruit, then poured over with a goodly ladle of rum to be left for the soaking until Christmas Eve.

The little ones emerged from the kitchen, faces smeared with chocolate from making their favourite Mars Bars Christmas crackles. Glazed fruit puddings wrapped in soft muslin cloth began to fill Mim's cupboards. Hand rolled truffles with the delicate aroma of vanilla and cinnamon stacked the empty cake tins and despite her protests, were eaten with gusto by her family. Sarah's favourite fruit mince pies were delights that sweetened our hearts.

Dad fashioned a beautiful floral wreath for the front door and Christian and I accompanied him to the pine forest to cut the Christmas tree.

'Just to do a wee bit of weed control for da council.' He smiled.

Christian found Sarah's favourite papier-mâché angel and sitting atop Dad's shoulders, carefully placed it on the tip of the tree.

'For Auntie Tha,' he declared.

Mim pulled out the cloves and the orange whisky marmalade to glaze the ham and prepared the chicken broth for the turkey. The larder was stocked with lemonade and oranges for the shandy and Dad raided the cellar for red wine and white rum.

As Christmas day drew closer, Auntie Mim kept a careful eye on the garden to ensure that the raspberry canes and the red berries that festooned the strawberry hillocks were ready. And the lights from the faerie lanterns twinkled from beneath the bushes, bringing comfort to our aching hearts.

After supper, we sat around the dining table, cutting silver foil and cellophane snowflakes for the windows. We twisted handmade party crackers wrapped in bright ribbon, tied with brown string. When the little ones had gone to bed, I sat silently helping Auntie Mim and Dad write Christmas cards. And once the day was done, they knelt close together at the side of their bed praying; silent tears streaming down their cheeks.

~

Nimbin, 15th December 1977

The Store's oak front doors slammed heavily behind me. I placed the key into the large copper keyhole and turned it. A satisfying clunk signalled the internal bolt sliding into place, securing the shop.

I'd worked late, oblivious of time as my mind and body buzzed with the pleasure of a job done well. Rows of produce and tools had been counted and sorted. Shelving tidied and cleaned. Christian sorted and stacked, singing to himself.

Finally, the ordering system added up and my tasks were complete for an early start the following morning. It was the nagging of my small hungry son for dinner that alerted me to the lateness of the hour.

Sarah's family were due back the next morning, after a camping trip to Surfers Paradise. It had been their first holiday since Sarah's death. I had wanted to go with them, but Dad asked me if I would look after The Store. I was overwhelmed with the trust he bestowed upon me by inviting me to take on such an important job. Dad understood more than anyone else my need for acknowledgement.

The excitement and challenge of looking after The Store had nurtured my confidence. My success over-shadowed my anxiety of being left alone without them.

Where's Chris? I thought.

Bending over to collect my parcels, I mused at how Christian could know so much about The Store. He was completely at home here. He had a photographic memory, especially for what lined his favourite shelves. Product was identified by colour, shape and markings. Boxes were emptied of goods and carefully put into their correct places. New items were piled on the floor next to shelving that was too high for him to reach. And inevitably I would find him babbling nonsensically and excitedly as he skipped and danced. Names and orders were of little trouble and customers were regaled with poems and songs. He incessantly asked them how they were or why they were there or what they wanted.

The hippies were his favourite. Our village was divided by

prejudice and there were some who refused to greet or speak to us. This was water off a duck's back to Chris, but at times I noted that his body would become uncharacteristically still. As if in the edges of his memory he had met with intense sadness. These moments always banished my hard-earned happiness, and I would cradle my son close to my breasts to shelter him from what he could never possibly understand.

Turning out onto the darkened street, I called to him as he hopped around the potholes, kicking small pebbles and sticks.

'C'mon, Chris,' I exclaimed, 'it's time to go home for supper. You hungry?' I asked.

He skipped towards me.

'Mumma, I wan' toast 'n vegemite 'n milo 'n peechas 'n cweem 'n toast 'n vegie 'n cweem,' he sang, dancing around me, tugging at my bag.

The cadence in his voice reminded me of Sarah. My heart skipped a beat, my breath caught in my chest. I smiled as I squatted next to him, holding out the cloth bag that I had filled with leftover bread, a glass pot of vegemite, a big tin of peaches and a super-sized can of milo.

We were both looking forward to a supper shared together after our long day of work.

Grabbing the bag from me, Christian skipped off up the deserted street, into the semi-darkness towards the far end of town. As I walked after him, my thoughts rested on that old, loving home with its huge bullnose veranda. In my mind's eye, I saw our tangled garden that fed us our every meal. Where the faeries lighted our path home and where Christian had found them in the corners of the raspberry canes as a toddler. Where shelter and nurture had been mine through the biggest of storms. And where love had taught me to feel safe.

I watched him as he played in his stride, arms swinging my bag from one side of the street to the other. The weight of it had little effect on the pace at which he moved.

'Wait for me, Chris. Be careful with our supper.'

Pulling up next to him, I grabbed his hand and reaching over, took the bag. He smiled up at me twinkling.

'Okay, Mumma. You're the boss.'

We giggled as the lights of the town dimmed behind us.

~

The semi-trailer ground to a halt at the crossroads north of Nimbin. The young man sitting in the passenger seat turned to the driver.

'Thanks for the lift, mate,' he said, shaking his hand.

'No worries, son. Anytime ya need help, gimme a yell. Sorry I couldn't take ya into town. I'm too big.' He grinned as the heavy passenger door swung open. 'And here. Take the rest,' he added, handing him a bag of pies.

'Ya gonna need it on that long walk, ay?' the truckie grinned. 'Good luck with that girl of yours.'

Dan smiled.

'Yeah. The walk will clear my head. It's good to be coming home. Been a while.'

Grabbing his backpack, he clambered down the steel ladder, dropping effortlessly to the edge of the road.

'See ya!' he yelled as the engine roared and the massive vehicle swung back onto the road, disappearing into the dark in a cloud of dust.

High up in the truckie's cabin, the kilometres had passed easily. In the full moonlight the east coast had been a picturesque landscape of darkening shadows and rolling hills outlined in silvery light. The ever-changing vista a reflection of tumultuous moods hidden within his heart. The Tweed River shone like a black mirror, its currents flowing strong towards the ocean

Danny hauled his bag onto his back and stood taking in the warm night air. The stars twinkled above, and the moonlight filled the trees with shadows. He heard the cry of a mopoke in the distance, this haunting call alerting him to the scurry of small feet in the bushes beside the road. The cattle in the fields raised their heads, gently chewing on their cud and watching him, their doe-like eyes filled with peace.

For Dan, the scent and freshness of the air was home. A place where his heart rested, even though contradictory patterns of happiness and regret gnawed at his soul. He stretched and massaged his lower spine. It was a long walk south to town. Over the old bridge and past the Butter Factory before turning onto the road east to home.

He had made a last-minute decision that night to hitch. Uni was done for the week and the trip home, a four-hour truck ride. It was a surprise visit. To see Rosanna. Mum and Dad were due back the next day and he wanted a night to be with her.

To tell her.

Before his family arrived.

His dug his hands into his pockets and whistling a tune stepped off the verge and onto the bitumen, striding homewards.

~

The full moon cast shadows on the road illuminating large potholes and sharp turrets from the flow and weight of the recent rain, channelled into the gutters.

I knew this path like the back of my hand. Christian's footfall carried him forward confidently. He too had walked its rough-shod surface every day and knew his way with the confidence of a small child, secure that he was on his way home.

The warmth that flowed through me as we walked together was a blanket of contentment. Life felt good. The shadows of my past and the always pain in my heart had dimmed. I was glowing with exhilaration from the honour at being the sole proprietor, book keeper, stockist and cashier for The Store for nine days.

I couldn't wait to talk to Dad.

The house stood alone at the end of the street. As we skipped around the corner, I could see the outline of the bullnose veranda. A dim glow shone through the windows where rays from the kitchen light escaped.

I had left the back door open and a light on as I knew that we would be home late. We followed the garden path around the side of the house and as we turned towards the back steps, Christian let go of my hand and scampered towards his destination.

It was then that I heard it.

The low scraping sound of a chair being pushed backwards froze me in my tracks. The raw stench of alcohol and cigarettes filled my nostrils. My senses warped up and out. Over the veranda railing. Into the darker recesses of the back porch, feeling the danger that lurked audibly in the shadows.

My skin crawled with the icy hand of doom as my breath came in short bursts.

Faerie lights dimmed their caution in the corner of the garden and in the distance the hoot of the mopoke owl called its warning. The moonlight waned as clouds gathered above me, hiding my face in sudden darkness as the heat in the night amplified to a furnace in my mind.

Silently, I reached forward for my son.

'Chris,' I breathed. 'Christian. Stop. Come here,' I whispered urgently.

Hesitating, my son looked back up at me, his first foot on the bottom step, his babbling cut short mid-breath as he read the warning in my voice. In two paces I had him by the hand, tugging him behind me, sheltering his body with mine.

He clung to the back of my legs, silent in the dark, feeding off my adrenaline. My right hand wrapped round the straps of the bag containing our dinner. The other reached back, holding Christian behind me, my touch warning him of imminent peril.

My breath stopped mid inhale. My body immobile as I waited, suspended in that moment of time.

~

The moon dipped behind clouds as Danny approached the last kilometres before The Butter Factory. An eerie stillness slowed his steps. In the distance a curlew called, its cry a melody of prophecy. Dan lifted his face to the sky. The wind had dropped and the clouds shielded him from the night. Pausing, he waited on the edge of the deserted road, many kilometres before the old bridge. His nostrils opened as he scented the air. Then, dismissing his thoughts, he shrugged his shoulders and swung his backpack to the ground. He squatted in the dirt at the edge of the road opening his bags and pulling out one of the warm pies. Chewing slowly, his thoughts turned to his family.

He hadn't been home for a year. The big city had consumed his life. Jobs and university absorbed his time with a colour and shape that formed a shield against the aftermath of Sarah's death.

He had called every Sunday. And the last Christmas had been the best ever. His family hadn't needed his earnings so he had set up home in Brisbane. The Whitlam government had given him liberty to study free of charge.

It had been a good year.

Hmm. Dad's right. Funny how time has a way.

He relaxed into his meal.

Of making things clearer.

~

The chair scraped again and the loose timber boards on the veranda creaked as a heavy weight landed. The night air burnt my nostrils as I held my breath, inching backwards. Chris against my legs. My heart, a drum of fear, beat uncontrollably under my ribs.

Out of the shadows on top of the steps, a dishevelled shape lurched towards us, stopping to lean on the railing at the top of the descent. I could just make out an unshaven face, heavy set features and long unkempt hair. The reek of alcohol rolled over the railing, spilling towards us; a menacing tsunami of danger.

Pa smirked down at me.

'Wal,' he drawled. 'If it isn't Rosanna.' His voice belched fumes of whiskey and beer.

I slowly released my breath. Pushing Christian backwards, I inched towards the side of the house, my feet feeling for the garden edge.

Dad's shovel... where is it?

My eyes sought the darkness for a weapon. For an instant, my mind was crystal clear.

Run, Rose, RUN!

Danny's whisper echoed in my brain.

I hesitated, steadying my breath, focusing my body for flight.

Then, that hidden child's voice tugged at my instinct, halting me. Echoing my lifetime's desperate bid for peace.

If I talk to him, maybe he'll leave.

'What do you want, Pa?' I asked, my voice even and low as I took another step backward, Chris gripping my legs.

Don't show him your fear, Rose.

'Aw Rosanna. Don' be like that,' he leered. 'Just come to say hallo. Wanna see the boy, don' I?' His thick voice was putrid with liquor.

'Ain't ya pleased to see me?' he whined, taking a heavy step down the stairs.

My mind raced as thoughts tumbled over each other.

Why is he here? Why is he out of jail?

Danger hung like a choking shroud over me, my legs heavy with horror. Here in the darkness was my most formidable foe. I was alone. Out of earshot of any neighbour. Mim and Dad's protective embrace absent in some sick joke of fate. In that realisation, from the bottomless pit of my suffering at this man's hand, a call for survival churned within me.

I skirted the corner of the house, Christian behind me.

'Don't want to see you, Pa,' I said, my voice thick with dread.

He sneered.

'Ree-lly?' Staggering down the last two steps, he swayed in the moonlight. 'Ya shud never lie. Not ever, girlie. Shud ya?'

Pa stepped towards us.

'Ya been at that shop. On ya own… aven't ya. Where's ma suppa, uh?' His eyes narrowed. 'Ya forgot ma cookies. Didn't ya. Yer just a selfish little bitch, aren't ya.' His voice dropped to a snarl.

My feet reached the edge of the house, my concentration pinpointed on the massive shape lurching towards me. Out of the corner of my eye I could see the twinkle of the village lights at the far end of the street.

Swiftly, Pa lurched towards me, clutching at my arm.

I leapt backwards, spinning on the spot, propelling Christian and myself towards the street.

'Run, Chris!' I screamed, gripping his arm as I sprung toward the front gate. *RUN!*'

~

It was well past midnight when Danny's footfall paused on the old bridge out of town. He leaned on the balustrade, looking at the water below. The Butter Factory formed a dark silhouette against the trees. Shadowy shapes played in the corners of his eyes.

Twenty minutes and I'm home.

Straightening, he turned to go when a soft whispering floated around him.

Christian?!

He paused. Straining to hear.

But a sudden cool breeze blew the voice past him. He shook his head and reaching down, shrugged his backpack onto his shoulders, the pie bag swinging from his wrist.

A solitary old man staggered out of the alleyway past the pub in town and reached up to him. A filthy hand begged for sustenance. Dan paused, handed him the pie bag and reaching into his pocket, emptied the last coins into his palm.

~

Christian's face was a mask of terror. Paralysed, he stumbled, sprawling out onto the path. My feet stopped dead beneath me, caught up under his body. Tripping, I somersaulted over him, landing on my side in the rough pebbles of Dad's path.

In one rapid movement Pa had me in his grimy clutch, ripping me up and off the ground, twisting my arm, digging his fingers into my hair, tearing at my skull. I shrieked in agony as a searing pain dug into my head.

'Run!' I screamed to Christian, '*RUN, Chris!*' But my son cowered on the ground, immobilised, uncomprehending.

A vice clamped itself around me, sucking the breath out of my lungs, clenching me against steeled muscle and a stinking sweat-soaked body.

Pa pinned my arm hard up behind my back.

'Let go of me.' I gasped. 'Let *GO!*'

Flailing wildly, my legs lashed out at his body, my free arm beating uselessly at him.

Pa dragged me backwards towards the rear of the house, cursing. One of his arms circled my chest, crushing me to him. The other hand punched at me. Steel fingers locked into my hair, twisting my neck sideways towards the ground. Struggling and kicking, my body wrenched and turned in his grip.

My teeth found his arm and I bit down fiercely into foul, fetid skin, blood filling my mouth. He howled in pain and momentarily his grip loosened. Kicking back violently, my feet found the rubbery flesh in his crotch as we crashed heavily to the pavers at the edge of the garden.

Pa doubled over, holding his groin, roaring like a bull.

Winded, I couldn't move. Sprawled out on the ground at the bottom of the back steps, I gasped for breath.

Christian screamed hysterically in the background, 'Mumm*AAA … AARMAHH…*'

Pa's hollering snapped into silence. Turning, he looked back at the huddled shape of my son pressed into a crouch against the wall of the house. Out of the corner of my eye I saw him straighten, turn and reel towards Christian, his fist raised.

'Ya fuckin… little… bastard.' Hatred filled the ether.

Fury ripped through me. A ferocious, annihilating rage consuming my agony, focusing my mind and driving me upright.

In one swift movement, I leapt to my feet and threw myself onto his back, wrapping my body around him. Clamping my ankles together, I dug the hard-steel capped heels of my work boots into his belly. Seizing his head in my fists, I jabbed my fingers into his eyes.

Pa screamed and jolted, spinning on the spot, grappling at my fingers, trying to dislodge me. I clung on with every sinew of my body, my hands and heels digging into him. And in the thundering darkness, as my son's anguish filled the air, a wild violent war cry erupted from within me. The screaming roar of the mother lioness against a deadly foe summoned my warrior leprechauns from the garden.

They rose up to protect us. With their swords slung from their hips, their helmets of gold and beards afire, they rushed at us, as I rode the back of the bucking, howling, roaring, flesh-eating dragon.

They threw themselves at his feet, grabbing his ankles. And they tripped Pa.

Fair and square.

And flung him backwards.

He caught his heel on the lowest step and came crashing down on his side, smashing his head on a concrete pillar. The fall knocked my breath away as Pa lay motionless, semi-conscious, half on top of me. Moaning, he opened his eyes, spittle running down his chin, blood gushing from the wounds in his head, his eyes scratched and gored.

'Ya… *fucking… whore*,' he gasped.

I scrabbled out from under him and staggered to my feet, pushing myself away from him. My lungs hurt like knives sticking into my chest and I bent double trying to breathe. Pa swayed to his knees and grabbed for my legs.

'Fuckin bitch… *cunt*.' He shrieked as I eluded his grasp. 'I'm gonna *kill* ya.'

Fire ate at my nightmare as survival and the demon of revenge bit into me. I spun away from him. Grabbing my bag, I wrapped it around my hand. Swinging it high above me, I brought it, full strike, down onto the side of his head.

A sickening, thudding crunch of glass and metal against skull bone filled the air.

Everything went completely still as Pa stopped dead in his tracks.

He looked at me, his eyes glazed and unfocused, then a strange sound gurgled out of his throat as he sank to his hands onto the ground before me. His gashed eyes rolled into the back of his head as he lurched face forward into the dirt of the garden bed and went absolutely still, blood soaking through his hair and pooling on the cement.

My weapon lay on the ground next to him. Glass shards from the vegemite jar pierced the cloth and stuck out of his head. The bent and mangled tin of peaches rolled out onto the earth beside him, and the air reverberated with the appalling, absolute hush of death.

~

The night surrounded me with silence as I bent double, gasping for breath, watching Pa for any signs of life. The moonlight flickered and dimmed, shadows dancing and receding into the black night sky. The air was still and close.

The warrior leprechauns watched from the side path, their faces impenetrable, their hands on the hilts of their swords, the battle done.

There was no sound anywhere except the rasping of my breath and the convulsive sobbing of my child. I waited for what seemed like an eternity on Dad's path to see if Pa would move. But he lay motionless. Face down in the dirt. Completely still. His huge, hairy, stinking body, a rotting disease-infested fallen tree in our forest.

My heart pounded as I slowly caught my breath, my mind grappling with what I had just done. I shook my head, trying to clear my thoughts, holding my sides as I struggled to steady the shock. Then, the enormity of what had happened hit me. I dropped to my knees, dry retching into the soft earth.

The moon disappeared behind the clouds and in the distance the curlews repeated their calls, eerie mournful tones that sent waves of crippling fear through me.

Then my heart broke, shattering into a million splinters of glass as I shook uncontrollably.

Why, WHY? I wept with disbelief.

And in the thundering of the locomotive and in the cataclysm of that night, I realised that there was only one thing I could do now.

Deep within me, Sarah's spirit stirred.

Rose, she whispered, *Rose Petal.*

Golden locks bounced as butterfly breath caressed my cheek. Her voice sighing soft within me.

Courage. Take courage. Fly sista. Fly.

And melded into Sarah's silken tones, the deeper timbre of Danny's voice.

Go upstream. I will find you.

I turned and stumbled towards my son where he lay cowering on the ground. Gently, I bent towards him, surrounding his body with my arms, pulling him to me. He held me fiercely, convulsive sobbing wracking his small frame.

'It's alright, Chris. It's all right,' I soothed. 'It's going to be okay.'

Tears drenched my face as I shuddered against the sudden cold of the night. Crooning and murmuring, I rocked Christian until his shaking settled.

Pa lay still on the ground close by.

'Come to me, my darling,' I whispered. 'We have to go now.'

Carefully lifting him, I swung him onto my back and turning, staggered out onto the road moving painfully and slowly away from the only home I'd ever known. Away from the love of my true family, the garden that had healed and inspired me and the memories of laughter and joy.

With the hand of my ancestors guiding my step, I carried my shaking son out into the night.

~

There were secrets in the shallow dells of clear water that reflected the footprint of the faeries. The scamper of little feet behind the trunks echoed sweet melodies of harps.

I could hear whispers in the trees as the forest bent to the night. Voices from the past, calling me from the centre of my consciousness. Where darkness and light reflected confusion in my mind. Where the present extended each moment as blood throbbed in my ears. And where events that were never meant to be, stayed attached to the deepest parts of me.

This is the landscape of your death… the voices boomed as I climbed deeper into the virgin rainforest.

My son clung to my back. My feet found the steady points on an unseen path as agony spun a web of resistance in my body and mind.

Christian was a dead weight, singing softly to me, his voice urging me on.

On the third day, the pain in my body stopped, blanketed with a numbness that replaced the searing jolt of broken bones. The sharp knife that had accompanied each breath dissolved into euphoric delusion, welcoming the icy water every time I slipped into the river.

Images blurred through my swollen eye.

At night the temperature dropped close to freezing. We found caves and hollow logs in which to curl our bodies. Thick bark from the eucalyptus and feathery fronds of ferns kept us warm. Folded in my arms, Christian shivered uncontrollably. I wrapped him in my jeans and pulled him tight into me, sheltering his body with mine, the fever in my temples keeping us warm.

As Christian lay whimpering, Danny's voice called to me. Telling me to keep going. Sarah's faeries played their flutes, lulling me into comatose, dreamless sleep.

During the day, Chris found his energy and following his keen sight, we crawled through hollows where the forest looked impenetrable. He clambered up and over huge logs pointing our way forward. I laboured with him over slippery boulders at the edges of the precipitous waterfalls. And prayed with every moment that we could keep going.

On the fourth day I awoke from dark dreams where an unforgettable voyage into a world of fantasy and light buoyed me up above the dark, freezing dawn. The lightest touch of Christian's small finger on my eyelid alerted me to my body curled up in a dank cave. His gaunt, filthy face looked intensely into mine.

'Umma. You okay?' he gently asked.

My mind floated into his words as they distorted into a blur, his face swimming before me.

'Mumma?' His voice drew me back to the numbing pain of my body, resting on our bed of leaves.

'I'm hunwee,' he murmured. 'You said Danny would give us food.'

'Yes, Chris,' I managed. 'We'll find it soon. Are you ready to go?'

As we struggled through the impenetrable forest, the voices from my past began to hum and catch me at the edges of my mind's eye. My soul pleaded for forgiveness, to understand the part that I played in death. To feel the promised joy of life liberated from the shackles of abuse. I saw Pa sitting in the dark, waiting for me. His vulture's breath burnt my nostrils. I felt his body as it had crushed mine and the nightmare of that life spun around in my mind.

Don't give up, Rose. Danny's voice softly urged me onwards.

In the middle of the fifth day my legs gave way beneath me and together we collapsed onto the forest floor. Christian crawled to me, too weak to walk. He rested his little head on my shoulder. A single spider wove its web in the sunlight as warmth seeped into me.

'Umma. It's okay,' he whispered. 'We rest here now. We wait for Danny.'

I nodded as unconsciousness called me. Struggling with the sweet lure of golden light that hovered around us, I breathed, 'Chris. Don't let me sleep.'

Through closing eyes, I looked up into a sky so blue that the sunlight blinded me and warmed my face as I rested in the soft earth.

The clouds scudded with white, fluffy shapes.

A soft smile began on Christian's lips as I watched my body drifting.

'Umma. There's a horse up there,' he murmured.

My eyelid flickered open. The billowing clouds had turned brown. Columns of smoke rose high above us, a chariot of horse-drawn carriages raced across the heavens. The smell of fire woke my senses, jolting me into reality as the deep, wild undying call of a life yet to be lived cried from within me.

Get up, Rose. Get UP. You must not give in to this. Its voice boomed into my semi-consciousness.

Do not desert him. DO NOT!

And the warrior leprechauns from Dad's garden stepped out from behind the trees, hands on their hips, their eyes ablaze with a love so fierce that my heart burst open, as the trauma of my life fled into a future of hope.

They pulled me to my feet. They lifted Chris and draped his feather-light weight across my shoulders. They placed a blanket of green around us, spun from gossamer and interlaced with determination.

They took my hand. Energy suffused my bones, knitting them together as the lead in my legs transformed into the lightest wings of angels.

And they drew me forward. Out of that forest and away from the pain of my past.

Brisbane, March 1988

THE room is still as I sit watching Rosanna, her profile backlit by dusk light. She stares out the window, motionless. Her chest rises and falls gently, her hands are folded neatly in her lap and her full skirt drapes her knees. The ringlets of her dark hair hang lightly to her shoulders.

There is a pulse in the air that beats with the rhythm of her heart. A sadness turns the corners of her full mouth. Her stockinged feet rest on the soft brocade cushion.

I quietly stand to prepare her tea.

When I return her hands are in front of her face, her fingers playing with the crystal light. I watch her carefully. Waiting. Observing the ebb and flow of her energy.

'I want to talk about the faeries,' she starts.

'Sure,' I reply as we settle into her session.

'I've been meditating.'

'That's good to hear,' I respond.

'Yeah. It seems to help. A bit.' She picks up the crystal she's chosen from the shelves.

'In what way?' I ask.

'It sorta makes me calmer. Rin reckons it's a great way to enlightenment. It's his Buddhist thing.' She smiles at me. In this moment, she's relaxed.

'But I see things differently.' She drums her fingers lightly on the arm of the chair.

'How do you mean, Rose?'

'Well. I hear and see things. Stuff most folk don't. I often know about people. When they don't know about themselves. Not just when I meditate. But other times.'

'Yes, we talked about that.'

'Yeah, but not that stuff. Not the crazy stuff,' she says.

'Not the voices?' I query.

'Not… those… ones. It's different to that.'

'In what way?'

'Well, in the forest I heard these echoes. Like muted rumours… they spoke to me… thought it was the wind.' Her eyes are distant.

'It sounded like… the river and the bird call. Like… a primordial language.' Her forehead creases. 'It was hidden by the noises around us. Blended into nature. I didn't realise I was hearing it. But… as the days passed, it got clearer. I began to hear murmuring. Strange whisperings. Deep in my mind.' She sticks her finger in her ear. 'I think it was some kind of faerie language… or maybe… maybe spirits…'

'Spirits?' I ask.

'The spirits of Indigenous folk.'

'Indigenous?' My voice inflects.

'Yeah,' she replies. 'I think I heard their voices. It's so confusing. I think… it was them. So… maybe cos I heard… maybe…' She looks at me, searching. I hold steady, but my heart rate goes off the Richter scale.

'I'm sorry Rose. I don't understand what you are saying. Do you feel the voices were speaking to you?'

She stares at me.

'You mean you found your heritage in the forest?' I try to control my breathing.

'Maybe…' Her eyes bore into mine.

'Were Ma or Pa Indigenous?' I ask abruptly.

'Fuckin' fuckers!' She glowers at me. Then, that impenetrable wall of suppression. She turns, her jaw clenching.

My hand shakes as I make a note.

Wrong question! Ma and Pa? Indigenous… What?

'Sorry Rose. Please go on. What did the voices say?' Tears sting the back of my eyes.

Rose flicks me a penetrating look. Then holding my gaze.

'I didn't know what it meant. Until… recently.'

'Go on,' I manage.

'Auntie Barb. Met her in Musgrave Park. I hang out there sometimes. She does too. She's taken me in. I started to tell her some of what you and I talk about. Some of the shit. She reckons them black fellas. They all go through stuff. Like mine. Them stolen generation.'

She looks away, distracted. Then…

'Did ya know that Prof Peter Read… wrote about that… in '81… studied it at Uni… reckon it sucks… anyways… Auntie says… I just have to keep walking with whatever it is… or whoever I am. Learn from it. Like their elders teach.'

She pauses and twiddles her hair. My heart rate refuses to drop.

'Okay,' I say slowly, making a note. Breathing deliberately.

Auntie Barb? Delusion / fact? Check it.

'Then I said about the forest. About that them faeries. About the voices. The words I heard. She got real quiet. Then said she knew those words. From when she played with her Aunties. From way back. She says it's the language of her people. So, I figure… maybe… because I heard too… that maybe… I dunno…' She shrugs a shoulder.

'What were the words?' I continue, shifting gears, mind racing.

'They told me not to be controlled by my fear.' She hesitates. Her face clouds over.

'I'm listening,' I say as I attempt to control my emotions.

'I live in fear. I've been ruled by it. It's my constant companion. Funny, but… except in the forest…' She fades into silence.

I wait as her breath deepens. Mine with hers.

'This guidance is really important don't you think, Rose?'

She looks at me.

'Yeah. Probably. It helps me understand stuff I'm worried about.' She stops, her hand opening and closing around the crystal.

'Ya know, there was no choice for me in that forest. I couldn't die. Had to go through it.'

'To understand your fear?' I ask.

'Yeah. It's like… when they spoke, it stopped hurting so bad. Inside. It's like I could feel… this love for me… from *them*.' She emphasises the last word.

'They told me never to give up. Not ever. That I was stronger than that. That the fear was bullshit. But I couldn't have walked alone from that forest. No way!'

Her voice is thick with conviction. I watch her more steadily. The steam from her tea is a soft mist rising between us.

Her fingers lightly trace the rim of her cup. The room fills with silence.

I make a clearer note. *Voices? Which ones?*

'The forest. It was so beautiful. It was like I was stoned.' She smiles softly.

'And Chris. He was incredible. Even when I hurt bad… and couldn't hear him properly… he kept singing. His voice was like the river. Pulling at me.' She frowns as her thoughts catch the edge of her deeper tale.

She looks at me. Her hands rest on the velvet of the armchair as she leans forward. Her face is steady, her eyes intense.

'And that smoke, Anna. I can tell you…' She shakes her head as the depth of her experience darkens her eyes.

We pause, gazing at each other as I take in the shift.

'Would you like to share what happened next, Rosanna?' I ask.

She rests back into the folds of the chair, crossing her legs, looking into the middle distance, gathering her thoughts.

~

It's late. I sit at my desk. My day done.

My notes lie open in front of me. Many lives, recorded in detail, unfolding in my care. But this one. Rose's story. *Why has this one cracked me open?*

Her clarity and confusion spin a web of indecision around me. Like rain on the red soil of my desert, Rose has opened me to a part of my past that has laid unattended for decades.

I spin the ring on my finger and watch as dusk sets the streets of Red Hill on fire. Before me lies my rudimentary crayon and charcoal sketch of the outback. The red of the waratah and the silver grey of the salt bush beckon me.

The two images in the small photo on my desk watch me.

I pick up my inking pen and begin to form the ghost like lines of a figure. Then another, a small child. The man leans into her as she squats on the red soil. Their dark curls frame a curious sweetness and intensity. Their heads and hands touch as she points to a mark, etched in the path in front of them. The footprint of a small marsupial. Behind them another figure begins to form. One of a blond woman. Holding a basket. Watching them.

I breathe deeply. Emotions swimming around me. My pen hovers above the markings as I suddenly pull back. Reaching for the Vermouth, I drain my glass. And as my mind refocuses, it hits me.

I pick up my phone and dial home.

The reassurance in the unhurried twang of his voice lightens the load of relief and shock that floods through me.

'G'day luv. How was your day?

~

New South Wales, 20ᵗʰ December, 1977

The sunflowers had grown huge that year, their golden heads reaching high into the noon day sky, turning slowly as they tracked the sun. The fields were a mass of colour stretching way back towards the forest. A solitary young woman bent against the taut of her hoe, her body tall and wiry, tilling the field with measured strokes. She smiled as she worked, her young back curving easily to the digging.

The earth was warm beneath her feet. Her naked toes dug into the soil. Wisps of long auburn hair, tied back and hidden under her scarf, strayed across her face. Straightening her back, Rebecca rubbed her hand across her forehead. The sweat trickled down her brow as she squinted in the heat, tilting back her broad, shady hat.

The creamy pale skin of her face shone in the light. Green-flecked hazel eyes, swept with thick black lashes, keenly watched the distant lines of the fields. Pale skin peeked out from under the protective cotton blouse. She rested her hands on her hoe, pausing to breathe in the rich aroma of the soil at her feet.

The garden bed was almost done. The last mulching needed to protect the soil from the drying scorch of the summer sun, one row from completion. Rebecca sighed in anticipation of the home-made lemonade that was her reward back at the house.

That December was unusually hot. The sunflowers were tall, proud. They stood close to her shoulders in height, the perfume filling her nostrils with the sweetness of their full bloom. Bees buzzed and hummed at their centres rubbing their tiny rear legs together and secreting large spheres of golden pollen. Rebecca smiled as she watched them pollinate her crop. She eagerly awaited the rich amber honey that would be her reward later that season.

Hitching up her long skirt and tucking it into her belt, she rolled the sleeves of her blouse up to her elbows and bent towards the ground. Shapely arms wrapped around the bale of straw as she straightened, stepping over the last hillock and dropping the hay to the ground. Pulling a wooden-handled knife from her belt, she cut through the binding, releasing the hay. It opened outwards onto the moist earth. Tugging at it, Rebecca spread semi-rotting strands over the surface of the manured soil. The scent of the decomposing straw drifted upwards. The heat of the day and the peace of her surrounds filled her with contentment. The sun beat down on her back. She was alone, her younger cousins having returned for refreshments and rest.

Her sweet humming filled the air with prayer as she worked, stretched and turned, shifting hay from one end of the garden to the other.

Finally, the last bed was tucked in and watered. She paused to view her work, massaging the small of her back with strong hands. The sowing of the final crop was done, her community ready to gather at the barn, to feast, sing, pray and dance.

Rebecca's eyes scanned the forest edge. A shadowy movement caught her attention. Shading her eyes with her hand, she squinted, bringing into focus the shapes moving there.

She paused, alert for the rogue fox that had attacked her chickens. Silently she moved towards the end of the field, her hoe over her shoulder. As she drew closer, two crouched creatures moved slowly along the row, hidden behind the vivid green and red of the last tomato and bean bushes.

'Halloo,' she called cautiously.

The figures froze, crouching close to the ground.

'Coo-weeee!' she sang.

The bigger of the two peered out at her.

'Hi.' Rebecca smiled. Slowly they straightened, stepping uncertainly out from behind the last tomato bush.

Rebecca stopped in her tracks. In one swift glance, she took in the scene. A young woman, close to her own age, clad in torn filthy clothes, tightly clutched a mud-spattered waif to her.

Her dark hair hung in tight, dirty wet ringlets down her back. Her boots were caked in mud. Her torn jeans rolled to the knee revealed calves with deep gashes. Dried blood soaked her clothing. Her perfectly oval face was swollen, her full lips lacerated. Her left eye hid behind a blackened bulging lid. Bruising covered her body.

Rebecca's pulse quickened at the apparition before her. The stranger was taut with fear, watching her like a wild animal ready for flight.

'Are you okay?' Rebecca asked hesitantly, taking a step towards them. The woman's eyes darted as she pushed the boy behind her.

'It's alright,' breathed Rebecca, pausing. 'I'm not going to hurt you.' She lay down her hoe.

'I've been working in the garden,' she gestured behind her. 'We're planting. The soil needs tending and mulching,' she added, closely watching them. 'See,' Rebecca said, gesticulating to the tomato plants.

'These are the last of summer's crops. Delicious, aren't they?' she asked, looking carefully at the child. A smile crept into the corners of his eyes as he peeped at her from behind the woman's legs, his face smeared with the red juice of ripened tomatoes

'Do you like tomatoes?' Rebecca questioned gently. 'These are my favourite,' she continued slowly. 'They are the sweetest, don't you think?' He gazed at her, a faint curiosity that began in the dirty streaks on his forehead.

Fugitives? she thought.

Squatting on the earth, Rebecca watched them. In all her life, she had never seen such a sight. Surrounded by steep rocky precipices and gorges, her community was in the furthest habitable part of the mountains. Pressed high up into an amphitheatre of cliffs, it was wrapped by impenetrable virgin rainforest. Their only access was via horse and buggy, back over thin steep trails the men had hewn. No one ever came uninvited.

Rebecca slowly stood; her eyes focused on the woman who watched her warily.

'My name is Rebecca. This is my home.' She spoke carefully,

motioning around her.

The young woman stared blankly at her, then with a slight shake of her head, dropped her eyes.

She is so young! Lord help me understand what is happening, Rebecca prayed silently.

'Mumma's hurt.' The small child stared up at Rebecca, patting the woman's legs.

'I'm hunwee…' he declared, fatigue written all over his face. Rebecca's heart skipped a beat.

'Would you like something to eat?' she asked.

"Ave you got vegemite?' His brow creased and his face lit with the soft glow of innocence.

'I've got fresh bread and butter and jam,' she reassured. 'Made it this morning.' A fleeting look of recognition crossed the young woman's face.

'Wanna eat bread 'n jam 'n cweem!' the boy chimed, stepping towards her. His mother grasped at his hand, tugging him to her and stepping further from Rebecca.

Rebecca straightened.

'It's okay,' she reassured. 'I want to help you. My house is up there.' She motioned towards the far hill. 'I live here with my family. We're farmers.'

Rebecca measured her words, taking her cue from the taut spring in the woman's demeanour.

'We live here together with many other families,' she murmured. 'You look like you've had a bad accident.'

The woman's hand fluttered at her face. She pulled the boy closer to her, grasping at his shoulders.

'Those cuts need cleaning and calendula to heal,' Rebecca persisted. 'And you need a compress of arnica for your eye.'

The woman's gaze steadied as she watched Rebecca, the veil surrounding her lifting for an instant.

'When was the last time this youngster ate?' Rebecca asked. *Please allow me to feed him, then you can go on your way if you wish.*

The young woman's gaze flooded with pain. Her mouth moved but no words came from her lips. Tears began to run down her cheeks.

The child's eyes implored her as he held her hand.

'It's okay, Umma. Please Umma. I'm hunwee,' he pleaded. The young woman bent to him then gasped in pain, doubling over, holding her side. The little boy hugged her, stroking her hair, trying to soothe her. Grubby hands caressed her cheeks. He looked earnestly into her eyes.

'Becca's good Umma. Good. It's safe here,' he lisped.

Rebecca watched this scene as her heart fluttered with apprehension.

'Please! Let me help you. My home is just up on the hill. Let me take you there,' she urged, reaching out to touch her.

The young woman's gaze froze on Rebecca's hand, then, as an ocean of torment flooded from her, she imperceptibly nodded. Rebecca gently circled her waist with her arm, helped her to her feet and taking the small child's hand in hers, turned towards the house in the near distance.

~

Mary and Jacob watched the three hazy figures inching up the ploughed fields towards the house. Rebecca slowly picked her way over the hillocky land, stopping to assist a tiny figure who clung to her companion's back. She repeatedly stooped to draw her arm further around the stranger as they stumbled closer.

From inside the kitchen, Mary paused, squinting into the distance as Jacob looked over her shoulder. She placed the heavy wooden spoon onto the smooth timber bench.

'Who could that be?' she exclaimed. 'Who's that with Beck?' Putting down the bowl, she wiped her hands on her apron and gathering her thick silver hair together, quickly plaited it into a long strand down her back.

'The children have all returned from the fields,' she said.

Jacob strode to the back door, swinging it open. It banged shut behind him as he stepped out onto the veranda. Mary glanced at her husband's back, her lined face questioning.

'She's carrying a child!' Jacob exclaimed. Reaching for his hat, he took the back steps two at a time striding out onto the fields towards them.

~

Christian clung to me; his arms tightly wrapped around my neck. Rebecca's arm held me up. The rich black earth begged me to stop. To pray. To fly free.

Christian's voice urged me on, his babbling registering in some part of me. My legs moved automatically. The field beneath my feet heaved and bent as my vision swam. Sweat soaked my face, blinding me. My hair stuck to my neck, catching in Chris's little fist.

In the distance, the outline of buildings blurred into the edges of the sky. The smoke from the fires melded with the white fluffy clouds. There was no shade from the sun as it spent itself upon my body. New voices penetrated the fog in my brain. A melodic brogue filled with concern and urgency blended with a strong resonant voice. Lifting my head, two figures swum into focus.

I felt Christian's weight being lifted from my back. Fear flooded its warning as I fought to stay conscious, to grip him to me.

'Mumma. It's okay Umma,' he murmured.

As concerned fingers pried mine from around him, my knees gave way beneath me and I released my hold on consciousness.

~

The small child held Mary's neck tightly, his arms circling her shoulders as his legs gripped her waist. He was beyond filthy, every pore in his skin was soaked with mud. His scrawny body was covered in scratches, his face a mask of grime. His intense blue eyes shone with a light that spoke a thousand stories as he looked, urgently, at the young woman at their feet.

'Mumma's hurt,' he entreated. 'Hurt!' he emphasised, holding out his hand to her.

'It's okay child,' reassured Mary. 'Your Mumma will be okay,' she added patting him gently.

Jacob crouched next to the young woman, touching her forehead, holding the back of his hand to her cheek. His eyes registered the concern he felt.

'We must get her back to the house quickly,' he commanded. 'She's burning up and not just with this noon day heat. She's in need of much care. Help me child,' he said, turning to Rebecca. 'Your prayers are sorely needed.'

~

My body floated in a sea of green as my spirit reached to the heavens to awaken a God that had forsaken me. I called long and hard to be taken. To find relief from the pain that wracked every fibre of my body. Whenever I hovered into wakefulness, cool flannels freshened my face and a soft, concerned accent held still my fears.

Christian's chattering drifted in and out, weaving a pure melody to still my shaking heart.

I prayed for release. For forgiveness. For the God that had left my side to return. Purple light took me to skip and dance in the fields beyond the horizon, where animals with soft, warm coats came to kiss and caress me. Butterfly breath touched my cheeks as soothing velvet wrapped itself around me.

And salted liquid ran down my throat as arms supported me in my delirium.

I danced and sang with Sarah. I held Danny in my arms as he wept. I screamed into the pain and ecstasy of childbirth, as my son's minute wet slippery body tore me asunder. Dad and Mim held my hands. Christian played in every moment of my dreaming, singing and dancing, calling me back to him. The searing heat in my body and the pain in my bones cut me to shreds.

Over and over, I prayed, *Take me, Jesus, away from my sin.*

~

Days later I floated back to consciousness, wrapped in a bed of textured cotton and natural thread, so soft I could hardly feel my bones. Clouds of luminous light shone through billowing white amorphous shapes. I was wearing a velvety flannelette night gown and my hair lay around me fragrant, clean and soft.

In the distance, I could hear a familiar tinkling, mixed with high pealing laughter that danced through my heart. The scent of hops, valerian and willow bark filled me as my head reeled in the sweetness of peace.

Children, I thought. *Sarah must have brought some kids home.* My smile froze as reality lodged itself into the vortex of shock.

Where am I? I panicked. *Where is this place? Why can't I see?*

I struggled to sit up before I felt firm hands on my shoulders, pushing me back into vast feathery pillows.

'She's awake,' I heard in the distance.

Muffled voices responded as I lifted my hand to my face. My left eye was completely bandaged with a cooling poultice. My right eye peeked out from under thick, clean cloth, soaked in the heady scent of arnica. My arms were strapped from the elbows down and my legs swaddled. My chest was bound lightly, holding my ribs steady for each breath.

Through the lid of my right eye a dim light shone. I could just make out a tall slender figure standing at the end of my bed and a smaller fuller outline of another woman seated next to me. A steady hand held my shoulder.

'Rosanna, can you hear me?' a lilting feminine voice asked.

That accent. I know that accent. I shook my head trying to clear my thoughts.

The woman spoke quietly, and I heard the silky swish of clothing brushing against my bed as stockinged feet moved across the floor, and then a soft click of a door being open and shut.

'Where am I?' I whispered.

'You're in Rebecca's bed,' a woman said. 'My name is Mary. I am Rebecca's mother. Rebecca found you in the far fields with Christian and helped you. Do you remember?'

Images floated in front of me. Searing sun. Hands helping me. Supporting me. Black soil. Golden sunflowers nodding in the sun. Chris's voice chattering in my ears.

I frowned, trying to remember, a euphoric haze floating around me. Pungent steaming herbs filled the air as my head swam and my body yielded to their balm.

'You have been badly hurt, child.' Her voice drew me back to the room.

'You have slept much and for long.'

I turned my head to face her, sharp pain radiating through my neck and shoulder.

'You're at The Farm, Rosanna.'

Her face swam before me. A blurred image. Long silver hair tied back in a bun. An oval face. White lace at the collar. A long-sleeved blouse with a small brooch pinned near the neck. Observant piercing eyes watching me.

'You're safe here now. The Lord guided you here. Your son is fine.'

Her words mixed confusion and relief within my heart.

Have I been here before? That voice. Whose is it?

'Your face and eyes need much attending to,' she said.

A tall young woman returned carrying a bowl of broth on a polished timber tray. A chunk of steamed bread sat next to it.

'How long have I been here?' I whispered.

'Ten days,' Mary replied. 'You're skinny. You must eat.' She turned and picked up the spoon, scooping it into the soup.

'Your bandages can be removed in a couple of days. Rebecca will stay with you,' she added.

'Where's my son?'

Mary's hand on my wrist was steady.

'He's outside. With the children. He hasn't stopped eating since you arrived. He keeps asking for vegemite. He sleeps at the foot of your bed.' The edges of her voice curled into a smile.

'Do you remember any of what has happened?' she asked, offering me the soup.

~

Rebecca slept on a mattress next to me. At night, when I woke, sweat drenching my sheets, her soft breathing reassured me. Christian slumbered with the rest of innocence. His little boy scent wafting up to me, filling my heart with hope. During the day he played outside, his chattering enchanting my room. The patter of little feet racing up the stairs to leap onto my bed and stroke my bandaged face was the light that would never go out in my life.

'I luv you Umma. You better now, aren't you?' he said as he cuddled my arm and placed wet kisses on my face. Then warbling tunefully, he clattered down the steps, squealing, out into the sunshine.

My heart lifted after his visits. I wondered how it was that I had begat a child so different to me. So like Sarah. Perhaps the leprechauns had bewitched him, leaving within him their magical touch.

Every day Rebecca nursed me, bringing me bowls of thin soup and fresh bread. She sponged me and changed my night gowns. She plumped up the pillows and smoothed the soft cotton sheets, helping me back gently into their embrace. Deep, dreamless slumber followed her night cap herbal brews, as the pain in my body eased.

Finally, she helped me remove the bandaging from around my head and held my hand as I plucked up the courage to look at myself in the mirror.

A pale gaunt face looked at me. Black-green circles surrounded my eyes and neatly stitched wounds traversed my forehead and nose. My left eye was still partially closed and through its swollen lid I peered at myself, wondering what it was I saw. Beyond the ashen face and the bruised healing abrasions was a woman, whom I did not recognise.

'Are you okay Rose?' murmured Rebecca.

Unable to speak, I looked at myself.

My eyes shone with a defiant light. As if the warrior faeries had left lanterns on inside of me and through my delirium, my prayers had been answered. A steely determination had taken the place of terrified trepidation. I watched, fascinated by what I saw, leaning forward to make sure that I was not mistaken. Reaching out, my finger traced my face in the mirror.

Then, as I watched, a coloured light began to play around my image, dancing around the perimeter of my head. In this mirrored hue, a soft glow swam about me. Behind my reflection a shimmering shape appeared. Golden curls ran down her back and pools of forever emerald-green eyes watched me with the deepest love imaginable.

She reached towards me, beckoning me to her. My heart broke with joy as Sarah appeared as a shining light in the ether. Tears ran down my cheeks as my hand reached through the cool surface of the glass touching the soft edges of her face behind me. Her warm lips brushed my cheek and silken fingertips traced the edge of my scars.

Rose… her voice whispered into my heart.

Love you forever, Rose Petal, you're safe now. Rest, Rose. Rest.

She stroked my face. Then the glowing edges of her shining form wavered, dimmed and were gone. I sunk to the floor sobbing with relief. Rebecca helped me back to bed, concern filling her eyes, calling to her mother to come and assist me.

'Are you okay, Rose?' Mary asked after she had settled me under the covers. I nodded. She studied me, then turning, left the room instructing Rebecca on the evening's treatments.

Rebecca sat, watching me.

'Rose,' she said gently, 'what happened just then?'

I looked at her, seeing her for the first time.

In the fog and pain within me, Rebecca had remained a figure of comfort. I knew her only by her gentle healing touch and skilful hands that massaged the pain away. Her soporific herbals at night and the quiet breathing of her slumber at the foot of my bed had reassured me that humanity still existed.

I was stunned by her physical beauty.

'Memories,' I murmured, 'of my best friend.' I turned away and closed my eyes.

8

Brisbane, April 1988

BY mid-afternoon the light casts deepening shadows onto my veranda. We sit together, either side of the coffee table. She relaxes easily this time, and her mood is buoyant. The breezes blow the last of the autumn leaves from the tulip tree onto the decking. She shrugs her wrap closer to her shoulders.

Waterworks Road is uncharacteristically quiet. I am working on a public holiday. Rose has asked to see me, so that she can join Rinpoche later at his temple to pray.

The swallows swoop and dive above us, their nest tucked into the rafters under the ceiling. The spherical rim is exposed to the outside. The parents attend to the gaping mouths of the baby birds. Their soft chattering floats around us.

'Would you like to talk about The Farm?' I question.

'Hmm?' She looks at me. 'Yeah, okay.' She's watching a car on the side road.

'It was quite an amazing time actually… but also…' she collects her thoughts.

'Go on.'

'There were heaps of rules. Daily stuff that had to be done. Designated jobs. The men often worked separately from the women. The kids were home schooled. All together. Up until their teens. The whole community taught them. Not just in the classroom but outside. Actually, it was a wonderful way for them to learn. Christian loved it. Mary was the main teacher. But it was Jacob who ran The Farm. I figured he was like… the boss.'

I make a note of the emphasis she places on "the boss".

'Then there were these white-haired men and women. Everyone was respectful and… sorta scared of them. I wasn't sure about them. They seemed to be… above everyone. Actually… they really were intimidating…' She looks up at the swallow's chicks.

'They're growing fast,' she comments.

'You were speaking of Elders,' I observe.

'Yep. That's who they were.' She turns to me, questioning, 'Have any of yer clients ever been in a cult?'

'Yes. They have.'

'So… ya know about them?'

'Yes. I do.'

'Okay. I didn't know that.' She looks away.

My response has interrupted her flow.

'Go on, Rose. You were talking about how the farm ran.'

She stretches her legs and pauses. Then a deep inhale. 'There weren't many fights. That I could see. They lived for the land. And Jesus. Reading the Bible was mandatory. But… they also worked incredibly hard. Always seemed to help each other. And… funny… but they just loved their home brew! And dancing… well… it was more… like… worshipping… if you know what I mean…' Rose reaches for her tea.

'But you weren't sure about it?' I query.

'Yep.' An audible sigh.

'Okay. So, what was it?'

'As I came out of that fog,' she shakes her head and raises her eyebrows, 'it was really hard.'

'Go on. I'm listening.'

She takes another long breath.

'It seemed that they were really concerned about me. But they never asked where I came from. Or what had happened.' She frowns. 'Except Beck.'

'Okay.'

'And there were heaps of religious rules. Weird stuff. I didn't get it. Sounded pretty fucked up to me.'

'Yes. You were saying.'

'Yeah. Beck said. Guess that morality crap made it easy for them to live together. The rules that is. But I felt like a stranger.' She laughs cynically.

I watch her carefully.

'Well, I guess I was, wasn't I?' She looks at me, her eyes dark.

'I wonder how they felt about you, Rose. It must have been something that they couldn't understand. The way you arrived. Christian. How was all that?'

'Well… I s'pose Mary was kind. But bloody strict. She helped Beck understand how to look after me. She didn't really interfere. Actually, Beck knew what to do anyway. Mary seemed more interested in Chris. And Christian took to her easily. That was good at first, I guess.'

Rose looks away. The tension at the corner of her eyes reflects deeper thoughts. She changes the subject.

I make a note.

'The Elders… they seemed to sorta… tolerate teens. Like… they wanted us to have a life. Wanted us to make up our own minds about stuff. The rules seemed easier on us. Some left and didn't come back. But most stayed. If there was gonna be an argument… well… it was between the teens. Then there was lotsa praying… talking… and mostly it resolved.' She smiles.

'I actually liked that part of it. Felt okay about it all. It reminded me of Dad and Mim.' Her voice trails off. 'And Dan…'

And Danny? I make a note.

'But you were a stranger to them. How did that sort itself out?' I regroup, focusing on her train of thought.

She stops and thinks.

'Well, it didn't really.' Her voice is soft.

'What do you mean by that?'

'Well, although I helped a lot, working with the animals, studying with Beck, helping in the Apothecary… I started to feel like Mary was… stalking me. Yer know… like… when I was alone with Christian…' Her voice trails off.

'And… I dunno… I just felt a bit creepy about how she latched onto him.' She shrugs her shoulders.

'In what way?'

'Like she owned him.'

'What did she do?'

'Well, she was like an Auntie but *so* different to Auntie Mim. She wanted him with her… most of the time. And then… when Beck and I had him… she… kinda… ya know… just used to stare at me. With this weird vibe. Not saying anything. But like she was angry… like she wanted him more. I didn't like it… didn't feel…' She pauses.

'Comfortable?'

'It just reminded me of…'

I wait.

Her eyes are sombre.

'I'm listening, Rose.'

'Of Pa!'

Pa? I make a note.

She looks away, picks up her cup and quietly sips her tea.

'What was the best thing about it all?' I ask, observing her carefully, aware of her rising anxiety. I want to keep things level today.

She takes a long breath.

'That's easy. Beck. The animals. And my…'

Out of the corner of my eye, up under the eaves I see a blur of movement. A tussle of sound and screeching followed by a light thud of a small body falling to the veranda.

The fluttering of feathers striking the floor takes our attention.

Rose stops mid-sentence as a large shape swoops past us. A magpie wings its way to freedom, a squawking baby chick in its beak. Rose rises swiftly to her feet, her attention on the small, twisted bundle motionless on the floor. She glides across the veranda, soundlessly moving towards the fallen mother swallow.

Squatting low, she concentrates on the bird. She reaches out. A soft tremor runs through her body. Carefully she scoops up the fallen creature and unhurriedly walks back to her seat.

The bird's wing lies at an angle, a sharp bend in it. The bone protrudes from the feathers. Rose settles back into her chair and lays the swallow gently into her lap as her hands run nimbly over its body.

'The wing is broken,' she murmurs. 'And possibly the neck.'

Her fingers move to the chest, pausing over the heart.

'There's the heartbeat.' She breathes.

Her fingers work skilfully and deliberately as she lays the wing out.

'This needs to be quick,' she murmurs, 'before she wakes up. Do you have a small pencil?'

I take one from my pencil case and hand it to her.

She snaps it in two.

'Can I use this cloth?' she whispers, picking up a table napkin.

I nod.

She deftly tears it into fine strips. Then, with the lightest of touches, she separates the two ends of the break, laying the wing out straight, positioning the ends back together. She places the pencil along the bone and takes the torn napkin, threading it between the broken feathers and around the pencil.

Her touch is tender as she works. Her fingers quick and skilled. Her focus intent on the bird. She weaves a fine stitched pattern along the ridge of bone until the wing is swaddled in cloth.

I sit silent, spellbound. I have never seen her like this.

The bird begins to stir as she completes her task.

'Now let's see if this littlun wakes properly,' she murmurs.

The bird opens its eyes and struggles to move. Rose gently places her hands around it, folding it into itself, covering its eyes. The broken wing protrudes from her fingers. The bird continues to move.

Rose closes her eyes. She goes completely still. Her breathing is slow. Then, a soft, almost inaudible droning starts deep in her chest. A warmth emanates from her – a tangible feeling of calm.

I watch transfixed as the small creature becomes completely still. Rose opens her eyes and looks down. The little bird sits peacefully in her hands, cheeping at her.

'Do you have a small box?' she asks.

I fetch it from the kitchen. She carefully lays the other napkin into the box and places the bird onto it.

'The wing will knit in three weeks,' she speaks. 'And she won't try to fly away until then.'

She strokes its neck as it ruffles itself and pecks at her finger.

'I think she's hungry.' She smiles.

Rose closes her eyes again. Her lips move silently. Then with her eyes shut, she addresses me.

'Just a little something that Beck taught me.' She opens her eyes.

Her gaze is filled with surrender. Her eyes glow as the colour changes to a soft grey.

'I really miss this,' she whispers.

~

New South Wales, Autumn 1978

The glowing red and gold light of the early morning dawn greeted me, a choral of bird calls from the forest nearby drawing me from my slumber. I had rested deeply that night, the magic of Rebecca's hop and valerian herbal brew sending me into a peaceful sleep.

Quietly slipping my arm out from under Christian's body and sliding from underneath thick blankets, I wrapped my shoulders in the soft woollen shawl from the foot of my bed. Watching Rebecca's slumbering form on the mattress under the eaves, I stepped onto the bright woven floor rug and silently stole out the half open door.

The wooden staircase creaked as I descended into the darkened recesses of the kitchen below, sneaking across the floor towards the back entrance. The far end of the house was lit with the faint glow of oil lamps and through the crack in the door I could see the outlines of Mary and Jacob kneeling in morning prayer before the cross of Jesus.

Noiselessly, I walked outside to the most glorious morning I could have imagined.

The far-off forest was backlit by the dawn light, silver and gold bathed in rich amber. Tall fluffy clouds reflected the sun's rays, splaying out into an arc of grey and pearlescent white. The sunflowers in the back fields stood like guardians. Bird calls saturated the ether, a symphonic melody cascading through the air, surrounding me in the music of nature.

I shrugged my shawl closer around my shoulders and walked out onto the grass. Dew soaked my feet, bathing me in crystal rainbow water. The cold of the earth wrapped around my ankles as freshness filled my lungs, its icy embrace sending pure mountain air into my chest. My mind hummed and slowly stilled in the tranquillity.

Beauty transfixed me as peace soaked into my pores. I moved across the grass towards the sown fields, taking in the vista before me.

I had never seen such unparalleled magnificence. The land sloped gently away, field upon field of carefully tended crops reached as far as I could see. Citrus trees dotted the landscape with colours of rust and gold, the rows between filled with the bright red of cayenne bushes. Marigolds turned their amber and yellow centres towards the rising sun. Coffee trees, carefully pruned to the height needed for hand harvesting, contrasted with the dark green foliage and mottled marbles of red berries ready for picking. Corn and climbing beans intertwined each other in a companionable hug, filling the far distance with shades of golden green. Further, the impenetrable forest circled the land in an embrace of thick shadows, hiding it from humanity in a shroud of secrecy.

~

Throughout my convalescence, I had been consumed with images of my last night on the steps of Sah's home, far down in the valley below. No one had asked how I had appeared out of the darkest recesses of that forest. The only expression of concern had been for the restoration of my wellbeing. Christian had immersed himself in the immediacy of life and never spoke of that last night, drawn instead into the throng of small children that played in the fields and meadows.

As I slowly emerged into life on the farm, there was safety in the embrace of silence. The uttered word threatened to open the sutures of my wounds. To engulf me in a darkness that was far from this valley of beauty and grace.

In my waking existence, my sanity teetered on the brink of self-destruction. I was deeply suspicious, fearing Christian's absence from my sight, clinging to him. When the choppers circled the mountains, I ran through the house with my hands over my ears, screaming in fear. Rebecca chased after me, calling my name and finding me hidden under the covers on my bed, shaking violently. At night I awoke her from her slumber as I ruptured into consciousness. Night terrors bathed me in cold sweat. Howling into a vortex of terror, I clawed my way upright as she finally crawled in under my sheets curling her body around mine.

~

The Earth had turned away from the sun. Night chased day too quickly. The fleeting warmth of August was well set before I truly awoke to life again and was freed to sleep deeply and restfully. And as the bird song at dawn called me that morning into the fields and Mary and Jacob completed their prayers, I began to open the door of my mind to the possibilities of a new life, hidden there in the shelter of that refuge.

~

New South Wales, Spring 1978

That spring, Mary decided it was time for me to fully join in with the community activities. She instructed Beck to take me to the kitchen to assist in making the evening's meals. With the older women by our side, we baked and fermented and prepared for the community. Familiar aromas of recipes akin to Mim's hearth filled my senses with delight.

Mary kept a watchful eye on me. Instructing Rebecca as to what I was permitted to do and how I could contribute to their community. The Farm was completely self-sufficient. The people, accomplished farmers, builders, musicians and educators. Their fiscal policy, one of bartering and exchange only.

During the day, Rebecca took my hand and together we would wonder through her gardens sharing common knowledge of what shapes and shifts a barren land into lush pasture sent from the heavens. The knowledge that Dad and Auntie Mim had instilled in me, and Rebecca's sovereignty and allegiance to her community, filled my life with a healing joy.

She explained the reason for the climbing beans clinging so close to the corn. How the parsley and the tomatoes yearned for each other's sweet embrace. Why dwarf beans and the filamentous fennel bear a mutual dislike. She stood by the pungent wormwood in solitary confinement in the corner of the garden and elucidated how it chases away unwanted flea beetles and moths that loved to share our common space.

She showed me the rough, sand-paper leaves of the broad comfrey that had knitted the wounds on my face. And took me to the golden orange calendula, to sing its praise as the queen of healers for deep muscle wounds. Valerian nodded its head as we passed, Rebecca singing her favourite chant, a smile of reverence on her face.

My first major chore was to care for the apothecary, the community's house of health, and to assist Beck in the fields. Mary had observed my love of nature and had witnessed my conversations with Rebecca about nature and healing. We were sent to the community's herb garden to tend to the collection of plants with which to make herbal extracts. The sleepy aroma of spherical hop heads induced a soporific afternoon as we prepared the strong night tinctures of this rough plant's flowers. We macerated and distilled. And soaked them with ninety-seven percent proof ethanol.

'Your knowledge of herbal medicine is extensive,' Rebecca commented one morning. We were turning and lightly shaking the hops as they soaked in their large, decanting jars. We had returned to the apothecary after the kitchen chores were done, to check on the tinctures. Christian had danced around us on his way to play school, demanding our attention.

I smiled inwardly remembering my days with Dad in his garden shed, washing recycled bottles for his home brew.

'Did you have a teacher?' she asked.

'The best.' I passed her each jar to confirm the changing colour of the pale-yellow liquid. 'Except, his use of this plant was for other means.' I laughed.

'You speak of the medicinal properties of home-made beer do you not?' She smiled at my rare humour. I had grown accustomed to her way of speaking – to the lyrical tones and the melodies of a poet and writer.

'Would you like to walk with me later, to see the men's brewing shed?' she asked, returning to her task.

'Is that allowed?'

'I will get Isaac to mention it to them. If he comes with us, it will be acceptable.' She peered into the large jar.

'Mm. These will not be ready until they turn to amber,' she murmured, holding it to the light. 'They will need yet another two weeks to be done fully.'

We had collected the pale green spherical hop flowers from the hessian sacks. The men had slung them around their shoulders, filling them as they climbed high on the wooden trellises, clad in leather to protect against the spikes.

'This is good for scared animals.' I said as I watched her. She was rotating the jars carefully, then replacing them on the dark shelf in the cool interior.

'How do you know that?' she asked, her back to me.

'I dunno. Guess it was when I was little. I used to look after the village pets.'

'Village?' She straightened.

I looked away, hurriedly replying, 'Yes. If they were hurt. And needed sleep.'

Rebecca stopped; her hands wrapped around the last jar.

'Which village do you refer to Rose?' she asked carefully.

'My village.' My breath quickened.

'Where is your village, Rose?' Beck's voice was soothing.

'Ahh… what… do you… use this medicine for?' I avoided her gaze.

She paused before answering, starting to gently turn the crock, watching me. 'Our mothers need this healing agent after their babies are birthed if their milk doesn't flow and when their breasts swell and redden,' she said.

We walked silently to the far end of the building. The pungent scent of the dried hop flowers, hypnotic. She reached up onto the high shelves taking down a cane basket. The inside was stuffed with small pillows of stitched tulle and filled with dried herb. She took one out and turning, handed it to me, smiling softly.

'Here. This is for you. For under your pillow. To help you to sleep and not to dream so much and so poorly.' She lay the pillow in my hand.

'Rose?' she asked, hesitatingly. 'Can you tell me why you never speak of your past? Why do you avoid answering me?' Her eyes were serious.

'You have bad dreams most nights. Can you not share these with me? Can't I help you?' Her voice was soft, questioning, reassuring me as my feelings tumbled.

I bent my face to the small gift and inhaled the calming scent.

'You have darkness in your past, Rosanna. I saw it when you first came. Your mind is full of shadows, my love. Your words are frozen in you. Can you not let me into you?'

I turned to walk away when her hand landed gently on my arm.

'Rosanna?'

~

At night we shared her small attic room. Christian slept on the make-shift bed on the floor under the eaves. We lay close together in twin beds and often I fell asleep with Rebecca's outstretched hand holding mine.

If I slept beyond the dawn she would be gone. Her bed still warm. From our window I could see her working in the fields. Her supple body bent to the task. I would watch her, entranced by the melodies that flowed through her as she worked. At the grace in her movements and the confidence in her stride

There was an ease in Rebecca that was a magnet to my soul. A place where peace always seemed to dwell. Her beauty was undeniable. Her stance alone stood her head and shoulders above all the other women, and the ease at which she commanded gentle authority and respect, belied her youthful years.

Her physical beauty was only a part of her attraction to me. It was that this woman was a healer. Born to lead. Born with a magnitude of graces and a depth of compassion that washed over me, taking the turmoil from my heart and the pain from my soul. Her spirit had met mine that morning in the fields. Where, through the numbing shock, I had laid my hand in hers and leant into a trust that drew me forward.

As that spring turned into summer, under Rebecca's watchful eye, I began to understand the full meaning of "safe".

~

It was on one of our companionable walks that Rebecca was uncharacteristically quiet. We had climbed up through the forest to a small pool of pure mountain water. The trickle of a clear stream that fed it and the soft breezes that bent the huge trees, whispered memories of my past through me.

We were completely alone.

She beckoned for me to sit close to her and lightly took my hand in hers.

'Rose, it is safe here to talk,' she said. 'I've been praying for your peace of mind. Can I please ask you again?'

I looked at her and toppled into the depths of her serenity. Her eyes, pools of safety.

'I can see your grief,' she murmured as I looked away.

'I… I… don't know where to… to… start,' I stammered.

'In your sleep you often call two names, Rose.'

I looked at her, pain welling up within me.

'Yes. They… they… were my friends,' I managed. 'My… my… best friends. I grew up with them.' I turned aside to hide the tears that stung my eyes. 'They helped me to find you.'

~

New South Wales, Early Summer 1978

'I'm interested more in your inner terrain, Rose.

Rebecca was tilling the soil close to me. We had been working side by side in the fields those previous days. High up in the paddocks. We had stayed on. More for the pleasure of each other's company than to continue working.

It was hot. Sticky, mid-summer hot.

The loose blouses clung to our skin and the sweat ran like rivulets down our backs. The sun had turned my skin a copper brown. Our hats were pushed down onto our heads, sheltering us from the sun's intense bite. The spring and early summer crops were almost harvested. Everyone had worked in stride, singing and chanting to keep the momentum going.

The rest of the community had eventually returned to the manor house to set up for the evening. To sing and dance long into the night. To celebrate the crop's magnificence and to ask for God's grace and abundance.

I paused, leaning on my hoe to catch my breath. The warm, fecund earth squeezed its moistness between my toes, caressing my naked feet. She turned to me. She had not asked again about my former life. My shut down, enough information.

'I mean not to offend. Am I not, without question, totally lacking tact at times?' Her good humour that day shone.

I smiled at her self-effacement, returning to my chores.

'But I do want to understand you more deeply.' Her eyes became serious. 'That forest has never seen a stranger through it. Especially one with a small child in tow.'

I continued to slowly till the soil, my heartbeat rising.

'Rose?' She reached out to hold my arm

I stopped and looked away. We stood for a short moment in silence, Rebecca's touch a life-line to my truth. My soul flying out into the safety of the clouds above me.

'But this really is not my business, is it?' Her voice soft, forehead creased.

'Rose?'

I lifted my hand to enfold hers.

'Then I am grieved that my persistence has hurt you. Forgive me Rose. Please.' Her voice was earnest, breaking through my escape.

I turned to her, unable to respond.

'Let's stop now, shall we? And rest,' she murmured, touching my arm.

She guided me to the shade of an old mango tree and reaching up, plucked two ripe fruit and sat, beckoning me to join her. The skin peeled easily and I sunk my teeth into the sweet nectar of the flesh. Mango juice ran down my chin as small sounds of pleasure arose from my throat. Rebecca laughed and wiped my face with the hem of her skirt.

'You've never had one before, have you?

'Not until now.'

'Well! What do you think? Aren't they the most delectable fruit ever?'

I nodded, overcome with the instant deliciousness of the ripe fruit, the fervour of her presence, and the confusing emotion that churned through me.

'There's a myth here, Rose. They say the mango is a gift from God.'

'What do you mean?'

'Legend says that they are sent to us to enliven our senses and alert us to the forbidden desires of the flesh.' She was smiling, the hazel pools of her eyes overflowing with feeling.

'I don't understand.'

She paused, looking down the valley. Then turned to me, her voice clear and passionate.

'In my community, the elders teach us that we are motivated only by our gratuitous desires. That we need to surrender to God's will, to understand them. That the pleasure of the senses is in essence our mortality and our downfall.'

She looked at me as if seeking a response. Then continued.

'Our doctrine forbids sexual pleasure.'

'I don't know what that is,' I muttered.

She turned quickly to me, her eyes questioning.

'Pardon? What was that?'

I looked down, trying to hide my feelings.

'But! Christian? His father?'

I shook my head. Trying to slide out from under what she now clearly knew.

'Rose?' She persisted.

I moved away. Rebecca's brow furrowed. She paused, then shaking the notion from her head, continued.

'Dancing in reverence to the Lord. In ecstatic worship. Well, that's something else. But it is servitude we are taught that enlightens us. Woman cannot reach God, except through man.'

I looked up at her, confused.

'That's oppression!' I blurted. 'And sexism.'

She studied me intently. 'Yes,' she frowned. 'Yes. You are correct.'

We sat looking at each other, the sun's radiant light setting in the west, shining in the corners of her eyes. Our bodies close. She continued to speak absorbedly.

'But since I have met you.' She reached forward and took my hand. 'Since then, I see things differently. Why is suffering right and pleasure wrong?'

I lowered my eyes, the heat in hers scorched me.

'Have you not suffered enough? Why would the teachings of my community apply to you? Or, now, to me either?' she continued. 'Since you have been brought to me, I wish to find my own liberation, Rose.

My way. The trials of being human are enough without this ridiculous notion about our bodies.' She looked away, anger flitting behind her eyes. Asking. Yet not.

'In this community I am obliged to understand the values of the Bible. But now I am confused. There is such hypocrisy in what I have been told. And you? You have shown me something utterly different.' Her hand tightened.

'I am perplexed, Rose. I love this family. I fear its control. But now my love, with you, beside me; I question what I have been taught.'

There was something in the tilt of her face and the glow in her eyes. Something new. Undefined. Something that compelled words to form in my heart.

'To me… it is much more…' I faltered.

'Go on, Rose. I'm listening.'

'What I think is… that God… is my connection to the planet. Something that turns my mind to sweetness and to soul. Without this,' I turned to look at the forest behind us, 'I would be nothing. The wilderness does hold secrets. And in the path it took me through… to you… I learnt… that love… love holds the deepest place. Kindness is always a gift, but a woman's touch… your touch… it heals and… and…' I lowered my head as my cheeks burnt. Her eyes blazed a trail into me, searing my skin and lighting a furnace in my belly.

'Rose.' Her voice was soft, her fingertips travelled up my arm.

'Rose?' She leant towards me, cupping my face in her hand, tilting my chin.

'Rose. What is it you feel? For *me*?'

My throat constricted as I tried to look away. She held my face in both her hands and leaning forward kissed me lightly on the cheek.

'What Rose, would you think if I told you that, since meeting you, there is one thing I am certain about. Despite all that the teachings have instructed, I know that intimate love lives between men and women. And between women and women.'

Her eyes held mine with an intensity that melted my body towards hers. She wrapped her arms around me, drawing me to her and gently kissed me again.

~

From the kitchen in the manor house, Mary and Jacob watched the dancers in the distance, the dust from the barn floor a cloud around them. They twirled and stomped and laughed as the musicians pounded out the beat. Rebecca and Rosanna sat close together at the door; their heads bent to their books.

'She is indeed studious,' Mary commented as Jacob squatted before the pot-belly stove, stoking the fire.

'A fine mind but a broken heart,' he replied.

She nodded her head. 'And the boy?'

He turned to her.

'He's a bright youngster. A credit to a mother so young,' she said, as Jacob stepped out into the night to chop wood. On his return, his arms stacked with dried kindling, he paused.

'Does she talk with you, woman?' he asked.

'Nothing. Not ever.' Mary stirred the large pot. 'They spend all their time together. Rebecca has helped to knit her trauma.' Mary picked up the biggest pumpkin and deftly split it in two.

'Does our daughter speak of her past to you?' he questioned, returning to his fire.

'No. She is tight lipped about it all.' She sighed. 'It bears well this way. I believe her trust is shattered and her voice mute because of her past.'

Jacob straightened, stretching his back.

'You are a good woman wife, but a little naïve,' he said, his steely grey eyes concentrated on her. 'She has a past. This will need to be spoken of to allow her to stay. When she is completely well, we will need to know what has gone before, so as to find her a suitable husband.'

She looked up at him, her palm on the handle of the knife. 'Jacob. I respect you in all ways. But this is between her and God. It is the law to not pry into such things. Besides, she may never speak of what has happened to her. We cannot force her lips open. This is her way, to remain mute. Rebecca has her confidence. I see it grow every day. This must not be ruptured, or I fear she will fly from us.' Mary turned towards the back door; her face filled with emotion. Her voice clear. 'And take the boy.

Jacob observed his wife carefully. 'You have become too attached to that little one.'

'I cannot deny my affection for him.' She bent to the larger pot under the sink, then looked back at her husband

'He is a strong-willed young thing. His resilience is remarkable. He is talented like her. He knows the names of the stars and the galaxies. He speaks with ease of the creatures of our land. His knowledge is profound for a child. And his memory is exemplary.' She sliced the pumpkin into small pieces. 'He will make a fine astronomer for our people when he is grown,' she said, taking the soaked beans and the squared pumpkin and adding them to the pot.

'This will be ready for tomorrow's dinner now,' she said.

Jacob quietly observed her. 'Has he spoken of any relatives? His father perhaps?'

She looked at him, her smile soft. 'He talks about them all the time. His father loved cars. He likes our horses but constantly asks where our vehicles are kept.' She smiled. 'I believe that his father may have been a mechanic. A fine one at that, to have taught him so much.' She reached for the salt and pepper.

'But there is another man. Someone that scares the wee one. He talks to him when he thinks there is no one around.' She bent to the sack of onions, taking the largest then slicing and adding them to the broth.

'Woman, there is something I must tell you. Isaac says there are posters in the village.'

Mary paused. 'What does this mean, Jacob?' she asked, wariness lining her face.

'They say nothing on them except that they are looking for someone.'

~

Beck and I were immersed in a large book on biodynamic gardening. The beat of the drums and the strident strumming of the guitar vibrated through our bodies. Tempos that lured the folk onto the floor to sway and gyrate to the pulse of the music, their bodies moving in ecstasy and worship.

Beck's revelation that dusk had opened a flood of feeling. Words had tumbled unrestrained from my heart. My emotions laid bare at the feet of my angel. My mind purged.

I looked up, drawn by the heat and throb of the dancers.

A crazy spirit had entered my soul and the cry for freedom called from the wildest part of me. From the green dales in the forest and from the sweet harps that had lured my Sah away from me.

…Dance sweetest sista. Dance into your life…

My legs seared with desire. To move. To stomp my feet. To feel the life that I had missed, pulsing through me. To turn and twist with Beck. To dance free from all that had held me back. To meld into the rapture that surrounded me.

And I yearned to feel the purity of her touch against my skin; to fulfil the aching between my thighs.

'Come on, Rose. Let's dance,' Rebecca urged, her voice jolting me back from my reverie. She looked curiously at me, tiny crinkles of delight lightening the edges of her mouth, turning it upwards into a smile that smouldered the fire in the depths of my belly.

'I swear that these bales were not meant to be sat upon. They are indeed spikey.' She grinned at me as I blushed, shuffling her hips and smoothing more of her skirt under her. The heavy book rested on our knees; our bodies pressed against each other for warmth in the cool drop of the dusk air.

'Nah. I'll wait here. Isaac wants to dance with you.' I looked towards the tall slender young man who hovered at the door of the barn, his eyes on Rebecca. Beck shot a glance his way. Her face flushed as their eyes met and she quickly lowered hers.

'Mother says it's time for our betrothal,' she said, looking directly at me with clear penetrating eyes. My breath caught in my chest as I glanced at her.

Isaac moved towards us.

'He's coming,' I stammered.

Rebecca turned to me, questioning. Her brow knitted.

'But I want to dance only with you!' She breathed, her hand brushing mine.

'I'll wait back in the house for you,' I mouthed, turning my head away from him as he approached. As they moved onto the floor to dance, hands held, I glanced back. Rebecca's physical beauty and the sensual rhythm of her hips was undeniable, as was the ache in my heart. Her revelation had shocked me from the heat of my fantasy and into a swirling mist of confusion and anxiety.

I closed the book, gathered my bag, and walked towards the house.

~

Mary looked closely at Jacob.

'Posters? Looking for someone?'

'A number of people.' His face serious

'Is there a name?'

'I cannot say yet, as I am unsure of what it is that Isaac has seen. Much can happen in that world out there.' Jacob watched his wife carefully.

Mary turned away, her face pale.

'Wife. Is there something you should share with me about Rosanna?' His eyes burnt into her back.

She stood still before refocusing on him.

'She has spoken with our daughter. About a question of great concern. I am not privy to disclose this to you, husband. Rebecca has alluded to it in prayer only. It is at this moment between her and God. It is not my right to share with anyone yet.' Her eyes were guarded.

Annoyance flicked across Jacobs's brow.

'You know that the Elders will not be pleased if you are harbouring secrets, wife.' He spoke sternly, staring at her.

Mary picked up the wooden spoon, stirred the pot and turned to her husband. 'I will of course. In time. When it is clear. I will inform you if it is needed. I know the law here.' Her eyes wavered as she glanced at Jacob.

'I will wait then, wife. But you need to know that I will be attending to the trade of our essentials next month in the village. I will be going after we have raised the barn. The men will be accompanying me. I will look more carefully into this when I am there.'

Mary dropped her gaze as Jacob turned to the fire box and hauled it onto his shoulders, striding out the door.

~

The light in the kitchen cast a glow on Mary's profile. Her back was to me as I approached the house. She was stirring the large dinner pot. I kicked off my boots and quietly opened the back screen as Mary turned to face the kitchen door. My feelings tumbled around me as I slipped towards the stairs. Mary's voice floated clearly along the corridor; Jacob's reply a testimony of disapproval.

I froze as I took in the intent in their words and pushed myself into the dark recess under the stairs, listening intensely as their conversation progressed. My breath caught in my chest as fear gripped my belly.

I heard the scrape of the wood box being lifted off the floor and the resounding of heavy foot fall moving towards me. Pressing my body deeper under the stairwell, I watched as Jacob pushed the kitchen door open and strode past me, his brow knitted with chagrin.

~

Beck came in later that evening, slipping between the sheets in her bed next to mine.

'Rose,' she whispered, reaching out, her hand caressing my arm. 'Are you awake?' The full moon shone on her face. I had left the curtains open, wanting to find some solution to the turmoil I was feeling, within the soothing light of the moon.

I lay silent, eyes tightly shut, hoping Beck would think I slept. I was alone. Christian's usual soft sleeping breath absent as he played with the dancers downstairs. He was eagerly expectant for a sleep over with his favourite friend

'Rose.' More urgent this time. 'I know that you're awake.'

I turned away from her.

'What's the matter?'

'Nothing,' I muttered.

'There is something. I can feel it!' Her hushed voice was insistent.

I rolled back towards her. Her eyes looked into mine, steady pools of liquid honey, rimmed with double rows of jet-black lashes.

'What's wrong?' Her voice more urgent now

'Isaac. You didn't tell me,' I muttered.

She paused, watching me carefully.

'They spoke of it only yesterday,' she said. 'We have been

committed since birth. It is the way here.'

'When?'

'It is not so soon. But it is written into the law.' A light crease knitted her brow.

I looked at her.

'For always?' I asked.

'Yes. Even. Even if I do not wish for this now.' Her face was an open book.

'You mean that, you have to?' My voice was rising.

'Shh. Yes,' she whispered, holding her finger to my lips and reaching out to take my hand. She turned it and kissed my palm, her mouth soft. Open. Then, looking into me she spoke that which I had wanted to hear for so long.

'Rose. My beautiful Rosanna. You must know by now. It is you I want, not him.'

Her words fell like butterfly kisses into my heart as my mind spun with conflict.

'I wanted to dance with you. I wanted to tell you. But there has never been the right moment.' She lifted my palm and with the lightest touch, caressed her cheek with it. She looked at me. Her pupils dilated.

'I have been in love with you, Rose. From the start. I have waited for you. For you to heal. To be ready. For us to have our time.' Her eyes filled with desire.

'You have been sent to me,' she whispered, 'by God. And I know now that God does not judge me for my feelings. I have prayed so many times, for an answer. And tonight, after we were on the hill. As he danced with me, I knew that I had to tell you. Before it's too late.' Her urgency was palpable

I stared at her, my heart racing with desire and confusion.

Then.

'They know,' I spoke.

She stopped.

'Who? What?'

'Your parents. They know what happened.'

Beck looked at me.

'About Pa?' Her voice rising.

I nodded.

'How?' She stared at me. 'How do they know?'

I looked at her questioning.

'No! No, Rose. I did not, Rose. I swear. As God as my witness, I swear I have never uttered a word.' Her voice shook.

'She heard you. Praying.'

Beck's eyes widened.

'No! This is against our law.' Her voice taut. 'This is a sin.'

She released our embrace, stood and locked the door. Then turned to me.

'It is them, not you, who have done wrong.' She knelt on the soft rugs beside my bed and took my hands in hers.

'It is forbidden, Rose.' Her eyes shone with sincerity.

'On our land. In this country. It is forbidden to hold the word of prayer against another. Or to speak of it.' Beck's words were filled with conviction. Her hands tightened around mine. I watched her, my heart aching.

'There are posters in the village, Beck. Looking for someone,' I whispered.

'Who told them this?' Her eyes scanned my face.

'Isaac,' I whispered.

Rebecca looked at me, incredulous.

'Mary said she'd heard you pray for me. She's figured out about Dad being a mechanic. There's only one in the village. She's going to work out who I am. Where I come from. And I'm scared she wants to keep Chris. Jacob's going to the elders. The posters. I know they are for me. Beck, what are we going to do? I have to go. The police…'

Rebecca stared at me, blinked rapidly, her lips moving in silent prayer.

Then leaning towards me, she breathed…

'Then this will be our time. Now my love. *Now.*'

Her eyes were filled with certainty and passion. She gently placed her hand under my breast as her lips met mine with the lightest touch. Her caress was like silk, her skin the smoothest peace resting on a twilight dusk. I kissed her back, the heat and confusion in my belly, igniting a furnace of desire.

The moon played shadows around us that starlit night, as I became a lover for the first time. And her soft voice cried out in pleasure as the whispered music in our union drowned out the voices from my past.

9

Brisbane, May 1988

ROSANNA'S legs jiggle up and down. Her thongs dangle from her toes. She sits on the edge of her chair looking at her feet. Her hands are tucked under her thighs. Her face, dark.

Her drug habit had worsened and the contrast from her last session is marked.

'I need to get something straight.' Her voice is hard. 'I wanna work out what was goin' on at the farm. What those bloody posters were about.'

She's agitated.

'Did you find out more?' I ask.

'Nup.'

'What do you think was going on?'

'I reckon Mary was up to something.' She looks at me, her eyes intense. Mistrust wages a war within her. Obsessive memories float just out of the reach of recall.

'What makes you think that?'

'Mary said when Chris grew up, he would be their astronomer.' She swings her legs in a wider arc.

'She was really evasive with Jacob. He was as mad as a cut snake when he walked past me.'

'Okay.' I observe her carefully.

Rose presses her fists into her armpits, then shakes her head.

'She also heard Beck praying for me. About… Pa…' she mutters, looking at her feet. Her eyes clam shut, then spring open as she turns her head away from me. She holds her breath.

'Rose?' I gently prompt.

'Fuck, I feel really paranoid about all this,' she vents.

'That's fine. This is clearly something that has been bothering you for a long time. Let's just breathe a little,' I reassure her.

Her chest shakes as she attempts to steady herself. 'I just don't get what those posters were about,' she mutters to herself.

'Do you think Mary or Jacob had a plan?' I ask.

'A plan?' She flicks a quick look at me, then shakes her head.

'How was Isaac behaving?'

Her breath steadies.

'Really creepy. I'd be in my milking bales and he'd appear. Out of nowhere. Spouting off from the Bible. Making out that there was hell, fire and damnation. That I was headed that way.' Her laugh is short and bitter.

She races forward.

'Then he kept trailing us. Looking at Beck. Really possessive. Wouldn't leave us alone. Men! They have this strange nose for other people in their territory.' She snorts, then looks at me. Her eyes are clear and bright, and I observe the high colour of her cheeks.

Medications too strong. I make a note for the psychologist.

'Guess Isaac was harmless though.' She rubs her face. Slows down.

'What about Mary?'

'Okay, I guess… Until she knew about them posters… then she changed.' Her voice is harsh.

'Did Mary ever say anything to you or ask questions about your past?' I ask her quickly.

Keep this on track.

She looks at me, her face a blank book. Then abruptly stands and paces.

'Rose. Can you please breathe and sit down?' I direct.

Her face has turned darker.

'It helps me think.'

'I know it does.' I watch her, aware of the combination of her meds and the street drugs giving her this edge.

'Fine! You know best.' She sits down heavily. Her breath comes in short spurts.

'So, you think. Mary was saying. That Chris was good. At stuff. Because he was? That she was just praising him? Not… that… she… wanted him?' Her voice inflects her anxiety.

I observe her carefully. She fixes me in her gaze.

'No! You think something else. Don't you?' She's piercing when she's like this.

'I'm uncertain. Was there anything else happening?'

'Jacob said he was looking for a husband for me. Buckley's chance of that.' She snorts, mood changing. 'He started to creep me out too. I kept catching him looking at me.'

'Do you know why?' I ask.

'Nah. But that felt even worse than Mary staring at me.'

'Did he say anything to you? Did he do anything?'

'Nup. Just looked at me funny.' She's wary. 'He didn't touch me or anything… if *that's* what you mean. But it felt like he could see… you know…'

'What, Rose?'

She drops her head.

'My guilt.' Her voice is low. Her head turns away.

'What do you mean by guilt, Rose?' I ask

She abruptly stands and opens the door.

'Need the dunny.' She vanishes down the hall.

When she returns, she's calmer. I make a note and wait as she composes herself. Then I change focus.

'What about the posters? What do you think Jacob was saying about them?'

She shakes her head.

'The men went to the village every month. To trade. I don't get why they didn't see those posters before?'

'How do you think Isaac knew and not Jacob?' I ask.

'Reckon he musta gone to the village on his own.'

'Was that usual?'

'It wasn't allowed. The boys had to be with the men.'

'Who do you think put them up?' I question.

She shakes her head, then goes quiet.

'If it was the cops, the men would have seen them much earlier.' Her breath is shallow. 'If they were new… then maybe… Who would do that?' She's disconcerted.

'Do you think Isaac and Mary were in on something together?' I remark.

'Like what?' She looks puzzled. I watch her as her mind clears.

'What do you think, Rose?'

She looks away from me, her features darkening.

Then slowly, 'Jacob said Isaac told him about the posters. Maybe Mary already knew about them. What if she told Isaac to pull them down? Why would she do that?' She's thinking aloud.

'Do you think it is possible that Isaac didn't want the posters to be left…' I stop as Rose's eyes widen.

'Mary set it up.' Her voice rises. 'That *bitch*. I was right.'

Rose jumps to her feet and paces madly.

'I always thought it was the cops. Looking for Pa. Or me.'

Cops? Looking for Pa/Rose? Why?

'What do you mean, Rose?'

She fires off, ignoring me.

'Isaac told her that the posters were there before he spoke to Jacob. She told him to pull them down. He didn't… because he wanted Jacob to see them. You're right. Isaac wanted me gone. And… she… she wanted me to stay. Or… for the cops to come and get…' She spins around, her body taut with conflict.

'He didn't pull them down 'cos he wanted someone from the farm to know… to know I was… wanted…' The last word is almost inaudible.

'What do you mean by *wanted*?' I interject.

She turns her back to me and paces aggressively.

Wanted? For what?!

'He was suspicious about me and Beck. He must have been freaked out that… that she… that we… But I still don't get why Mary wanted me to stay at the farm…'

Rose suddenly stops.

'Oh no… fuckin' hell… I get it. They lost a child. Beck's brother. Beck said Chris looked like him.'

She stands there, her hands to her face, her features highlighted as comprehension reins in chaos.

'That's why Jacob said Mary was becoming so attached to Chris.'

Rose is motionless. Her breath held.

Then the exploding outbreath.

'She did want Chris, didn't she?' She turns to me.

I look at her as some of the pieces of the puzzle begin to fit.

Rose sits back down heavily.

'That's why Beck said that I had to go. Not because we were getting involved, but…'

'Beck said you had to go?' I interrupt.

What?

She flicks a look of intense annoyance at me.

'Yes. Yes, she did.'

I watch her carefully, my mind searching for any clarity.

'Not because of us. She knew… she understood… that her mother was obsessive… about my boy.' Her body shudders. Her eyes ache with memory. Her shoulders hunch.

'And not because someone from outside was looking for me. Mary knew about what happened… because Chris… Beck…'

'What part of *what happened* are you talking about Rose?' I respond quickly.

She flicks her eyes down. There's no traction here. Not yet.

Rose leans forwards and holds her head in her hands.

'I never saw it before. Never. I thought we had to go because of…'

'Pa?' I finish. She stares angrily at me. In full fight mode. The pendulum swings quickly today.

There's something else here … justification / projection?

'Did you ever ask Beck what she thought?' I persist.

She doesn't answer.

I make a note.

'So, what happened after that?'

'What do ya think? The shit hit the fan.' She's furious.

'What happened, Rose?'

Steady.

She ducks her head, controlling her outburst. My guidance has not been futile.

'That fucking bitch. She stole from me.' Her voice is intense.

Narrow.

'How, Rose? How did she do that?' I ask.

'Danny!' she spits it out.

~

New South Wales, Early February 1979

Rebecca teetered on the edge of the chair reaching high up into their between-wall closet. Her parent's bedroom, on the first floor of The Manor, was impeccably neat. Each item placed in order of preference and use.

'I cannot see it, mother. I will need the ladder,' she called, stretching further. 'Please come and assist me.'

'Then leave it, daughter.' Mary's voice was clear. Marked with annoyance.

'I will look for it later. Your father must have used it in the bales for the calves. I'm going to the cows now.' She was in the kitchen below, wiping her hands on her apron, untying it and hanging it on the back of the door

Her voice was loud up the stairwell.

'Please make sure you knead the dough strong,' she commanded. 'And do it before you attend to your other chores. Do not leave it long, you hear. The yeast is ready.' Her voice was filled with irritation. She shouted back over her shoulder. 'You must stay here after your chores. Isaac will be joining us for evening prayers.'

'Wait, mother. I need the torch. I think I can see…' The back door banged as her mother's footsteps receded into the distance.

Goodness she's in a mood, Rebecca thought and, sighing, jumped off the chair.

~

I heard the soft thud of her feet landing.

'Rose?' Beck called, her voice muffled, reaching me in our attic room above.

'Can you please come down? I need you to help me.

Mary had been looking for an old winter eiderdown in which to wrap the ripening cheese. The milk from the dairy was abundant that year, yielding vast quantities of delectable cream.

As I neared their bedroom door, I heard Beck clattering around at the side of the bed, hauling the wooden stool out from under it. She looked up as I entered, her cheeks flushed from the effort.

Her smile lit my world.

'Here,' she said. 'Come and hold the stool for me. So that I don't fall and break my neck.' She grinned at me impishly. 'I will be of no use to anyone in that occurrence.'

It was the day after our first embrace. My mind was filled with euphoria and turmoil. Beck's touch lingered on my body. Her scent filled me. Her breath on my belly had lit a furnace of aching need in my womb. Entwined in each other's embrace, we had talked the night through. About Sarah and Danny. About us. About what to do, about Pa.

She insisted that we bide our time. She knew that the men were due to leave for the village at the new moon, after the barn had been raised and all the produce harvested. She wanted to find out more about what Mary knew. About Jacob's true intent. To secrete provisions for me to leave. And to keep me by her side longer.

She placed the stool on top of the chair and clambered up, swaying on her toes, her torso disappearing into the closet above us.

'I think I can see it. It's at the very back. Lord knows why she would have pushed it so far.' She wriggled further. 'Hang onto both of them please,' she called as I leant my weight to the chair and steadied the wobbling stool.

'Help me. It's a bit further.' Her voice flowed down to me. I reached up, placed my hand on her bottom and pushed hard. Rebecca disappeared into the closet giggling, her feet hanging over the edge.

'Great. Thanks. I've got it.' The requested eiderdown came tumbling over the edge, toppling onto the floor.

'Now I need to get myself off this lofty height.' Her eyes were filled with fun as she peeked at me over the edge.

'I will turn around now. Can you please move the chairs?' She flipped herself onto her belly and was wriggling her feet over the edge when she stopped.

'You alright?' I asked.

Her feet disappeared again.

'Beck?'

Silence.

'What's happening, Beck?' I called more urgently.

'There's other stuff up here. Mother said there was only the quilt. But. It's…' her voice was muffled in the dark recesses of the loft.

'It's right at the back. Behind these… Oh Lordy… Pass me the torch.'

I heard a dragging sound and Beck's face appeared at the edge.

'Look,' she exclaimed. 'It was hidden behind the eiderdown and under these bags of old clothes. Here. Can you get it?'

She hung precariously, reaching down and handing me a large, sealed cardboard box. Then she swung herself back over the ledge and dropped easily to the floor. The flaps on the plain container were tucked neatly into each other. On the outside was written one word.

'*Private.*' We both spoke at once. Beck looked at me puzzled.

'That's Mother's hand,' she exclaimed, lightly touching the inscription. 'I had better return it to the loft.' She placed her foot on the chair, steadying herself to clamber back up.

I reached out to her.

'Wait,' I said. She turned to me, her eyes enquiring.

'What would she put in a box… that needed her to write private on it?' I asked. Our eyes met as my question floated between us.

'And why store it so far back in a loft where it's hidden and no one but her knows it's there?' she slowly voiced my question.

She looked at the copper plate script, her thumbs idly caressing its curves.

'Father has been looking for his extra summer shirt for this hot weather,' she murmured, giving the box a gentle shake. A rattling sound came from its depths.

'But whatever is in here, I doubt it's that!' she declared. Her fingers slipped between the flaps, probing its interior.

'This is paper. No wait. It's…' Her voice was hushed in the silence of the house.

'It's private, Beck,' I whispered my hand more urgent on her arm.

'Let's see what the Elders think about *private*.' She looked at me. A new light of defiance shone in her eyes.

'*Private* means I need to know.' Her lips moved in silent prayer,

173

then she deftly flipped the box open.

Laying at its bottom, wrapped with string, was a pile of envelopes. Each neatly sliced open at the top. Beck reached in and pulled them out. Unravelling the string, she turned them over. Her hand froze as the envelopes cascaded to the floor.

'Rosanna,' she read aloud, her voice a hoarse whisper.

~

The door to the barn swung shut behind Isaac. He thrust the bolt into place to keep the horses safe for the night. Whistling for his dog, he trotted back towards the Manor House.

Rebecca was due to meet him later that night for their first pre-nuptial gathering. His forehead creased with perplexity as he thought about her. The perfect wife-to-be by all accounts. Intelligent. Chaste. A hard worker. Beautiful. Definitely ripe for breeding. But so strong willed.

He strode towards the milking shed, for the final check on the poddy calves.

But there was a feeling. A thorn in his side that itched to be pulled. It was this new woman. "The Girl from the Forest," as he liked to call her. His groin knotted in mortification as he thought of her.

There's something not right. Beck is too fond of her. And the child. It's not natural.

His thoughts trailed like a black cloud after him, his pace fuelled with perplexity in the growing dusk.

Those posters. The elders must know.

'Come on, boy,' he called. 'Keep up for heaven's sake!'

~

Beck and I sat on the floor of our room, surrounded by letters. Some open. Some still secreted in their envelopes. Written as I climbed the forest. As I healed in Rebecca's arms. As I watched the seasons pass in the fields and as my son grew taller each day.

They reached out to me into that valley of secrets. Reassuring me. Begging me to come home. My heart burst open as I read *Always with love* inscribed at the end of each. I looked at them repeatedly. Danny calling me in the night. Dad asking why I had run. Auntie Mim reassuring me of her love.

And money. Hidden. Folded into their creases.

I read until I couldn't see any more for the tears in my eyes and the flood of realisation. Beck sat beside me as I wept. Holding my shoulders. In those moments where betrayal sank like a lead weight into me and where deceit replaced my belief in Mary's human decency, a void too wide to cross had changed Rebecca too. Her heart broke with the undeniable truth that had laid hidden in her parent's bedroom. In that lofty secreted space.

'So, this is your family, Rose. The ones that you had to leave behind.' Her eyes were filled with pain. 'Their words are beautiful. Their love so great for you. Now I understand your anguish. Your dreams.' Her fingers caressed my face.

'But why did Mary do this?' I implored.

'I cannot answer that. But Mother has acted with unconscionable treachery. I am convinced now that she is a threat. To you. To Christian. To us. You are truly an innocent.'

I looked at her, fear flooding me.

'But I have done such wrong,' I exclaimed.

'No Rose. You have never wronged another. It has never been a part of you. Not ever.' Her eyes filled with understanding, yearning. 'But you have to leave. It is not safe here now. They will know. They know me too well. And we will never be one here. Not ever.'

And for the first time, I saw my beloved weep.

~

Isaac drew close to the house. The kitchen lights glowed softly from behind the cloth curtains. He could hear Mary attending to the evening supper. The light in the attic room was off. He slipped through the back door and ignoring the sanctum of The Manor House, took the steps two at a time. His ire had risen on the walk from the dairy as he focused on his betrothed and her friend.

I have to know what is going on.

The landing before their bedroom door squeaked at his foot fall. He hesitated a second, decorum and the learnt scriptures calling him to his integrity. Then, banishing civility, he pushed the door open and stepped into the darkened room.

~

Beck held me close. Her naked breasts pressed to my lips. Her nipples hard with desire. Her body wrapped itself around mine as she moved her hips against me. My fingers explored her depths. Salt and tang and sweetness filled my senses.

Her back arched as she moaned, our bodies writhing in the heat and the passion of our embrace. Our love making obliterated all time.

Her eyes were closed as I drew her face down to mine. Her rose scented hair fell like a shroud around us. I kissed her hard as her open mouth drew me into her. The scent of our bodies filled my head as the ache between my legs engulfed me. The blankets around us fell away when I heard her gasp and her body went rigid.

'Rose!' she breathed. '*Stop.*'

I froze as she looked past me. Our door shut abruptly and a fast footfall descended the stairs. The back door slammed shut behind him.

~

'Who?' I urged. Beck placed her finger over my lips as our bodies parted.

'Shh! Isaac!'

My eyes widened as her pupils dilated.

'Mother must not know,' she mouthed. Her fingers lingered over my body as she lightly stepped off the bed and slipped on her clothes.

'Where are you going?' I whispered.

'After him, I have to stop him.' Passion and urgency filled her voice.

'I'm coming too.'

'Hush. No!' She leant to me and her lips pressed into mine, her mouth open in a last kiss.

'Why?'

Rebecca hesitated. 'Trust me, Rose. Please.' And within the cloak of darkness, she slipped down the stairs, leaving me in the warmth of our love.

I sat upright, my mind spinning.

Throwing the sheets from me, I stepped into my mended jeans and a shirt. I reached for my backpack. Grabbing the torch, I found all my letters and stowed them inside, shoving it back under my bed, hidden behind my books.

My boots hung from my fingers as I noiselessly descended the stairs and stepped out into a moonlit night. In the distance, I could hear the sound of Isaac's dog barking. The lantern in the barn on the hill shone dimly. Pulling my boots on, I ran towards it.

As I approached, I could hear hushed voices. I slid up to the door pressing my ear to it. Through the crack I could see Isaac and Rebecca. Isaac was pacing the straw strewn floor, his hands clenched in fists. Beck stood to the side, her face a mask of concentration.

'How *could* you?' he growled.

'You don't understand Isaac. This is not what is seems.'

'With a woman? *That* woman?' He turned to her, his face red with rage. 'You will be put aside, Rebecca. Your life will rot in *hell*.'

'You cannot condemn what you do not understand Isaac. You do not know that God wants that for me,' her voice was low, controlled. Each word marked in time.

She watched him as he paced.

'You are unworthy of me,' he growled. 'Of us. You have behaved like a harlot.' His voice was loud as he faced her, his body contorted with humiliation.

'What has happened here is out of your control.' Beck stood her full height against him. 'It is not your right to speak to me like this. You must control yourself, Isaac.'

'But you are my betrothed. *My* wife to be. How can I look at you without shame now?'

His voice was clear as I shrunk back against the wall.

'Then do not marry me, Isaac. If this is your belief, I cannot have you. You know not what has happened. It is not me who has betrayed us. It is another.'

Isaac turned to her.

'And who do you speak of, Rebecca? *Who* could have ever done worse than you?'

I stepped out from the shadows.

'Rose!' Beck breathed.

Isaac spun around, his fists clenched.

'So! You come now to show me your face.' Isaac spat the words at me.

I stood still.

'You have *stolen* from me!' he cursed, moving quickly towards me, eyes blazing.

Beck leapt between us, shielding my body with hers.

'This must stop,' she commanded, her arms blocking the blows meant for me. Isaac halted inches from her. His fist raised.

'You don't understand, Isaac,' she spoke softly, a visible cloak of love pouring around us. Isaac froze, riveted to the floor.

'You know nothing of her story,' Beck continued, slowly lowering her arms, her eyes affixed on Isaac's.

'You know not what she has endured. You cannot condemn her or me. You are not the judge here. Only God can do that. You *must* control yourself.'

Her voice was laced with compassion, drowning out the anger and the pain that filled us all in that cavernous lofty building. Isaac looked at her.

'Please. Please listen to us. To her.' Beck stood shoulder to shoulder with this tall young man, whose life had been turned upside down by my unwitting entrance into it.

I watched. An observer. Knowing that as we stood there our paths were crossing. That we were entering a junction where destiny dictates the human will.

Isaac's face was pale. Rebecca looked at him. Their energies meeting like a current in a fast-moving stream, then separating and re-joining around the obstacle of confusion that was between them.

'Is it not written into the scriptures, Isaac, that we must in time travel with sin?'

'But I trusted you, Rebecca.' His voice rose to a sob.

'Do not speak to me of broken trust, Isaac. You have no idea of what this means.' Her words were a measured beat of authority.

He looked at her.

'You must listen to us. We need your help.'

~

The shadow of the moon hid behind the earth. The barn had been raised. The women had cooked up a feast. The carousing had begun. The coveted liquor was finally released from its barrels as the community celebrated yet another success.

Beck and I had pleaded study as our excuse to slip away, Christian's hand in mine. He followed us, his curious eyes asking questions that I could not answer.

The horse was saddled. The provisions stowed in our backpacks. My letters tucked securely. In the dark of that night, wrapped in cloaks against the cold, I fled again from my life, my son seated between my lover and me. And the hooves of Isaac's gelding drummed a repetitive beat, pulsing with the echo of Danny's voice.

It's time, Rose. Time!

~

New South Wales, February 1979

A cool breeze flowed in under the door of the solitary red phone booth. The dial tone rang clearly in my ear, twin chimes synchronised with my heartbeat. Silence in the emptiness. Vacant moments weighted against intervals spaced three seconds apart.

Chris clung to my legs. It was well past midnight, in that isolated locality. My heart beat a contra refrain as I held my breath.

~

The train had stopped just south of the border. The guard sauntered past as we sat in the cramped interior of his rear cabin.

'Wanna stretch your legs a bit, miss?' he growled.

I stepped out into a fresh night, Christian sleeping soundly on my shoulder.

'Is there a phone here?' I asked.

He tilted his chin in the direction of the dirt road that ran beside the lines and stomped off to the grey Besser brick toilet block. A single streetlight illuminated the telephone box.

~

The music from the Nimbin hippy commune echoed in my mind as the train clattered north. I had thumbed a ride in the last carriage. Thick columns of black acrid smoke belched out of the locomotive and floated over us. Like a cloud-shaped plume of my past burning memories into moments that rattled forward towards my future.

From where we sat, I could see shadows in the night of the familiar countryside flashing past. Chris was perched on the edge of his seat, his small face pressed against the window.

As the kilometres sped by, my body was lulled by the rocking of the carriage. The streets of Nimbin and the undulating fields of The Farm were behind me, fading into a rich tapestry of my past.

I was free.

My mind reeled with confusion.

~

'I will never forget you, Rose.' She had sighed, kissing me intensely. Huddling me into her body.

We had melted into each other. Her voice liquid honey as she kissed my cheeks.

'Dive deeply into your life,' her eyes shone as she held my hands to her lips. 'You are gifted. Talented in ways most are not. You must study. But remember me, Rose. Send your love. Even when there is no possibility of them allowing it,' she whispered.

'Can I write?' I breathed.

She shook her head.

'*I* will write. Mother… her plans for you are…' She paused; her eyes grieved as the pressure of my hands on her belly drew her away from her thoughts.

'I love you, Rose. Your touch… forever…' She sighed, pools of light in her eyes diving deep into me.

'Come with me, Beck,' I urged.

'I cannot do this Rose. Not now. I must return. To keep you safe. Isaac is watching them. He will distract them. He has prepared our bedroom. They will think we are studying late tonight. That the barn took the time that we needed to learn from the books. I have to go back. My place is there for now, with him. But… the future… I promise…' Her words paused as I kissed her, her mouth, soft, open.

'Hold me, Rose,' she breathed.

We laid across each other that last night. Our hands, lips and fingers traversing the sacred spaces in our bodies as our parting drenched us with tenderness. The scars in my armour melted with our tears, the pain within the memories of my life vanishing into her soft caress.

~

'Mumma?' Chris's voice interrupted my reverie.

'How far is it to Bwith-bane?' he lisped, his face peering through the carriage window, eyes squinting into the dark.

'A while,' I responded, wanting to get back to my thoughts.

'Will we see Becca soon?' he said. 'I wanna see her.'

'Beck will be back at The Farm.'

'Will we go to The Farm too?' he persisted.

I bent over and pulled him onto my lap.

'We are going to the big city, Chris,' I explained, 'to get a job and make a new home there. Danny is waiting for us. Remember?'

He pulled back from me, looking earnestly into my face.

'But why do we have to leave? I wanna see *her*,' he complained.

'I know my darling. But the cold winds blow at The Farm. And I don't want to run away again and hide. Beck will be here when we come back.'

'What will Danny do?' he asked.

'He will help me find what I have lost Chris.' I smiled. 'Remember how he loved to sing to you?'

Christian looked at me, a small smile tickling the corners of his mouth. Then as quickly as the smile had formed, the petulant five-year-old returned.

'But I mith Beck.' He frowned, cuddling into my shoulder.

'Me too.' I sighed.

'Wrap me up, Mumma,' Chris ordered. Closing his eyes, he buried into me and drifted off to sleep.

The train rocked and vibrated under me, as my thoughts lingered towards Beck.

~

Beck had held me tight as I said goodbye.

'Go Rose,' she urged. 'Go to your life.'

Reaching up, I pressed my face into her neck and wrapped her in my arms. Her soft thick auburn curls encircled me. Breathing her in, I drew her scent into the deepest part of my brain.

Then, in the distance, we heard the hoot of the approaching train.

'I must go,' she said, her face now dry. 'Before I'm seen.'

Her hand squeezed mine as she bent to kiss Chris, wrapping her arm around him. Then she was gone. Her cape flowed behind as our steed carried her away into the inky black night. My lips kissed the darkness that had held her, as a wave of her heat filled my body with the soft memory of her promise.

As the headlights of the train lit up the forest surrounding the station, I once again turned to face an unknown future, Christian's hand held tight in mine.

~

The sound of the phone being picked up roused me.

Silence. Then the buzz of static. The sound of fumbling. A sleepy, grumpy voice.

'Watsa matta, Dad? It's so late.' Irritation slurred the inflection of his unmistakable voice.

My heartbeat accelerated.

'Dan?' I whispered.

A pause.

'Who is this?' His voice sleepy. Annoyed.

'Danny!' My apprehension reverberated against the icy glass of the phone booth.

'Yeah! Yes. This is Danny. Who is it? What do ya want?' Impatience tempered with curiosity.

'It's me, Dan.' My voice caught in my throat.

The sound of a sharp inhalation.

'Rose?' Loudly. Disbelief inflected the tenor voice that had called me in the darkest of my nights as he reached out and into that cold chamber.

'Rosanna! What? *Rose!* His voice filled with urgency.

'Yes, Danny. It's me.'

'Oh… my… God…' He breathed. 'Rose… Where are you?' Down the line I heard a lamp clicking on. Feet striking the floor. Animated movement.

'At the siding.'

'What? How?' His voice filled with disbelief.

Then.

'Are you okay? Christian…?'

My voice choked.

'Yes, he's with me…'

'Wait. I'll come…'

'No, Dan. The train. I'm on the train. I'll be there in the morning.'

'Oh… my… Rose! Rosie-rose!' His voice was thick with emotion. 'How?'

'Can you meet us? The morning diesel?'

'Yes, yes. Of course.'

'I have to go,' I whispered.

'Rose. Rose…' His words stopped, tears resting in their cadence.

'I'm alright, Dan. See you there.'

'Rose! Please wait… I…'

The coins fell through the slot as the line went dead.

10

Brisbane, February 1979

WITH the thunder of the locomotive still ringing in our ears, we stepped from the train. Danny stood in the dawn light, waiting for me. I could see him straining to find me from the far end of the platform. His eyes met mine and held them steady, the corners crinkled in recognition. Sarah grinned at me through his smile.

His likeness to Dad took my breath away.

He pushed through the crowd towards me, his face flushed. His body had grown in size, his stature akin to one of the giant trees of the Nimbin forests.

I let go of Chris's hand and my bag dropped to the ground. In an instant I was gathered into strong arms. His thick, red beard tickled my face as his firm lips kissed my cheek. His eyes sparkled and brimmed with feeling. My feet dangled above the platform as he stood there holding me, murmuring nonsensically, absorbing the endless time that had flowed between us.

Tentatively, a little hand tugged at me.

'Umma?'

A small face peered up at us. Gently, Danny placed me back on the platform and wiping his nose with the back of his hand, squatted in front of Christian.

'Well then. Who might this be then?' His rich Gaelic brogue lit a fire in my heart.

For once, shyness overcame Chris and, ducking his head, he pulled in behind me, pressing into the back of my legs. I bent and stroked his head.

'It's Danny, Chris,' I said. 'Come and say hi.'

Christian buried himself into me, the strangeness surrounding him and the earliness of the morning confusing him.

'Remember?' I prompted.

Danny began to hum a soft tune as Chris peaked out at him.

'So how are you, little man?' Danny enquired, reaching out his hand to shake Chris's.

Chris looked tentatively up at Danny.

'Good,' he replied. Then, recovering his self-assurance, he frowned.

'Umma says you gonna help us,' he declared.

Danny grinned.

'I reckon!' His voice filled the air with tangible confidence.

'Remember the wild herb garden, Chris?' Danny said 'Well, that's where we'll be going.'

Chris looked at him, puzzled at first, then smiling.

'Our garden?' Christian asked. 'With Auntie Sah?'

'Yep, cobber,' Danny replied. 'We can visit her there, whenever you like.' Reaching down he swung Chris up onto his shoulders, collected my luggage and took me by the hand, striding out into the Brisbane dawn.

The streets were deserted as Danny's old Holden spluttered across a flat wide bridge not far from the station. We turned towards the muddy, slow-flowing river. A few cars drove past as we waited to cross the main road. We turned into a long street lined with small timber homes and huge warehouses. I had never seen so many dwellings packed into such a small space. Narrow blocks of land where windows looked into neighbour's backyards and where clothing, draped on Hills Hoists, flapped in the wind.

The scent of frangipani was heavy in the air as we cruised noisily to a halt in front of an old house. Two identically painted windows framed an open front door with a long corridor disappearing into the darker interior. Rotting cornices decorated the sides of a shady veranda. The front steps were chipped and cracked. An old bicycle leant against the far corner. And the sweet floral waft of incense with a musty undertone of cannabis greeted us.

Gold and cream rays of sultry heat lit the space within.

The front lawn had been converted into a vegetable garden, not unlike Dad's. Small cherry tomatoes crawled over a makeshift frame of bamboo. Basil and parsley poked up through weeds that threatened to smother them. I recognised the pungent aroma of onions and the leafier greens of a mass of carrots. A passionfruit vine choked the far fence and extended towards an overgrown backyard. Golden fruit hung in clusters, dripping with the richness of a warm subtropical morning.

Danny smiled as he turned off the engine. We sat in silence, absorbing our surroundings.

'Here we are,' he finally said. 'Welcome to Brisbane.'

He was different, but the same. Self-assured. Steady. I looked at him, remembering that final farewell on the streets of Nimbin. When my life was a chaos of grief and confusion. He faced me as my thoughts silenced and watched carefully as I breathed in our new home.

Then, turning, he opened the car door, tugging my backpack easily onto his shoulders and called to Christian as he disappeared into the house.

~

That night, we sat in the dark on the shabby couch in Danny's loungeroom, Christian draped between us, absorbing his surroundings. Danny's hands idly stroked Chris's hair as he hummed softly, murmuring responses to his sleepy questions.

There was a strange familiarity to it. The lullaby. The man. The conversation. The warmth in the air from the early evening humidity. The aroma of the baked beans and fresh toast from the kitchen stirred a deeper memory of lamb stew and freshly baked bread and the shrieking laughter of children tumbling, chasing and playing on Mim and Dad's wide, bullnose veranda.

The strains of the John Coltrane trio floated around and the pungent sweet fragrance of Danny's evening reefer soothed my tired nerves. The low light from the kitchen semi-lit the room, casting shadows into the corners. Piles of books covered the floor. Dirty mismatched teacups were stacked high on the kitchen bench, half-filled with cold tea as milk and cream stains ran concentric circles towards their chipped rims. Cracked plates with half-eaten pizza lay strewn on the coffee table amongst edited essays and library books. A jazz guitar leaned against the wall and a trio of drums stood neatly in the middle of the floor.

In the gathering twilight, the screeching argument of flying foxes and the pungent smell of bat urine stung my nostrils. And somewhere along the banks of the Brisbane River, close to Danny's front porch, a mopoke owl called, sending soft shivers down my spine.

Christian's rhythmic sleeping breath comforted me. I quietly collected him into my arms and carried him to Danny's bedroom, laying him on the large mattress in the corner, kissing his downy curls. I crept back out to the sofa.

Danny watched me approach. I stood before him as he reached out, offering his hand, gently pulling me next to him. I rested against his side, my legs curled up between us. I breathed him in as my thoughts spun with the events of the last week. Danny's hands soothingly stroked my arms and back. His fingers trailed images from the forest faeries of our youth, speaking to me of Dad and Mim and Sarah. The touch of his hand on my shoulders sent waves of comfort through my body as he brushed my hair away from my face.

The night lengthened and finally his lips caressed my head. Standing up, he drew me to my feet and wordlessly beckoned me to follow him onto the back veranda. A mattress lay there, covered with a mosquito net and piled with cushions and rugs. Parting the corner of the net, we crawled in and lay facing each other. Infinite pools of blue gazed into me.

'Rose.' He reached out, taking my hand in his, the velvety brogue of his voice soothing me.

We had chatted throughout that day as Christian played, exploring his new home. We walked through the parkland close by to look at the river. It was swollen with recent summer rain – muddy and deep. I had never seen such a broad watercourse. Small vessels motored up and down its length and breadth. The current ran swift and strong. The banks were covered with mangroves. Strange trees that I'd not seen before, their fat tubers extending around them.

'Look Umma,' Chris called to me. He had disappeared over the small wall that stood between the embankment and the river. 'Look, there's sticks in the river. Lots of 'em!' he declared.

We clambered over onto soggy, tidal mud. Chris squatted at the river's edge, his fingers pulling on the upright grey roots. His clean clothes were covered in sludge.

'Chris!' I sighed, exacerbated.

Danny grinned at me as he tugged my small son up onto his hip.

It goes with the territory… I thought as I smiled shyly at Danny.

'See those sticks, Chris?' Danny asked. 'Well, they are a part of the trees here. And when the river goes down more, there will be hundreds of them. They come up out of the water and breathe the air.'

Chris looked solemnly at Dan. 'Trees don't breathe. Only animals do,' he declared.

~

The night was filled with the muted sound of the river and the inner city, the background hum from the freeway competed with the cicada's drumroll. Somewhere a cistern flushed and the sound of running water caught my attention. A back door banged shut and muffled voices receded into the neighbour's house, reaching out to me through the night.

A single mosquito buzzed around the netting, drawing me back to the veranda. Dan watched me as my senses traced the unfamiliar suburban noise.

'So many questions, Rose.' The fiery red of his beard caught the streetlight. I watched as his eyes travelled my face, trying to read my answers.

We talked into that night, tracing the patterns of our lives. We lay close, the heat surrounding our bodies, Dan's reassuring presence easing my uncertainty. Then, in a heartbeat, Beck's face filled my mind and I turned from him, curling into a ball, rocking myself into a dreamless slumber.

~

The sound of dishes rattling in the sink and the clatter of little feet along a corridor woke me. Danny's deep tones answered Christian as he excitedly explored his new territory. I lay there in the warmth, waiting for sleep to clear. Through the lattice on the side of the veranda, the sun beat dappled patterns of golden heat onto the foot of the bed. The buzzing of bees was the background to Christian's delighted shrieks.

'Umma. UMMA,' he called. 'Come look. There's bees 'n a bike 'n tomato…'

I rolled onto my side trying to ignore this intrusion, before a small frame thundered up the stairs and Christian threw himself at me, pulling the mosquito net aside and leaping onto the bed.

'Mumma. Where were you last night? I looked for you,' he complained.

'I was here, in my new bed.' I smiled as a wet kiss landed on the side of my nose.

'Danny slept wiv me. We slept together,' he exclaimed, bouncing on the mattress

'Umma. Get up. Now. I wanna show you.' He pushed through the mosquito net and scampered down the back steps, a trail of glee following.

'He's taken to it like a duck to water.' Danny's brogue caught the edge of my reverie. He leant against the back-door frame, a large cup of steaming coffee in his hand. A grin across his face.

'Did you sleep well?' He lifted the netting and sat down next to me. 'They could hear you snoring across the bridge.' His eyes twinkled with amusement.

'Breakfast is on. Fancy eggs and bacon?'

I managed a thank you before my ball of mischief came flying up the stairs.

'Danny. Danny. Come now. I wanna show you. *Now.*' He hopped from one foot to the other impatiently.

'No problems, cobber.' Danny chuckled as Chris dragged him down the steps.

~

The aroma of roasting Arabica beans floated around me as I sipped the sweet hot coffee. The heat of the February morning was a soporific blanket of humidity. I watched as Danny swung Christian up onto his broad shoulders and spun him around the overgrown garden, chanting nonsensical poetry and tickling his naked feet. Christian's squeals of delight accompanied their play, a medicine reaching deep inside me.

As the coffee drew me from sleepiness, I wondered if Danny thought of Christian in our absence. I didn't realise how much I had yearned for his friendship. For the life woven into the fibre of my soul, the threads of which had intertwined magic and tragedy, knitting my past and present to this new life. Sitting in my shroud of white cotton, Brisbane and Danny were as natural as the ripples in the water of the great old river at our doorstep. I breathed the fragrance of the frangipanis, mixed with the musty smell of damp clothing drying on the Hills Hoist in a moist-laden summer air.

The languid heat softened my heart, drawing me onto an unknown path to my future, as a gate opened, beckoning me to walk through.

~

'I prefer the Tanzanian variety.' He took a swig from his coffee. 'But in this parochial town, all you can get is the Indo stuff. It's got no body. Tastes like that bloody fruit. The one in Bali that smells like a sewer.' Danny beamed at me over his shoulder as he turned the eggs and bacon.

'Sunny side up?' he questioned.

I nodded.

'We grew coffee. On The Farm,' I said, watching Christian turn Danny's lounge into a bomb site.

'Chris. Come on. It's breakfast,' I called to him. 'Hungry?' I asked as he raced through the door, grabbing Danny's leg as he moved around the kitchen and standing on his left foot.

'Umma. Can we go to Uni today?' he asked, bouncing up and down, his eyes sparkling.

'I've been telling him about my course. He wants to come and see.' Danny smiled broadly.

'Can we, Umma, can we?' Chris nagged

'Well, I guess we could take the ferry.'

Danny's voice bounced off the interior walls of the fridge as he bent to find the butter. He hobbled back to the stove, Christian clinging to him, giggling.

'This is Mum's butter,' Dan said, extracting Chris from around his leg and tickling him under the chin. His hand held a large, round knob of butter impregnated with herbs. My heart skipped a beat as my mind's eye tracked the length of dirt road that swung over a railway line.

Danny turned to me.

'Yep. It's Mrs Flan's milk. Mum has a butter churn now,' he said, his eyes riveted on mine.

I blinked and looked down.

He knows my thoughts.

Danny watched me carefully. Then softly.

'She's everywhere lassie. Thought I could get away from her. Here in the big smoke.' His eyes filled with pain. 'But she's a pesky little thing. Worse than before she carked it.' A lopsided grin. 'Do you ever feel her?' he asked.

'All the time.' I said, looking away.

He paused.

'Sorry, Rose. We don't have to talk about her.'

'No. That's okay,' I murmured. 'I… I need to.'

~

The small river ferry collected us at the rickety old pier and with Danny's hand tight around Christian's, we clambered inside.

'The bloody campus, it's huge,' Danny shouted over the din of the engine. 'Yer gonna love it,' he said. 'There's a lake in the middle. As big as 100 houses.' He grinned at me.

'And a pool. For the students. I'll get yer in.' He beamed. 'Just watch this little fella for a tick while I pay me mate here.' Danny dug his hand into his pocket, retrieved some small coins and tossed them at the ferry driver.

Christian's face was pressed to the window.

'Look Umma,' he squealed. 'There's a boat. And another.' His small finger traced the image of the row boats that dotted the water surface.

'I wanna go on that one,' he demanded.

'Later, little man.' Danny picked him up and held him close as he carried him to the rear of the boat.

'Look at the water, Chris,' Danny said. 'You know those engines? They can pull 100 horses.'

Christian looked at Danny, puzzled.

'How?' he asked.

~

The ferry pulled into a stop, close to a wide expanse of bushland and mown playing fields. Holding my hand, Danny led our way off the boat. He put Christian down and we walked along the road that ran beside the river.

'Want a swim?' he asked, as we came alongside an enclosed Olympic sized pool.

'I wanna. I wanna,' sang Chris, pulling at my hand. 'Come on, Umma. Let's go. I wanna swim.'

I gathered my bag and reached up to kiss Danny on the cheek. His eyes met mine, lingering in a surprise embrace.

'Have a good one, Rose.' His voice was husky. 'See yah after my lecture.' His long bronze hair blew in the breeze as he strode off.

~

That evening we lay on the back mattress, listening to the sultry sounds of the Graeme Bell All Stars. The pool, and the adventure into the grounds of the University, had tired Chris and he was splayed out between us asleep, his breathing soft and deep.

Danny's eyes travelled over my body as I got up to move my son to the front room. When I laid back beside him, his silence filled the night with questions. His finger reached out and traced the scar above my left eye.

'Who?'

'Him. He did,' I mumbled.

Danny's eyes widened. 'He did it! Fuck that bastard. He deserves to be dead.' His voice a low growl. His eyes narrow. 'When?' he asked.

I looked away.

'Did you go to the river?'

'Yes… yes… I… I waited… for you.'

'Where?' His forehead creased.

'Under the bridge. Near the butter factory.'

Danny stared at me.

'So, you *were* there…' Shock flooded his face and he abruptly turned away.

'Dan? What's going on?'

His hand reached out and gripped mine. His face colouring.

'How did you know I was coming home?' he breathed

'Dad spilt the beans. It was supposed to be a surprise. That's why I waited, Danny. Like you said. Like you told me.'

The corners of his mouth tightened.

'But I don't understand. I looked for yer… early that morning. Everywhere. I looked…'

I watched him as the implications of this information sunk into my brain.

'But… but… you didn't come, Dan…' Tears pricked my eyes. 'It was… too… I left. I was so scared. I didn't know what to do. It was so dangerous.'

Danny stared at me, swallowing hard. He took both my hands in his, his eyes troubled.

'Rose… I… what happened was… he… Pa…' Danny shook his head, his breath agitated. His mouth tightened as he ducked his head and sat tight.

'What happened, Dan? What?' I pleaded, sensing his all-familiar silence.

'Dan! Please talk to me!'

'Posters…' he muttered.

'You know about them?' I interjected.

He looked away trying to speak. 'Because I couldn't find yer, I thought that… Dad was right. About yer running away. I wouldn't have kept trying if I thought yer were… were…' His voice inflected with turmoil. I watched him, confused by the change in his energy.

Forbidden questions filled the night.

'I don't understand, Dan.' Bewilderment chased the corners of my memory. He turned to me, his face pale, refusal in his eyes.

'But where did yer go lassie?'

'Up river… like you said.'

'How? How did you get through that wilderness?'

'I listened, Dan. I heard your voice inside my head. Sah too. Chris led the way. I listened to the forest.'

He took a breath, shook his head.

'We found our way.' I watched him as the neighbour's back porch light cast irregular shadows across the contours of the mosquito net.

'That's impossible!' Danny breathed heavily.

His eyes flicked away and then back to me. He reached out and lightly caressed my face.

'So! He did hurt you.' His cadence was raw and angry.

'Bad.'

'Chris?'

I shook my head. Danny's outbreath was filled with relief. He gently lifted my arm. The shadowy light clearly illuminated the thin scars that traced across my forearm and the deeper ones on my hands.

'This too?' he breathed.

I nodded again, trying to pull my hand away.

'That fuckin bastard!' His face flushed deep. 'What happened, Rose. What happened then?'

'I found it,' I whispered. 'Way up high. Like you said. Where no one could find me. They looked after me. Got me well. Chris…'

'Who? Who helped you?' he interrupted me.

'Rebecca. The Farm.'

'What farm?'

I watched Danny. My thoughts spinning with uncertainty.

'Up high. The place you thought was there.'

We looked at each other in the semi lit shrouded space, both uncomprehending what had happened. Danny shook his head, then taking both my hands, he kissed them.

'But. How did you find me?' His gaze softened.

'Your letters.'

'My letters?' His voice was amazed.

My heart wanted to speak it all. My mind filled with caution.

'Yes. They were at the Post Office.'

'You went to the Post Office?'

I took a deep breath.

'It's complicated, Dan,' my voice trailed off.

'But I wrote for so long. So many letters. Dad and Mum too. We never heard back. The postie. He said a woman told him you were… so I thought that… that you were…'

I looked away. He reached out and turned my face to him.

'Why didn't you answer them?' Gently.

'I couldn't, Danny.' Tears filled my eyes.

'Rose,' he whispered. 'I need to know these things. So that I can understand.'

'They were delivered to me,' I lied.

'Then why didn't you answer them?' he probed.

'Because I only got them five days ago.'

Danny's sharp inhalation filled the quiet. His face was shocked.

'But why? Why didn't you get them earlier?' He looked at me, seeking answers as memories flooded me and tears drenched my face. His eyes flashed with pain as he reached for me, folding me in his arms.

'I'm so sorry, Rosanna. So sorry!'

~

Brisbane, March 1979

Small feet thundered past in the early sunrise. I heard the scrape and then the loud bang of the door on the outside toilet as Christian greeted the dawn. I awoke sleepily, stretched out next to Danny.

'Good morning,' he murmured, as Chris charged back up the stairs and flew past us. We heard him squealing from the front of the house.

'Mumma. Where are you?' he demanded, his voice anxious.

'Out the back,' I called. 'Here, Chris.'

Christian screeched to a halt in front of the bed and tugged at the mosquito net impatiently.

'That's where you are!' He clambered in and sat on top of Danny. 'I was looking for you. Why didn't you come sleep wiv me?' he scowled.

Danny reached up and rubbed his back.

'We slept out here, Chris.' He smiled.

'But, what about me?' Christian's lower lip quivered. 'I was scared, Umma.' He looked at me, his face petulant.

'What of, little man?' asked Danny.

'Of that nasty man coming.'

'What nasty man?'

'You know, Umma. The one back there.' He flicked a hand

randomly towards the city.

'You mean back at The Farm?' Danny guessed.

'No. That's where Beck is. I mith Beck,' he scowled, the lip going again.

'Where then, Chris?' Danny persisted.

'Back there.' His voice rose in annoyance. Danny looked at me, an eyebrow raised.

'Mumma. I'm hunwee,' Christian announced. Pushing himself off Danny's lap, he scuttled back to the kitchen.

'I'd best go check.' Danny watched me. 'Before he burns the house down.'

The cotton sheets draped over my knees as I gazed out to the jungle garden. Chris's voice babbled in the background. The sound of kitchen cupboards being opened and closed and crockery landing with a resounding thud on a bench filled the interior of the house. The smell of burnt toast and Danny's laughter wafted out to the veranda.

I smiled.

If Danny had grown unaccustomed to the rampant chaos and energy of a five-year-old boy, he showed no signs of it. As much as Chris was already a limpet on his side, Danny seemed to be lapping up the adulation of my son.

That last night, Danny had wanted to know more about The Farm. I told him as much as I could, including the letters and Jacob and Mary's betrayal.

'But I don't understand where it is,' he kept repeating. 'I know that forest like the back of my hand.'

'That's what they wanted, Dan. Secrecy. That's exactly what they wanted,' I emphasised.

The early hours of the morning found us cuddled into each other. His thumbs traced my lips as he leant towards me. I looked at him, the roller coaster of my life drawing me into his embrace.

'What about you and Beck?' he murmured.

I swallowed hard, avoiding his gaze.

'She said she could only be a part of me for a short time. She says my place is not with her, but in Brisbane now. She said I would never survive The Farm.

He looked steadily at me.

'What about me, Rose?' he spoke with reverence.

I took a long breath.

'This is so new, Dan. You. The city.'

He watched me carefully, his face softening.

'I need time. Time to think. To feel what is right for me and Chris.'

'Oh, Rosie-rose!'

I ached as he called me by my childhood name.

'Then let's wait. Let's see how this all goes. How Brisbane shapes up for you. And how that little man settles.' His eyes glowed with affection.

'You're safe here, Rose. Always.' His fingers lingered on my face, and he kissed my cheek. Then we wrapped our arms around each other as the heat of the night and the background symphony of the big city lulled us into slumber.

~

The squealing of delight roused me from my reverie as the clatter of my son in another room of the house awakened my curiosity. His voice was accompanied by the tinkling of a piano.

I sat up and swinging my naked legs over the edge of the bed, pulled on my top, wrapped a sarong around me and padded into the kitchen. The musical notes of something I remembered filled the house, the sensitivity in the playing sending shivers up my spine.

I heard Danny's baritone voice answering the high-pitched tones of my son's questions. Then I remembered the strains of Debussy's 'Claire de Lune'.

The morning light peeked along the hall. A glow in the spare room shone into the darker recesses of the house. Gently pushing the door open, I found Christian sitting on Danny's knee in front of a baby grand piano. Underneath it was a thick mattress, pillows and blankets. I stood quietly watching this scene, basking in the delight of the music and of the man and the boy.

Danny brought the piece to its superb finale then sat quietly, Chris's hands resting on his arm.

'Didn't know you could play, Dan,' I said, softly.

They turned to face me. Danny's features, a mirror of bliss. Chris's little upturned nose and eyes, focused and calm.

'Mumma, Danny said I could learn. To play the peeana.' He looked at me, his face questioning.

'Bruce is the pianist.' Danny smiled. 'I just dabble.'

'Bruce?'

'Now that's another story all together.' Danny's eyes twinkled.

Brisbane, May 1988

IT'S a cool, late autumn afternoon. Rosanna strolls into my office on time. Her hair is clean. She wears low-heeled sling-backs under tight jeans. She drops down into the chair and begins to braid her hair.

'Rinpoche wants me to be his lover,' she says, wrapping the end of the braid into a knot and stretching her body. She flicks her heels off and tucks her feet under her, relaxing into the soft cushions.

'He's a Monk, isn't he?' I ask.

'Yep. In Tibet. But not here,' she replies.

'I didn't know that,' I say.

'He says he wants a girlfriend. He wants me to show him how to do it.'

'To make love?' I ask.

'Yeah.'

'How's that for you?'

'I dunno. Thought I'd talk to you about it first.' She fixes me in her gaze.

'Go on.'

'He says he wants me to stop though.'

'Working?'

'Yeah. He hates it when I go. Waits all night for me to come home. Then he's sad the next day. Even if I'm okay.' Her voice is soft as she speaks. 'He says he understands. That I have to do what I need to do. But… I know it's really hard for him.'

'Do you talk to him about it?'

'No. He never wants to know.' She rubs her thighs. 'Do ya think I'm weird?'

'Because of your work?'

'Yep. I mean… it's not normal, is it? Not many women could do what I do.' She continues. 'But I know about sex. Men want to own women. Women prostitute themselves to men. It's in marriage, isn't it? Women stay married for the money and the lifestyle, so they don't have to work. Then they have sex with their husbands, even if they loathe them. There's not much difference between me and them.' She stares at me.

'What do yah think? You're married, aren't ya?' Her gaze is steady.

'Yes Rose, I am. But I feel very differently about my marriage.'

'Uh-huh.' Her eyes flicker as she contemplates me.

'What's he like? Yer hubby I mean?' she persists.

'I'm interested in why Rinpoche has made this decision,' I say, changing the subject.

'Yeah. Yer don't wanna talk to me about that, do ya Anna?' Her gaze is piercing.

'It's my private life, Rose. And a long story.' I reply. 'One day we can share that journey of mine.' I hold steady whilst she studies me.

'Okay. So, yer got issues too, haven't yah, Anna?' She examines me intensely.

'That's very perceptive of you, Rose.'

'I wasn't studying law for nothing.' Her eyes sparkle with warmth.

'You are right. I have had some big issues, Rose. And a huge learning curve. But now is not the time.' I watch her as I make a note. *First positive assertion.*

'Hmmm.' Her gaze is disconcerting. 'Okay then. No drama. I'll butt out.' A warmth fills my room as Rose smiles at me.

'So, ya want me to talk about Rin, ey?'

I nod.

'I'm listening, Rose.'

'Well, he's got family in Tibet. He sends money home. To a friend. A Chinese friend. To give it to his parents. It's really dangerous. Rin can never go back. They'd kill him if he did. But his family needs the money. He finally got a letter from his Mum. She said she wants him to get married. Have a family. He wants to know what it's like to be with a woman. He's never done it before.' She pauses, pushing her hands under her legs. 'He's really sweet about it. Very respectful. Reckons it can only happen if I like him that way. And if I really want to.'

'So, what do you think you will do?'

'Well, I couldn't do it… if it was like work,' she says.

'Yes, I can see that.'

'I mean. It'd be different. With him. Wouldn't it?' She's reflective.

'That would depend on you, don't you think? And where you are coming from.'

She looks at me.

'So, yer think that if I'm really honest, that it'd be alright?'

I watch her as she looks down.

'Do ya think I am honest with myself when I go to work?'

I choose my words carefully.

'I believe that this is more than your honesty. It's your integrity that needs to be considered here. And your commitment to make wise and safe decisions for yourself. I believe that Rinpoche is asking something of you that you need to carefully reflect upon before you enter into.'

She stops. Thinking. Her body hunches slightly. I watch carefully. Then the deep inhale, the pause and the softer exhale.

'Yer right.' She smiles. 'Yer really are very good at this, Anna.'

I watch her silently. She blinks at me as we gaze at each other, then flicks her eyes down.

'So, yer saying that… being with Rin… it couldn't be like… like…' Her voice trails off. 'Like Danny.' She takes in a slow breath.

I nod.

'So, not like that.' She speaks slowly, a slight crease in her forehead heralding the change.

She unravels her feet and stands, stretching back. She walks to the CD player and picks up her favourite disc. Slips it into the slot and slowly clicks it shut. Pressing the play button, she turns and walks to the window. Another measured breath. Then returning to her chair she slowly lowers herself.

The soothing tones of John Coltrane float around us. Her chest rises and falls, deep in thought. Then a soft shuddering as she lifts her head, smiling.

'He wants me to get a normal job.' She looks up at the CD player. Her eyes clear.

'How would that be for you?' I ask.

'I think it could work. I could get a job in the pub. The owner is cool. But the money wouldn't be as great. But. Yer know. We could look after each other if there wasn't enough.'

She turns and looks straight into me. She is completely comfortable today in her own skin. And with me.

'And yer know,' a sparkle starts up in the corner of her eyes, 'he really is very cute!' Her eyes are full of mischief.

~

Brisbane, March 1979

It was late afternoon during my second month in Brisbane. The front doorbell rang. A loud chime repeated three times, echoing through the house and out onto the back porch. We were sitting on the mattress, sipping coffee, playing dominos with Chris.

'Who could that be?' Chris asked, as he swiped the board of all its pieces, gleefully stacking them next to him.

'Why don't you go see?' Dan smiled, ruffling Christian's hair. 'Maybe it's a surprise.'

'Oooo… Mumma. You come too!' Chris demanded, grabbing my arm, hauling me up.

'Yer better go, lassie.' Danny smiled at me, reaching out to touch my hand. I looked at him curiously, then Christian's shout of recognition filled the house.

Approaching the hall, I could hear the sound of Chris's excited voice and an unmistakable brogue. I paused, my breath quickening, the dappled afternoon sunlight casting shadows along the hall.

Mim and Dad stood in the arch of the open front door. Christian was wrapped in his Auntie Mimi's arms, enthusiastically patting her. Dad stood with tears running down his face, his arms around them both. My heart ached as I watched them wordlessly. Dad looked up, over my son's head. His eyes met mine and handing Christian to Mim, he strode towards me.

'Rosie-rose.' His voice cracked as he held me by the shoulders. His beard was almost completely white. His hair streaked with silver and copper. A youthful agelessness shone in his eyes. The cragged lines that traversed his features marked the history I could never forget.

Time stood still in that moment. His hands were strong on my arms. His body straight and sturdy as the massive trees in our beloved forest. I burst into tears as he enfolded me in his gigantic embrace, engulfing me with a heart that held the only place I knew as home.

'Hi, Dad,' I managed, my face buried into his shirt. He stood back, his eyes travelling my face. 'Good to see yah again.'

'Mumma, UmMA. It's Auntie Mimi,' Chris's happy voice rang out as she stepped towards me, embracing me to her soft breasts.

'Rosanna,' she murmured kissing my hair. 'Danny-boy rang us. Told us you were alive and well. We packed and left as soon as possible. And Christian. Oh my. He has grown into such a bonnie wee laddie.'

Aunty Mim smiled, her face wet with tears.

'He knew who we were as soon as he saw us.' She kissed his cheeks.

He reached up, his little finger tracing her tears.

'Why are you crying, Auntie Mimi?

'Because I didn't think I would see you again.' She stroked his face.

'But I knew. I knew you were there. With Auntie Sah. In the garden.' He looked perplexed as her eyes melted. Then wriggling to get free, he called out, 'Danny. Dada and Mimi. They are here. Come see.'

'Hi, Dad.' The two men grabbed each other in a bear hug as Dad pounded his son's back.

'Yer still the man, son,' Dad beamed.

'And yer still the oldie, Dad.' Danny's eyes twinkled with love as he extricated himself from his father's embrace.

I watched, Auntie Mim's arms around me as Christian tugged at their hands.

'C'mon… C'mon. Wanna show you my bed,' he nagged.

They disappeared into Danny's bedroom as Mim smiled at me.

'Let's see what's on in the kitchen, lassie,' she said gently. 'Dinner will be needed soon enough and that little fella of yers will be starving.'

~

'So, what's happening son?' I heard Dad's voice on the porch.

We had eaten a splendid meal. Auntie Mim prepared her famous stew, her home garden basket overflowing with produce. Dad and I helped cut the vegetables and brown the meat as Danny and Chris chased each other through the house. The ensuing feast was filled with the flavours and nostalgia of their kitchen at home. Christian animatedly told them about The Farm, Beck, the horses and lack of cars. His comments caused Dad's brow to furrow and Mim's voice to disappear. Danny sat close to me, his hand reaching for mine in my silence.

After dinner, Mim and I attended to the dishes as Danny and Dad sauntered out into the twilight, cigars and whiskeys in hand.

'Well. She rang. In the middle of the night,' I heard him say. 'They were at the siding. Then they arrived. On the dawn train.'

'How on earth did they get there?' Dad asked. 'And what's this Farm all about?' I heard the glasses on the coffee table and the creak of the men sitting in the wickerwork armchairs.

'She can tell yer about that,' Danny was evasive. 'We're sortin' stuff out.'

'I see.' Dad's voice was serious. 'But what about yer, son?'

'I'm just taking it slow, Dad. She's been through a truck load of shit. She's only just landed. Just finding her feet. I wanna wait mate… not scare her off like… don't yer trust me?' Danny's voice was defensive.

'I know yer Danny-boy. She's very attached to yer. And it looks like yer are totally there for her. But, how is this going to work?'

'I know what I'm doing.' Danny was short.

'So, what are yer doing?'

'Like I said. Going slow. Honest. I've got it under control.'

'All right son. Here's the thing. Yer know how badly she's been hurt. Yer've been up the bloody shit creek cobber. Those crims! Remember what yer've been through.' His voice stopped suddenly. Danny's chair scraped hard as he stood up.

'Dad.' His voice was low and angry. 'Give it a break mate!'

Tension warped the air as the two men met in the conflict of father and son. An awkward moment of silence, then Dad's voice. 'Son, it's just, yer know what's happened. Yer'll have to get honest one day. And I get yer going slow with that. But this! Yer know how you can be with women. Don't yer think it's too sudden?'

'Look, Dad.' Danny sat down heavily in his chair. 'She's not like the others. She's special. She's a part of me. Part of us. Sah, yer know they were like sisters. But she's different to me. Much more than a friend. I want to be a father, Dad. And not just to Chris. To our own.'

'What about the others?' Dad asked

'There's been no one for ages. There really was never anyone else. Never. She's always been in the back of my mind. I knew they were alive. I've been in love with her since Sah went. I've just been waiting. Yer know I dreamt about her all the time. In that hole, and here.' I heard him draw on his cigar, my forehead creasing with confusion at his words.

'I wouldn't have kept trying if I thought she was dead.' My heart skipped a beat as he continued, unaware of the volume of his voice

'And now, well, she's here. I love her. And Chris? He's such the little man, Dad.'

I felt Auntie Mim's hand on my arm.

'Come on, Lassie.' She smiled knowingly. 'Let's get this pudding a-cookin.'

~

It was the afternoon of the following weekend. The heat was heavy on my shoulders as we picked the long cylindrical beans for dinner. Chris, Dad and Mim had disappeared, and Danny and I had some time alone at last.

The leaves glistened with the rain from an earlier thunderstorm, small droplets of rainbow moisture cooling my hands. Before me, two butterflies flittered in a mating ritual, the turquoise on their wings spinning patterns of laced silk in the afternoon light. The humidity hung like a moist blanket. It was one of those languid late afternoons that arouses the mind to wonder and calms the body in an effortless request to relax.

Danny reached up to pick the pods from the very top of their climbing frame. His naked muscular torso gleamed in the heat, soaked in sweat. His auburn dreadlocks were plated into a ponytail and straggled in clammy threads down his back.

'It's bloody hot, eh, lassie? We'd best get these beans picked before they run up higher.' His eyes sparkled with mischief. 'Hot enough to seduce the sleep out of any fellow needing rest.'

I looked at him, puzzled.

'Just one of those sayings from Dad's Grannie.' He grinned as he passed me a handful of the crisp beans.

'Look at those Emperor butterflies. They only come out at this time of the year. They lay their eggs on leaves. Then hatch into those magnificent creatures.' He pointed as the two shimmery butterflies danced around us. 'I love watching these mating rituals. It's a dance of intimacy, eh? And the sky. Its brightness. See how beautiful it all is, Rose,' he murmured.

The vitality of the garden and the closeness of the man travelled through my body and into the earth below.

How often have I felt this?

'Did you mean what you told Dad last week?'

He gazed at me, his eyes serious.

'About what, Rose?' his brow furrowed.

'About me, other women, and Chris. And wanting my babies?'

He looked carefully at me. Then reaching for my hands, turned my palms to his lips and kissed them.

'With all my heart, Rose. Forever. This is what I have always wanted.' His eyes were sincere. His body still. He held me steady, his energy gleaming with an intense magnetic light.

And then, the wheels of my life began to turn again.

'Then there is only one thing missing, Danny,' I whispered.

I reached up, my arms circling his neck and as his pupils dilated with surprise, I kissed him, my mouth open to his. His arms travelled around my body and he held me to him in an embrace that dissolved my doubt.

~

Brisbane, July 1988

It's quiet for a Saturday afternoon. The midwinter sun shines through the open door when Rose arrives on time for her appointment. She is neatly dressed and carries herself with a fragile air of self-assurance.

She sits before me, her legs entwined at the ankles, her hands resting on her thighs. She manages to smile as she looks at the rug between us.

'Hi, Anna. Nice to see you again,' she says, not looking at me.

'How are you, Rose?'

'Yeah. Good.' Her thumbs move up and down against each other.

'Shall we start?' I ask, after a pause.

'Yeah. Sure.' She remains disengaged.

'Last time you were here, we were talking about your arrival in Brisbane. Would you like to share more about that time?'

She looks at me, her smile crooked.

'That was the best year of my life,' she manages, taking in a deep breath and deliberately unravelling her legs.

'Danny was at Uni and I found a job. In town. In a vegetarian café. When I was at work, Dan hung out with Chris.' She begins to relax.

'How was it with him?' I query.

Her smile deepens.

'Amazing.' She breathes more easily. 'I could feel him everywhere. It was such a new, scary feeling. We were mad about each other yer know. He was as passionate as he was deep. And…' She uncrosses her feet and places them on the floor, looking straight at me.

'God, sex was good!' Her face glows pink. 'We didn't stop. Just couldn't get enough of each other.'

'Danny was your first man, wasn't he?' I ask.

'Yup. He was,' she answers.

'How was that?'

'Well, when we made love, it was like… all the good stuff was there. Everything from my past that was beautiful… was inside of him. In his big, generous heart. His body…' She shakes her head as she reaches for her cheeks.

'His hands when he touched me…'

Rose's voice trails off. She becomes silent again as I watch her carefully.

'What are you remembering, Rose?' I disturb her thoughts,

breaking up the pattern of her inner dialogue. She looks at me, her eyes distant.

'Just about how we made love everywhere.' Her eyes begin to re-engage.

'Everywhere?'

'Yeah.' She nods. 'Down by the river. At night under the stars. In the backyard. In the kitchen. Whenever Christian slept. You know. He was always completely there for me. It was…' She shakes her head.

'Words?' I ask.

'There are none to describe it… and…' Her fingers lightly brush her chest. 'Things started changing. In here. It began to melt. That defensiveness. You know that shit. It stopped.' She glances at me as I listen.

'And the stuff that started up in the forest? That changed too. Like. I started to forget about it. It stopped being so strong. Being with Dan, well… as I got soft in here… I buried it.' Her hands clasp over her breasts.

'Buried it?' I query.

'Yeah. We didn't talk about Nimbin much. Except The Store… and the garden… We never spoke again about the stuff that happened that night. At his house.'

She stops and looks at me.

'And the voices, Anna. Those voices in my head. They went quiet.' She trails off and lowers her eyes. The sharp edges of memory and pain loom in front of her.

I pick up the teapot and pour her another cup. Handing it to her, I settle back into my chair, my notes open in front of me. Rose is silent. Her legs still. Her hands are folded neatly in her lap.

Her effort at self-composure noted.

'Rose,' I say, 'you mentioned that Danny said he wouldn't have kept trying if he'd thought you were dead. What do you think he was referring to?'

She looks away, her eyes remote.

'The posters.'

'Did you ever ask him or Dad that again?

'No.'

I make a note and pause, watching her carefully.

'What does that mean to you now?'

She takes a deep breath, leans forward and picks up her tea. The fragrant aroma of chamomile wafts through my office as she speaks.

'I want to tell yah about Brien.'

I watch her as the walls go up.

'Go ahead.' I make another memo.

She backs into her seat, crosses her legs and outlines small circles with her foot. The teacup sits precariously in the saucer, tea spilling into it as her foot moves faster.

'Rose. Remember your breath,' I say gently, pointing to her cup. She takes a noticeable inhale and imperceptibly moves her head.

'You were about to tell me about Brien,' I prompt.

'Hmmm? Yeah? Okay. He was the proprietor of the Sauce Café in town.' Rose slowly sips her tea, avoiding my gaze. Her pace slows.

'I'm listening,' I comment.

She pauses.

'He was huge. He really dug vegetarian food. Reckoned meat sucked. He loved the vegetarians. But. Actually. I reckon he was a closet meat eater. No veggo could be that big.' She grins as the pendulum swings. She continues faster.

'He had a wicked sense of humour and he really looked after us.' Rose smiles broadly. 'I ended up putting some aside. You know. To buy Christian stuff and to spoil Dan when I could. Danny and gifts!' She shakes her head imperceptibly and pauses, her face unreadable. Then a deep breath.

'You know. In those days. In Queensland. The workers always had to fight to be paid proper. But not with Brien. My money was in my account. On the dot. Sometimes with extra. And he insisted I take all the left-overs. Yer know. For Chris and me. And Dan. He just loved his food…' Her face is a complicated picture of pain and joy. Her internal anguish profound.

'It's so good to remember, Anna. So good.' Her eyes ache and brim with it.

~

Brisbane 1979

The first half of 1979 flew past. Dan was enrolled in music at the University of Queensland and our lives hummed with the sounds of his guitar and drums. The evenings in our South Brisbane squat were filled with gatherings. Bohemians, students and fringe dwellers came to eat home-made pizza, smoke pot, debate politics and jam into the night. Our flatmate appeared randomly in our lives, his grand piano swinging into action with nights of operatic magnificence.

My life overflowed with colour, love and sex. Danny and I were inseparable. By June, he insisted we enrol an increasingly wayward Christian in the local primary school.

'He'll be painting this town red before we know it.' He laughed. 'He needs other kids and an institution to keep him clean. And besides, his brain is exploding with questions.' Dan's eyes twinkled as he hugged me. 'And it looks like yer and I can't possibly answer them all.'

I looked unhappily at him as he gathered me in his arms and kissed me.

'I know yer want to keep him here, but honestly, Rose, how are yer ever going to study with this little ratbag running amuck?'

Christian loved it. As he sped from my arms into the embrace of a throng of first graders, my heart ached with uncertainty. His short life had been a journey that few could possibly comprehend and his photographic memory of it troubled me.

His shrieks of delight echoed in my brain as I walked slowly home from the school.

As Chris blossomed it became clear that my time for education had arrived. With Dan's and Dad's insistence, I went back to night school. I wanted to apply for university and needed to finish my formal secondary education. Whilst the musos gathered in our colourful pad at night, I studied. English, maths, history and economics absorbed my mind as our life buzzed around me with the good-natured banter and argument of like minds.

There on the banks of that great old river, my world came alive.

~

Late the next summer, we were home early afternoon and hungry after the first day of Chris's school year. It was close to his sixth birthday.

Danny was ducking him as they shadow-boxed.

'Looks like it's soup tonight,' Dan said as he patted me and fended off Chris.

'That market, the one I told yer about. It's out at that grunge suburb, Rocklea. It's got the cheapest food. Yer can buy stuff by the box-full. We should go there once a month.' Danny shooed Chris off to the lounge, pointing to his favourite book. Then he started packing vegetables from Brien's café into the fridge, filling old, cracked bowls with fruit and ducking Christian's attention.

'What about the veggie patch?' I asked.

'Ya can't grow much at this time of the year. What with the bloody heat and the bugs? Man, it's warfare out there,' he chuckled.

'Good thing the rocket, tomatoes and basil grow okay. Rocklea should fill the gaps. Let's go next week.' He grunted as he lifted a huge bag of potatoes and cabbages and strode off downstairs.

'It's cooler and drier down here and we'll never starve so long as these are cheap. And Brien's charity reaches us,' his voice trailed off as his footfall faded into the dark interior of the underside of the house.

Christian raced into the lounge and grabbed a book, splaying himself on the cool floorboards, reading. I went to the kitchen to start preparing the evening meal. My hand drifted to my belly.

'We got any rice, Dan?' I called.

'Yep.' His distant voice shouted, 'In the back of the pantry.'

I opened the slatted wooden doors and squatting in the dark, reached for the sack filled with grainy brown rice. Dan appeared a while later, a cask of Lambrusco hanging from his finger.

'Hope yer don't mind cask. What with school starting and yer heading off to Uni, we can't afford bottles this week.'

'I'm okay for today,' I replied, looking at him, then at the label.

'What? Those Farm evangelists still on your case, huh?' He kissed me as I smiled.

'Well, lassie. If yer want. Otherwise, it's cool.' His fingers traced my shoulders, lingering at my neck, kneading me. I sighed involuntarily.

'Yah need a good massage, Rose. There's lumps in that neck that haven't seen the light of day for a long time.' His voice was tender.

'Mum. MUM!' Christian's voice broke through our communion. 'What's this word?'

Danny squatted beside him and peered at his book.

'Yer know that one, Chris.' Danny smiled, his arm around him. Chris pointed at the page and together they read. I watched the man and boy, my heart aching with the joy at the bond between them.

I wondered when was going to be the best time to tell him.

'Dan?' I said.

'Yep.' His head bent to Chris. Their voices blended together, Danny's deep tones weaving contrasting melodies with Christian's sweet soprano.

"...He *climbed and he climbed and he climbed,*
And as he climbed, he sang a little song to himself.
It went like this:
Isn't it funny?
How a bear likes honey.
Buzz. Buzz. Buzz.
I wonder why he does..." (A. A. Milne).

I watched Christian's hands playing in the air, painting pictures of his favourite insect. As they finished A. A. Milne's classic *Winnie the Pooh* prose, Danny looked up expectantly.

I held up the small square of plastic with a faint red line across it. Danny looked at me, then taking it, turned it to the light. The corners of his mouth twitched with surprise and as he turned to me, his eyes widened and filled with tears.

'Hey, Chris.' His voice was husky. 'Wanna watch the tele for a bit matey?' he said, ruffling his hair. Then standing, he faced me and ran his hands over my belly.

'Well, lassie,' his face smouldered with emotion, 'it looks like we are up the duff.'

He bent into me, his body warm, his heart beating strongly as I melted into him. Then lifting one foot at a time Danny walked me to the bedroom as Christian giggled at us.

Closing the door, Danny helped me to the bed.

'Danny!' I protested, running my hands through his hair. He

unhurriedly removed my jeans and stripped off his shirt. He knelt between my legs, unbuttoning my blouse and enfolding my skin to his body. His hands stroked my hair and cheeks.

I pressed myself into him, drawing his face to mine.

'At last,' he murmured. 'Thank you, Rose. Thank you.'

And his hands found the small of my back.

'I want to see for myself, lassie.' His breath was hot on my breasts as he slipped my undies from me and kissed my flat belly, his fingers travelling lower. I moaned as he lifted his eyes to mine. He was flushed with pleasure.

'I guess we had better go slowly now.' His mouth met mine and I heard Christian's muffled squeal of excitement as the TV went to full volume.

~

Brisbane 1980

I awoke suddenly that morning to the sound of thumping on the roof above my head. The muffled shrieking of laughter and the booming of voices followed the discordant muted strumming of a guitar.

I struggled out of bed, my swollen belly protruding from my night top. My heavy breasts stretched against the buttons of my cardigan. Pushing my feet into my Ugg boots, I waddled down the hall to the back veranda.

The garden was empty, the air chilled. Struggling down the back steps I saw the extension ladder propped up on the guttering of the house.

'Dan. Chris?' I called.

'Mum, I'm here.' The sound of Christian's voice echoed out over the house.

There on the roof were Christian and Danny. His guitar rested precariously on the corrugated surface. Christian was cavorting along the ridge line, Danny's hand holding him steady. They beamed down at me.

'What on earth are you doing, Dan?' I called out, my heart in my mouth.

'Giving him a guitar lesson.' Danny's wide smile lit up the morning as my heart pounded with fear.

'Up there on the bloody roof?'

'Yeah. He wanted to see the river mist. From up here. Wanna come up? It's spectacular.' His mischievous grin filled my heart with lust and annoyance.

'Bloody hell, Danny. How on earth am I going get up there with this belly of yours?' I exclaimed. 'Get down now,' I commanded, stomping back up the stairs and into the kitchen.

I lit the stove and reached for the coffee pot, musing at how irrepressible they were as a team. The ladder rattled as Christian descended, then his shrieks of delight filled the air as he leapt on his push bike and rode swiftly out onto the street, hollering to his friends.

Danny's softer foot fall glided into the kitchen. His arms wrapped around my belly, his strong torso bent into me, embracing my spine as he fondled my hair.

'Barefoot and pregnant, huh, lassie?' Danny's cheeky whisper tickled my ear.

'I just want you to be more careful,' I complained. 'He's still very little.'

I ducked my head as he nibbled my neck.

'Stop it, Dan,' I complained, leaning into him, trying to hide my pleasure. His warm lips kissed me more firmly.

'Sorry, lassie, but it was completely safe. He saw the ladder there and climbed up. I was in the kitchen when I heard him on the roof. Took my breath away.' He laughed.

'Figured it was better to act casual… so…' His fingers traced the line of my neck and down into my blouse, lightly stroking my cleavage.

'I grabbed the guitar and shot up after him. I guess I need to take him to the cliffs. If this climbing bug isn't handled properly, we could have a problem.'

He nuzzled me. I turned to him, my body twisted to the side, my belly too large for a full-frontal embrace. His hands caressed my neck and back.

'Mm… that feels good.' I sighed. 'This bub is gonna be a whopper.'

'Yer need more than a massage, me love.' His voice was low and passionate as his hands travelled down my belly around to the small of my back and cupped my buttocks. Reaching up, I caressed his chest. He leant into me. I could feel his hardness on my swollen body. Closing my eyes, I melted into him

'So! They reckon a pregnant woman gets hotter by the month.' A bemused voice spoke from behind us.

Danny lifted his head from my breast. A portly, bald-headed young man, clad in stripey pyjamas, an oversized poncho and rainbow-coloured socks, lounged against the spare bedroom door.

'Sorry, mate. Didn't know yer were back.' Dan sheepishly replied, reluctantly drawing away from me and making an indiscreet attempt to rearrange my clothes.

I peeped out from behind Danny's chest, trying to hold my open blouse shut over my naked breasts. The intruder stretched and scratched himself, smiling broadly before strolling into the room.

'Yep. Got in last night. You guys were all asleep. Who the hell was destroying the roof this morning? If I wanted an alarm, I would have set one.' He grinned at Dan.

Danny grabbed him, slapping him on the back.

'Bruce, babes!' he enthused, placing a resounding smooch on his ear.

'Phew! Sure you don't wanna cross the floor?' Bruce tittered, holding Danny at arm's length. 'You're such a spunk-rat. No wonder she's glowing.' He smiled, pinching Danny's cheek. Danny punched his arm as Bruce winced, extricating himself from his embrace. He looked at me, his smile filled with delight

'And who might this be?'

'This…' Danny stepped towards me, encircling my swollen waist. 'Is my very pregnant, very beautiful Rosie-rose.'

Bruce pulled himself up to his full height, threw his arms open and drew me into a bear hug.

'You are absolutely radiant, my darling. May I?'

I nodded, and a gentle hand reached out and lovingly caressed my swollen belly

'Hi, Bruce. Good to see you again,' I smiled.

~

Danny spooned into my back, his breath warm on my neck. His

fingers trailed the curves of my belly. The silky doona tucked in around us as the wintry night wind blew through the cracks of the old house. Christian's sleeping breath floated up to me from his mattress on the floor.

'Wow, this joint is in dire need of bogging,' Danny said. 'That wind is bloody freezing.' His hands travelled to my breasts, cupping their fullness and tenderly squeezing my nipples.

'But a spoonful of loving and a pregnant belly will keep us warm any night.'

I relaxed into him.

'What's with Bruce today?' I asked sleepily.

'He's just fussing again. He'll get over it.' Danny's mind was only on us, as his hands found the knots in my shoulders.

Our baby stirred.

'She's waking up,' he whispered, his warm hand cupping my belly.

'How do you know it's a girl?'

'Irish intuition.' His voice smiled.

'Mm. That'd be nice. One of each.' I sighed as Danny lay still, his fingers playing with the movements of our baby kicking.

'So why is he so nervous?' I persisted.

'Yeah, well… there's been another gay bashing. Bloody homophobes.' Danny's voice was pensive. 'Mostly he takes it on the chin. But today he was really rattled.'

'You're worried about him.'

'Yep. He's brilliant. And he's a brother to me. He was the first one I talked to about Sah. And Pa. And you. I bloody love him.'

In the background we could hear the rumbling snores. Danny's hand rested on my lower belly.

'Jeez these walls are thin.' He chuckled. 'Guess we'd better keep it quiet while he's home.' His voice was filled with desire.

I turned to him and stroking the back of his neck, pressed my face to his.

'Dan?' I exhaled, my throat softening.

'Yeah,' he murmured.

'Can I talk to you about something?'

'Sure.'

'If something happened to you, what would I do?' I asked.

Danny's eyes deepened as he watched me.

'Yer a worry wart, that's for sure, Rose lassie. Must be all those hormones making yer freaky.' He kissed me gently.

'I'm not going anywhere, except right here. With yer.' He was serious. His body still. 'It's taken all this time to get us together. Nothing's going to change that.' His hands stroked my face as his lips brushed mine.

'But I hear yer, mother ship Rosanna.' He grinned at me. I could see the wheels of his mind ticking over.

'I could catch a nasty Asian virus and cark it. Or fall off the roof onto that blackberry patch and get spiked to death.'

'Dan!' I protested, digging my fingers into his ribs. 'Stop it. I'm serious.'

Danny's mouth found mine as the eruptive snorts from Bruce's room paused, our tussle breaking through the quiet in the house.

'Shh. Yer'll wake the snake,' he whispered. 'I love yer lassie. I'm not ever going to leave yer.' Danny's hands found mine. He kissed them and resting our palms on my belly, he said, 'Besides, this wee lassie needs a Dada.' And running his hands between my legs, Danny warmed my heart and lit the fire in my belly, his desire for the child, resting in my womb, chasing the fears from my mind.

~

Isabella came into this world with little fuss. I was heavy with child late into my fortieth week of pregnancy. Auntie Mim had been sent for and had set up my birthing space in our lounge. The heater was on, taking the chill off the afternoon.

On her instruction, we had set out on a ride to stimulate my contractions. Dan and I meandered along the banks of the Brisbane River. Christian was seated on Dan's handlebars just behind me, his voice ringing out over the parkland with melodies harmonically exact from Dan's repertoire.

I relaxed into the warmth of the mid spring sun on my back. The cool breeze smelt of the muddied, littoral swamps close to our home. A growing euphoria opened my womb and spread through my legs. As we rode together, my body softened. My desire was only for this man and his child as the deeper parts of me beckoned.

By the time we arrived home, my labour was in full swing, the song line of my unborn child calling me.

I squatted on the lounge floor, rocking and moaning, a concerned Danny massaging my back and whispering words of encouragement. His strong arms held me steady, as the oceanic waves of birth flooded me. Chris sat quietly in the corner of the room, his face an open book of curiosity. Auntie Mim moved between us, softly reassuring Chris and instructing Dan.

Then taking my hand in one as soft as the deepest velvet, she crooned the tongue of her ancestors. A melody sweet as honey transported me to a life of hope and freedom. And the compassion from a mother who had birthed so many and lost the one she loved the most, infused my heart with joy. Her voice melded into the background flow of the mighty river at our doorstep and the far distant cry of the curlew winged its blessing into my soul. My life was about to change forever as Isabella sang her silent voice into me.

As the contractions of my labour carried us into the night, my body melted, and my mind disengaged into a forever space. All I could feel was the urging warmth of my daughter, resting at the opening to her world.

The moon ascended into the night's sky and the stars led the faeries from Dad's garden to sit on our porch in wonder. My voice rang out three times in the greeting of birth as Isabella's head crowned her glory and broke a tidal wave of salty liquid. Hot torrents of tears poured from her father's eyes as he held her close to my birthing canal, her fire red hair signalling his paternity.

12

Brisbane, August 1988

ROSANNA arrives late for her appointment. She is dressed casually. Her thick hair is pulled back from her forehead, tied high in a ponytail. Curly strands hang in a straggle of sweat down her neck. She wears joggers, a tracksuit and no make-up.

'Sorry about being late. It took longer than I thought to get here.' She sits in her chair, catching her breath, pulling out her scrunchie and tugging her heavy black ringlets back into a neat, tighter bunch.

'Would you like tea?'

'Just water thanks,' she responds. 'My Naturopath reckons if I keep up this jogging I'll need to drink more.' She smiles at me as she draws off her hoodie. I pass her a glass and she gulps it down in one hit, handing it back for more.

'Anna. I need to talk to you about something.' Her hand swipes the corners of her mouth.

'Sure. I'm listening,' I reply.

Rosanna takes a deep breath and places her feet on the floor.

'It's bad.' She looks at me seriously.

'Go on.'

'I've been wanting to say this for a while. And now… well… now that I don't do it anymore, it shouldn't affect the kids coming home. Should it?' She looks at me nervously.

'That will depend on what you have to tell me,' I reply.

She watches me, chewing on the inside of her mouth, her hands under her thighs. Silent as she thinks.

'You were studying law, Rose, so I guess that you have researched this for yourself. Is that right?' I ask, observing her anxiety.

'Yeah, I've looked it up. The court order shouldn't be affected by it,' she says, looking at me seriously.

'Okay. So, if you think it will help, let's talk about it.' I sit, waiting

219

for her courage to build.

'It's that. Well… I don't do it anymore. I stopped before last time. Ages ago actually. Rin has really helped me a lot with it. But…'

'Go on, Rose,' I gently prompt.

Rose inhales quickly

'You know how I used to always come in here with those headphones on?'

I nod as I watch the thin wisps of her smoke screen rise between us.

'Well. I used them to try to kill myself.'

'What do you mean?' I ask. *Steady.*

'It started ages ago. You know. After the kids were sent away. When I started coming here.'

'Yes?'

'Well. It was like this. I had a weird bet with myself. It was those voices actually. They told me to.'

I watch her carefully.

'Like, they said, if I could get away with it, that they'd let me keep going. And they'd give me Chris and Izzie.'

'So, you had a deal with them?'

'Kinda like that.' She looks at the rug, buries her hands under her body and flicks her legs up and down. An agitated gesture.

'What happened?' I ask.

'It was like they said that if I could outsmart all the trucks then… they would let me have my kids back.'

She glances up. Her dark eyes clear, her face blank. Her drugs are low dose now. I watch her.

'I'm not sure what you are talking about. The voices have been quiet for ages, haven't they?' I ask.

'Yup. Yer know that.' Her eyes change. Hard.

'Yes, I do. So, I assume that now you are feeling grounded, that what you are telling me is coming from a clear space. Is that right?'

'Yeah. Basically.' There's her annoyance.

'Is that anger, Rose?'

Her body tenses as she attempts to control her feelings.

'Sorry, Anna. It's just…' She looks at the floor. Shakes her head.

'So here it is.' She pulls herself upright.

'The law reckons that because of the work I do… 'cos I hear my ancestor's voices… 'cos I behave differently to others… and I've had a substance abuse, that I can't be a parent. That's what makes me so mad. I love my kids. I'm a bloody great parent. I'm doing my best. And I'm fucking smart. So why can't I have them back?' her voice snaps at me.

I look at her, watching the pendulum swing hard.

'Let's breathe, Rose,' I say.

She shakes her head before a tense exhale.

'I mean. Everyone has addictions, don't they?' She flicks a look at me.

'Yes, that's very true.' *Careful.*

'How about cigarettes or compulsive eating? Or love addiction… there's one they all talk about now. And sex addiction… that was fuckin' Pa!' she rants.

I watch cautiously.

'I can see that you have a lot on your mind today. Would you like to…'

She interrupts me.

'Anna. Can I say this please?'

'Go ahead.'

'I really rattle you, don't I?'

Once more, I'm taken aback at her honesty. It's my turn to hesitate.

'Yes, Rose. Sometimes you do.'

'I want to say sorry for that. You are the only person I know that is incredibly straight with me. It's like, yer don't let me get away with much and I can't get to yer… except when I lash out.'

I watch her.

'You have this look in your eyes and I really see you.' Her eyes have softened but her mouth is still hard.

'I wasn't always like this you know. It wasn't as shitty in here.' Her hands rest over her belly. 'I wasn't always the complete bitch. But it all changed. After Dan…' She pauses.

'I know, Rose. I do.' I gently reach out to touch her. She looks down at my hand resting on hers. There's a tremor in her voice.

'This is about me trying to kill myself. But it never fucking worked!' She laughs cynically and takes her hand away to wipe her nose. I hold the tissue box out to her. Her energy softens. My heart reaches out.

'I'm just chicken shit.' Her voice is muffled as she loudly blows her nose.

'I don't see you like that.'

'There you go again, believing in me,' she smiles though her tears.

'Dan always believed in me.' She is still again, as the wheels turn.

'Would you like to continue about these suicide attempts?'

There's the shaking inhale and the sigh as she releases.

'It sounds really stupid now. What kind of crazy was I doing, huh?' She looks up, her face is clear. Her eyes moist.

'Okay. So, this is what I used to do. And Rin helped me to stop it. I used to walk along this road. On the way to all these appointments. And I'd put my earphones on real loud. And turn my back on the traffic. And then. When the voices said *now*, I'd... I'd step out onto the road.'

The room goes very still. Rosanna sits motionless. I can feel my feet on the floor. My heartbeat is loud under my ribs. The rush of blood in my head subdues the sound of the traffic on Waterworks Road. I look at her, speechless, as she slowly looks up and smiles a soft loving smile.

'Yer've got that look in yer eyes again, Anna,' she says quietly.

~

Brisbane 1982

I watched from the door as Dan and Bruce sat close on the piano stool, playing a duet together. Isabella was perched on Danny's lap, her little fingers resting on his arms, her feet bouncing up and down in time to the music.

Christian lay flat on Bruce's mattress under the grand piano, his fingers interlaced behind his head, his face a picture of raptured delight.

'Wow, Dan. I can hear the notes running around inside the piano,'

Christian called. 'They're all through it. In different places. It's like feet dancing.'

'Can yer see pictures? In yer mind?' Danny replied, bending to kiss our daughter's curls. Then he executed a pitch perfect chromatic scale with Bruce's baritone accompanying him in contra harmony, an octave below.

'Yes. It looks like the ocean. Rolling onto the shore,' Christian declared.

It was Christian's fourth year in primary school. I had entered Uni as a Law student and Dan was close to finishing his Music and Politics degree. We continued to live in our old ramshackle home, down by that vast, broad river.

A rich tapestry of colour blended the operatic magic of Bruce's genius on the piano and Danny's improvisation on guitar, sax and trombone. Our evenings were a melody of classical repertoires from the concert halls of Europe as Bruce and Dan rehearsed together.

'Hang on then. Here come the trolls,' Bruce exclaimed. Chris's face lit up as he spread his arms, pressing his fingers into the mattress, squeezing his eyes closed.

'Great. That's my favourite. Okay. I'm ready,' he called as the first strains of Peer Gynt's, 'Hall of the Mountain King' floated up and out into the room.

Danny and Bruce's hands moved in a portrayal of musical synchronicity, plucking at the notes. Under the piano, Chris's face melted into the perfect resonance. Then as the tempo increased, Danny's hands chasing Bruce's over the keyboard, Grieg's magnificent piece came to a resounding finish.

Christian leapt up, stomping his feet, his face burning with intensity.

'I'm going to learn it,' he cried. 'I can do it.'

I turned back happily to my studies, making my way around the chaotic mess of children's books and toys, Danny's diaries and textbooks that scattered around our lounge room.

When Dan wasn't rehearsing or instructing Chris on the finer points of rock-climbing or musical improvisation, he would dance around the house, our red-haired daughter balanced high on his shoulders. His foray into freedom was still our rooftop. I heard the squeak of the rickety ladder and the thumping of feet above me, announcing their climb and conquest of its heights.

'Chris? Izzy?' I called. 'What are you doing?' My thoughts interrupted by the cacophony of sound above me.

'They're up here with me,' Danny's muffled voice floated down to me.

'Mum, come up with us,' Chris called.

I moaned inwardly.

'I'm studying, Chris,' I yelled back.

'Yer know what, lassie?' Danny's deep voice boomed out over the neighbourhood, 'I'm going to put the Brisbane cityscape into the final bars of this PhD. It'll be done next week. And you kids? Yer are my bloody inspiration!' His guitar squealed with intensity as the thunder of Chris's footfall echoed along the ridgeline.

'One day this town is going to be on the map of international cities,' he shouted. 'Mark my words, son, by the time yer kids have grown up.'

His words sent a shiver through me. My breath caught in my chest as time slowed and my entire world rested there, precariously on our roof's apex.

~

Drugs had become the backdrop in our lives, a euphoric rebellion that snubbed its nose at the conservative government of the time. A tribute to his Irish blood, Danny protested the regime with a fire in his belly.

'Times are changing, Rose,' he declared that day as he dismounted his pushbike and limped into the house. His jeans were torn, his face bloody and his jacket ripped at the shoulders.

'Dan, you're bleeding.'

He glanced down at himself and grunted.

'It's this fucking government. It's not just finding books to read that haven't been banned, it's fighting for our ideas to be allowed. To be heard.' He grimaced, gingerly touching his head. 'This government is a bloody joke. They've recognised same sex partnerships in South Australia and up here in the banana bender state, we can't even walk three abreast or wear dreads without them threatening arrest.' He

224

gingerly touched a thick strand of his hair.

'Dan, stop.' I reached out to take his arm. 'What happened?' I searched his face.

'Don't worry, lassie,' he muttered. 'It was the cops.'

'The cops? But Dan,' I protested, 'you're badly hurt!'

'It's just those brainless developers. The cops… they…' He winced as I led him to the bathroom and helped him sit down on the closed toilet.

'They want to ban ideas. Not just our actions.' He flinched as I touched his face. 'We must have the right to think for ourselves, Rose. To have our autonomy. This fascist, sterile, anti-everything government can't remove our constitutional rights,' he ranted.

'Sit still, Dan,' I exclaimed, holding his arm as I cleaned the congealed blood from his face, my concern palpable.

'I don't want to hate people because of their values but I bloody think that I'm headed that way,' Danny muttered. Then, reaching up, he held my hand, gazing intensely into my face. 'Rose, they want to tear down South Brisbane.'

'What?' I exclaimed. 'South Brisbane?

'Yeah. Expo 88.'

'Expo?' My hands rested on his shoulder, shocked.

'Yep.'

'Wha… our home?' I gasped.

'All of it.'

~

Something about the wounds on Danny's body felt very wrong in me. So that night, once the children were safely tucked into bed, I sat with him in the warm night air on our back porch.

'What really happened, Dan?'

He looked at me, his eyes uncertain.

'The less yer know about this, the better, Rose. For the kids' sake.'

'What do you mean? Don't keep me in the dark.

He reached out to hold my hand.

'Rose, lassie,' he murmured, 'this is more than the cops. It's more than the developers. I want to keep yer and the kids safe.'

'What are you talking about, Dan?' I pulled away from him, my heartbeat rising.

'There's some really bad stuff going on out there. It's very political. And dangerous.'

~

The next afternoon, as I walked home from work, Danny's words rang in my ears. I passed the newsagency and stopped to chat to the elderly proprietor, Mr Jacobs. The sandwich board out the front shouted the news.

'Protestors Rally Expo!'

There on the front, was a photo of Dan.

I paid for a copy of *The Courier Mail.*

'Here you go, luv,' Mr Jacobs said, giving me a concerned look.

I raced towards our street, my head bowed against the hot wind. I turned into the vacant lot close to home and crossed the wasteland of old warehouses and deserted factories.

Rounding the last rubbish dump, I looked up, halting quickly.

A short heavyset man in black jeans and a denim jacket stepped out in front of me, blocking my way. The air hung heavy, the sound of the river booming in my ears. My heart pounded in my chest. Parked on the opposite side of the street with the engine idling was a solitary car, passenger seat door ajar.

Danger hung in the air.

'He's a mighty fine fighter, that hubby of yours,' the man said, flicking a lighter and cupping his hands around his cigarette.

I watched him, my senses exploding into hypervigilance.

'You're the missus, huh?' he drawled.

'Don't know what you're talking about, mate,' I replied steadily, my eyes holding his.

'Hey, don't be scared. I've just got a message for ya.' His accent was rough. His voice nasal.

'Yeah? Well, next time you can tell me without being such a dick about it.' And turning, I ran as fast as possible towards home.

~

'So, what's going on, Danny?' I bristled, later that evening.

'What do yer mean, lass?' He looked at me, his eyes evasive.

'On my way home, this fuckwit tried to intimidate me.'

'Where was he, Rose?' Danny's forehead creased.

'Back there. Near the waste dump. What aren't you telling me, Dan?

Danny's face was filled with confusion.

'What did he say, Rose?' he deflected.

'That you're a good fighter. They knew who I was,' I exclaimed.

'What did they look like?'

'I only saw one of them. Short. Dumpy. Foul looking face. But the car…'

'What car?' Danny's voice was sharp.

'A big black car with tinted windows.' I glared.

'Did he say anything else?' Danny's concern was tangible.

'No. Just that he wanted to tell me something.'

Danny turned away. He lifted the lid from the hash tin and slowly rolled a joint.

'Come on, Rose. Perhaps we should talk.' He held out his hand and drew me gently to him. We walked out onto that cracked rotting deck and climbed into the shroud of white mosquito netting on our soft, back bedroom mattress.

~

Dan and Bruce faced each other, embroiled in conversation. The pre-Christmas afternoon light shone with intensity on their faces. From where I stood in the hall, they couldn't see me. I was still smarting with annoyance from Danny's avoidance the night before and I wished I could lip read.

Danny's shoulders were hunched as Bruce spoke. He was puffing quickly on a cigarette, his head down. For once, Bruce's face was serious. He spoke long and earnestly to Dan, trying to persuade him. Placing his hands around Dan's neck, he drew his forehead to his. They stood together, silently in the embrace of men. The tall one, my lover and saviour, the shorter, my best mate.

Then hugging close, they turned and walked up the stairs.

I stood in the hall, watching them approach. Bruce saw me first and stopped abruptly, the look on my face speaking volumes.

'Hi, Rose,' he said, tentatively.

I nodded at him, watching Dan's eyes.

'What's going on, guys?'

They exchanged a guarded look.

'And don't hide it from me again.'

'It's the developers.' Bruce's voice was evasive.

'No, it's not Bruce. Don't fucking lie to me,' I raged. 'Dan gets beaten up all the time. You're both hiding something from me.'

They looked at each other. Danny's head shook imperceptibly.

'Dan, stop. What is it? You're scaring me,' I ranted.

Bruce stepped towards me, his hand held out, his round, gentle face full of concern.

'It's Pa, Rose,' he spoke softly and gently.

I froze, my heart racing.

'What about Pa?' My voice was loud with shock.

'I should have…' But Danny's voice was interrupted as a light tone rang out along the hall.

'Pa? That idiot.' Christian's foot fall padded towards us. 'I remember him. He's that really mean one. The one you all hate.' Chris's open face looked at us.

Controlling my fear, I reached out.

'How was school, Chris?' My voice wavering.

'Good.' He held my eyes. Seeing me.

Then, his face shining with the luminosity of our truth, he continued. 'Pa's evil, Mum. Don't go there. Ever!' And turning, he trotted into the kitchen and opened the fridge.

~

The cliffs' striking façade stared down at the winding river, the murmur from the passing water muted by the distant roar of traffic on the Captain Cook Bridge. Brisbane's only skyscraper, the Town Hall, extended its steeple towards the heavens.

The small ferry deposited us at the southern bank of the river. With Isabella tugging my hand, Bruce fussing around us and our Christmas day picnic basket in the crook of my arm, I stood in awe of the mighty face of the Kangaroo Point Cliffs.

Christian gazed upwards.

'Look, Mum. There are faces up there.' His loud voice bounced off the rock wall.

Carved rock masks from eons of time glared down at us as we made our way towards the base of the cliffs.

A small group of our friends were gathered. They eyed the slanting horizontal crevices, necks strained at its colossal height. Ropes, helmets and crampons scattered at their feet. Estimates of climb times and sequences drifted through their conversations. There was an aura of reverence as they readied themselves to pit their bravery and strength against its rugged edges.

Belay points dotted the top, firmly anchored into the rock face. The only signs of vegetation were small tufts of grass that held out against the hot buffeting wind. A dry waterfall streaked dark incisions of stained vertical lines, a poignant reminder of the power of tropical storms and the devastation of floods.

Danny arrived, spinning to a halt. He pulled off his bike helmet, releasing untamed red hair to dance around his shoulders. As he propped his bike against the steel grey ochre-flecked granite, his profile reflected the wildness of his surrounds. He swung Isabella onto his shoulders and kissed me passionately, stroking my cheek and grinning.

'Cool!' he exclaimed. 'There's some good climbing in that today. The view's worth the scramble, son.' His eyes sparkled with excitement as he rested his hand firmly on Chris's shoulder. Chris gazed upwards, his eyes filled with the wonder of his first cliff-face climb.

'Good to go, cobber?' Danny enquired, beaming at Christian.

Chris nodded his head.

'Want to climb too, Mum?' he asked, eyes shining with equal portions of eagerness and anxiety.

It takes one hundred and fifty seconds to abseil from the top to the bottom of the Kangaroo Point Cliffs. Up to thirty minutes to climb up. And if the ropes don't hold, or if your belay loses concentration, then it takes two seconds to plummet to your death.

I was acutely aware of the risks Danny was taking, but his tutelage of Chris on the ropes had already been extensive. There was a clear code of respect for the dominating force of nature and when it came to rock climbing, Danny was uncompromising. Although he was fearless on the ropes, if he had his way, he would climb free.' His gigantic stretch enabled him to swing from toes and hands, spinning a web of access across any interface of rock or crevice.

I smiled at my son's concerned face.

'Just do exactly what Dan says, matey. We'll watch from here.' I reached out, patting his arm, in awe of his courage.

But as I watched Chris take his first hold on the rock, a feeling of foreboding gripped my belly.

~

Brisbane, December 1988

The languid December heat hangs around like an oppressive sauna. In the distance, thunder rumbles. The dusk sky briefly flashes with lightning. A gust of wind momentarily buffets the house.

Rosanna sits on the edge of her chair. Her hair is pulled off her face, tied into a messy bun at the back of her head. She wears a peaked cap shading her eyes. Her face is flushed from running here. Her features dark. Agitated.

'Do you think I should go back on them?' she launches into our session.

'Your drugs?' I ask.

'Yep.' Her heels drum the floor.

'That depends on how you're handling the changes,' I respond.

She looks at me.

'So, how's it going?' I continue.

'Not so good.'

'How are you feeling?'

'Edgy. Buggered. Not sleeping properly.'

'When did you last take them?'

'Last week after our session. I felt so good that I figured it was time to stop. The doctor agreed.' She fidgets with the hem on her shirt and reaches between her legs, running her hands up and down the inside of her thighs.

'It's a tough call to go cold turkey.'

'Yep. Most folk don't know how bloody addictive they are.' She snorts derisively. 'And they reckon the recreational stuff is bad. These are far worse.' She scratches her chin and swipes at the trickling sweat.

Then sits still. Far away. Eyes intense.

'There's something I should probably talk to ya about, Anna.' She looks at me, her eyes watchful. Wary.

'Okay.' I observe the darkening of her cheeks and the tightening in her jaw.

Rose looks away. Her words trapped. She glances back at me, looking for traction. I watch her quietly.

'It's about… yer know… him…'

A large butterfly flitters into the room and lands on the bookshelf. Its colours meld into the shades of blue on the cover of the book. Rose looks up, distracted. Her pupils dilate. She stands, slowly moving towards it as its wings wave softly in the warm air. I watch enchanted as she and the butterfly meet. It lightly lifts off before landing on the tip of her outstretched finger.

'See. They're not afraid,' she whispers, 'yet I've always been so scared.' Her eyes are intently focused on the creature's iridescent gold and turquoise markings.

'Scared of just about everything. Not many folk know that, Anna. Yer've seen me,' she says. 'I have such a big crappy front, don't I?' Her fingertip caresses the butterfly's wings, barely grazing its soft surface. It rests motionless on her hand.

The butterfly floats from her hand and flutters out the open window. Her gaze follows it as she walks to her chair.

'Would you like to continue?'

'It's about Pa.' Her voice is so soft I can hardly hear her.

'Yes?'

She stops and slides her hands under her thighs. Her breath quickens as the memories bubble to the surface. I watch her carefully, wary of the tipping point.

'Rose,' I say cautiously, 'I can see you're uncertain about speaking of him. Perhaps it would be more helpful if you shared about Danny and Chris.' I watch as she looks at the floor. Her mouth forms a thin line. Her shame and pain reflect in the micro-movements of her body.

'Last time we talked about Chris and Dan's passion for rock climbing,' I continue.

She flicks that look back at me, coughs and wipes her mouth.

'Yeah.' Rose clears her throat speaking slowly. The clipped sentences reflect the inner resistance.

I make a note of the sudden mood change.

'Chris still loves to climb. When Dad lets him. In the forest. Any cliff he can. Loves it. The same as he loves surfing. Competing next year. Down the coast. Can I have water?' She looks at me, her eyes screw up.

'Sure,' I respond. I make my way to the water filter on the side cabinet, my back to her.

Behind me I hear the scrape of her chair and her feet hitting the floor as she stands up quickly. My office door is wrenched open and the sound of runners on the wooden floorboards in the hall echo with her panic. The heavy thud of the front door shutting behind her heralds the abrupt termination of her session.

Exhaling sharply, I turn, staring at her empty seat, holding the full glass of water in my hand.

~

The pavement bit into my runners as I fled along Waterworks Road heading for Southbank. The traffic was loud in my ears, the setting sun blinding me. Overhead the sky was dark. Tall thunderclouds towered over Brisbane in the looming of a tropical thunderstorm.

I picked up my pace as my breath met my footfall in a rhythm of pain.

Why did it happen… WHY?

I can't do it… I won't tell her…

A car horn blared, warning me that I had veered into the traffic.

Fucking drugs. Fuck 'em…

I bolted across the road as her voice chased me, my tears falling freely down my cheeks.

Rosanna… Rosie-rose…

The rising wind and the lightning above Mt Coot-tha shone an eerie green light over the inner city. A clap of thunder in the distance almost drowned out her voice.

Trust my love… This too shall pass… Silken caresses whispering hope.

I gulped at the air, the pollution stinging my throat.

How do you know that, Sah? I raged silently.

Soft lips brushed my cheek.

Because I know you, Rose. Forever sista…

I sprinted towards the bridge.

But if I tell Anna, I will lose everything…

I stumbled heedlessly on the curb, sprawling onto the edge of the road, the hot bitumen ripping into my knees. The traffic exploded into a cacophony of sounds assaulting my body.

Ya fucking suicidal idiot… can't even get that right… Pa's voice snarled at me.

Heavy droplets of rain began to fall as I picked myself up and limped along the bridge.

Wait, Rose lassie. Yer nearly there. This is not yer way…

His love spun a mantle of protection.

Danny… my heart ached… *What do you want me to do?* I sobbed.

Lightning and thunder filled the sky as I turned towards the streets of our former neighbourhood. New buildings had sprung up everywhere. Where character and history had once steeped the suburb with the tenure of the artisans, flat earth now laid bare its soft belly to the imminent summer storm.

I stopped at the end of our street, gasping for breath, bent double with the pain in my sides. Our old home stood alone, a legacy to Danny's last fight. Razed blocks of a featureless moonscape surrounded it. A wasteland from the dismantling of Expo 88. As I approached, the heavens opened and the torrential tropical tempest broke open. In seconds I was soaked to the skin

The old wrought iron gate squeaked the melody that I knew so well. I pushed it open and fled around the back. The garden was a jungle of weeds. The outdoor toilet door hung at a rakish angle, its edge pressed into the dirt.

I shook my head as visions cascaded through my mind.

Bruce's infectious laugh filling the air.

Danny and Chris chasing each other in a game of tag.

The ancient gum tree hung its sheltering limbs over the house. Remnants of the rotting timber of the children's treehouse hung vertically next to its trunk.

Mumma, stop it! Isabella's giggling wrenches at my heart.

Danny's lightning rod bent sideways atop the roof, a vestige to his overzealous desire to protect us. It twisted and scraped at the corrugated iron in a tuneless squeaking dance of metal upon metal, the growing wind conducting it in an eerie comforting memory of Dan and Bruce's musicality

Shivering, I crawled in under the veranda, scrambling deeper into the dark belly of the underside of the old house. The light in the sky transformed into a murky green blackness as I found an old crate and sat down heavily, shaking the chill from my bones, my soaked clothing clinging to me.

I rubbed my body to keep warm. Shivering. Trying to collect my thoughts.

Get a grip, Rose. You have to talk to her about this. My inner dialogue danced with the rhythm of the wind as it began to shake the house.

But if I do, I will lose it all. They'll put me in. Forever. I'd rather die than be there.

If you don't, you will always live with it. And then, they will keep the kids. You have a chance!

The house shook as thunder crashed.

'Danny, help me!' I screamed.

The sky lit with intense white light. The roar of the cyclone filled the air. Forks of silver light engulfed the dark space in which I huddled. Then a violent shudder burst open the heavens.

I clapped my hands over my head and shrieked.

A shockwave arced through me as the epicentre of the gale struck the old eucalypt, splitting it in two. The massive overhanging limb twisted and jerked as it fell, ripping free from its mother tree. A yawing crunch crashed over the back deck. The shattering of timber and steel screeched its warning, as the entrance to my retreat caved in front of me. My body flew through the air, crashing into a cement pillar.

I lay there stunned for a timeless moment. The deafening sound subsiding, as my breath flooded back into me. A strange tingling filled me.

Slowly I sat up. My mind clear and still.

The small crate on which I had been sitting lay tipped over by the force of the deck collapsing at my feet. It was crushed. Its contents sprawled out onto the dirt.

I crawled towards it.

There in front of me lay a torn and faded book. I picked it up. Danny's diary fell open. His writing a notational cleft of familiar security. Words spilled out. His voice a rich, resonance of hope. Pictures of our lives together played in my mind.

I turned its frayed and worn pages to the last one.

Dec 15th, 1977. Hitching home today… have to see Rose… she must know the truth…

I read back, my heart beating faster. Memory tears blurring his words.

A piece of paper, used as a bookmark, fluttered onto the dirt. I picked it up. It was in a foreign hand. I squinted in the dark, the storm crashing around me. A flash of lightning illuminated Pa's flat square writing. Three words. Repeated.

'He's my son, MY son…'

My heart stopped, as the message fluttered unhindered to the ground.

~

The heavy metal door-knocker thumps three times, echoing along the corridor. I look at my clock. It's late. Rosanna's case lies open in front of me, the notes from her abandoned session this afternoon incomplete.

Rising from my desk, I head out to the front door. My heels echoing the emptiness of the clinic.

'Who is it?' I call, from behind the locked door.

'Anna. I Rinpoche.' A thick accent in a soft, deep voice.

'Rosanna's friend?' I ask.

'Yes. Please open.'

I unlock the heavy bolts and swing the door open.

A small, youthful-looking Tibetan man in soaked joggers, jeans and a t-shirt stands in front of me, bowing low. His thick black hair is plaited down his back in a wet ponytail. His face is flushed. His breath quick.

'Rinpoche. How nice to meet you. Please come in out of this rain,'

I welcome him.

He moves from one foot to the other, agitated.

'Anna. So sorry. I know it late. I run. Big storm. Rosanna tell me where you working. She not know I come. She say me not come.'

I watch him, concern rising.

'Is Rose alright?' I ask.

'No. Not okay.' Catching his breath.

'What's happened Rinpoche?'

'She bad.' His fingers slice through the air above his wrist. His face in shock.

'Where is she?' I ask, registering a crisis.

'At house.'

'Come in Rinpoche.' I reach out, taking his arm, leading him into my office.

'Wait here please.'

I walk quickly, gathering my car keys, phone, bag and umbrella. I resist the urge to dial 000. Flicking the night light on, I shut my office door and turn to him.

'Why is she not in hospital, Rinpoche?' I ask.

'She say she good. Not go. She say Chris, Isabella, never come home now. She say not tell you.'

We walk through the front door, it shuts automatically, the lock sliding into place as we dash to my car. Thunder rumbles and crashes around us.

Red Hill to West End is a ten-minute drive. Especially late at night. My wipers speed across the windscreen, chasing the heavy aftermath of the severe storm. The road is deserted. I avoid the water flooding the gutters.

My mind is on hyperalert as we drive, Rinpoche's agitated chattering a background noise as I mentally check over my last, brief session with Rose.

In five minutes, we are through the Normanby Five Ways, over the William Jolly Bridge and pulling up in front of a deserted pub on Boundary Road.

Rinpoche ushers me up the dimly lit stairwell and along a corridor of doors. He slips his key into number three and swings the door open.

The room is dark. Spanned across the ceiling is the inside of a tent. Clothing hangs neatly from hooks on the wall. A door to the left is backlit revealing a small, spotless kitchenette. A timber-framed queen size bed almost fills the room. A shape huddles underneath the sheets.

Rinpoche approaches, sits gently on the bed and reaches out his hand.

'Rose?' he whispers.

The huddled shape stirs, and Rosanna looks up. Her eyes swollen; her face puffy. An empty bottle of whiskey sits on the bedside table. She peers at me, struggling to sit upright as her heavily bandaged hand appears from under the sheets.

Dried blood soaks though the strapping.

'Told you not to bring her, Rin!' she flashes at Rinpoche, her voice shaky and slurred.

'I scared, Rose.' His eyes plead with her. Rosanna flicks his hand from her arm.

'Rose? It's me. Anna.' I interrupt. 'What's happened?'

Rose looks at me. Her face filled with anguish.

'I won't tell you, Anna. I just can't…' Her voice fades, as tears drench her cheeks.

I reach over to lift her wrist.

'What's going on, Rose?' I ask neutrally.

She tries to withdraw her hand.

'It looks like you have cut yourself,' I say softly.

Her arm goes limp in my hand as her body caves in on itself and her sobbing fills the room. I turn to Rin.

'Could I have a moment alone with Rose please, Rinpoche?' I ask gently.

He nods. The door shuts softly behind him.

13

THE low rock wall on the top of the cliffs offered little challenge to the long stride of the young man walking along the road immediately adjacent to it. It was a single swing of his leg to the top, then a short drop down onto the narrow shaley ledge of rock and rubble on the other side.

The lights of the city twinkled in the foreground, lighting up the low-level skyscrapers and bridges that spanned the river. The water below, an inky darkness as it swirled and eddied and flowed out to the ocean.

The street behind was in full swing, raucous now with late New Year's Eve revelry. Fireworks on the river splayed flashing lights, filling the air with the crashing of pyrotechnics. Merriment and partying wrapped his senses with delight, as the sultry warmth of the humid midnight, clung like a sweaty mantle of moisture around him.

Over the rooftops of the houses lining the river's upper embankment, he could see for miles. The cliffs were backlit by permanent safety lights. Scanty shrubs clung to its surface, offering little protection from the sheer drop to the footpath and the scattered boulders below.

Standing there in the euphoria of the night, looking out over the vista that shone before him, the man could only feel the delight of the pot. The acid. The booze and the party that had spun a web of soporific fantasy around him. His feet gripped the edge of the drop, as his mind played with the unheeded danger of a descent.

He saw only the delight and the freedom of this hard-edged, vertical place that had so often seduced him, calming his mind.

His fingers tingled to climb. To drop. To descend the cliff face.

Like a spider… he had always said to him.

Use your fingers as if they are a part of the rock. Let go of your head. Feel for the cracks. Toes dig deep. Stretch the legs. Reach into it. Until it's part of you.

Feel for it. It's always there.

Half closing his eyes he felt the hardness of the rock against his belly. Pressed into it; part of it. Absorbed by it; secreted into the escarpment of stony shelves. His body spread-eagled. Melded. One with it.

Great view… easy drop… best place in Brisbane.

A half smile turned the corners of his mouth.

Squatting to take it all in, he reached around, releasing the bulk in his back pocket, removing his wallet and car keys and placing them next to him.

Won't be needing those for a bit…

Crossing his legs, he sat there on the shale and rubble, pebbles digging into his ankles. The night deepened as he wrapped his arms around his legs. Chin on knees, watching. Keen eyes scanned for shapes in the corner of his mind. The lights of the city playing in the blue of his iris.

He leant forward.

Hah! The raptors can fly this one…

Then. That familiar warmth in his groin. Excitement spinning a web of freedom. His cock strained against his jeans.

I could reach in there now, wouldn't be the first wanker up here.

In that momentary distraction the first light of a dawn twinkled.

It's the best time to climb. It's a pinch. A real pinch. No ropes?

Yep, no ropes.

His breath deepened.

…tinkling laughter… chicken breath… smiles in the corners of emerald-green eyes…

Butterfly wings caress… soft breath…

Ah! Ya wouldn't know a dare even if yer could see one.

The city lights dimmed a little with her voice. A cool river mist swirled his thoughts. Casting a pall of confusion around him.

Why did she do it?

Arms hugging legs.

Why?

The night lengthened. The festivities of the first day of the New Year continued around him. A new potential.

Youth has a habit. One of survival at all odds. And invincibility held his mind as he watched his city.

The Chinese New Year forgives everything? This too? I don't think so… yer so bloody stupid… she never deserved that.

And reaching into his pocket he pulled out the last tab and slipped it under his tongue.

Stay here. Till the morning. It's easier then… to talk.

The heaviness of the night hung on him. His head throbbed as he watched and waited for it to kick in. He rested against on the hard surface. Knees bent to the heavens. Fingers interlaced behind his head. Mind chasing the colour and the shapes of the trip. Breath held in the vibrant river of life.

When you drop hold your arms out. Spread eagle them. Then fly…

He wanted to sleep, a deep sleep. No longer accountable for deeds done. But remaining in the twilight of memories. Gardens.

Loving arms wrapped around him… *yer chicken shit… peeling laughter…*

The edge seemed steady as he turned to face the cliff. Sliding belly into its curves. Feet finding crevasses. Fingers reaching into it. The drop below close. The rock yielding to him.

There! There's that ledge…

Thoughts stilled as the young man swung himself over. Took a breath.

And let go.

14

Brisbane, December 1988

IT'S early. The storm has left debris everywhere. I trip on a fallen branch as I walk from the coffee shop to the clinic. Righting myself, I head for the entrance. The front door swings open and I step into the cool interior. I flick the switch in the darkened corridor, illuminating the hall and the many paintings from clients and friends adorning the walls.

Rosanna's exhibition sits neatly stacked around the waiting room. Charcoals and nudes intermingle with highly abstract fragmented figures and geometric rhythms in oil. Transparent shapes and patterns adorn images in a surreal flight of fantasy and reality. There is a convincingly focused atmosphere of emotion in all. A narrative that runs through them that enlivens me.

Rose's inspiration from her subjects is profound. Beautiful. Tragic. My connection to her, a poignant journey of personal and professional challenge.

I pause at her last painting. The two delicately sketched female figures of a mother and daughter are woven between stripes of dark and light, melded together by blotches of ink. A struggle for some kind of secret disclosure, hovers just below their surface. There is a rudimentary lack of finish and in the chaos of the marks, dwells a mystery.

The single word *Discovery* takes my attention.

I gather it up and walk to my office. Crystal light floats around my room, reflecting the intensity of the dawn. A familiar comforting space after the challenges of the night before. I sink into my armchair, my hands wrapped around my coffee. I put my feet up, resting on my desk.

Through my window I can see the city buildings sparkling brightly, scrubbed clean by the force of nature, contrasting with the scene of destruction before me. Piles of hail stack the edges of the gutters, melting in the early morning heat. Cars are parked end to end on footpaths and under shop awnings, seeking shelter from the massive spheres of hail that pummelled the city. Jacaranda trees are stripped bare of their foliage and lay smashed on roads and houses, a vision of annihilation.

I sip my coffee and breathe, reflecting on how the human spirit mirrors its environment. How, in the devastation of the storm, Rosanna has unintentionally found a way through to her hidden beliefs. As the cyclone ripped our city apart, her life was laid bare. Its roots pulled up from the earth and smashed into pieces in front of her

I pull my notes out from her folder and flick back over them. Records of a life profoundly challenged by the unwitting circumstance of birth and of a culture that sanctions hidden abuse and incest. A story confronting the unconsciousness of the norm, that places most experience into the realm of the insignificant. It is one that defies the capacity of the human spirit to forgive and move on.

As I sit alone, I see the profound changes that have occurred for Rosanna and how her healing has taken a course which, for most, would not have been possible. I understand, now, that she has been sent to me as a gift for closure. That in the story she has shared, I have found myself.

Danny's diary lies open before me. I read, searching for a link. For the thread to pull it all together. To reconstruct it into a comprehensive whole. My intuition nags me. There is one thing I don't get about her behaviour. About her patterns. It tugs at me. At my full understanding. Rose's drawing leans against her chair, the questions in my mind burning into its surface.

I look at the clock. I register the hour. The early-bird public servants will be opening their computers, readying themselves for a day of work. The answers I seek are written in their files.

I reach forward and pick up my phone. I dial the number and wait.

'Corrective Services. How can I help?' The voice at the end begins my day.

~

Rosanna sits in her chair. Her face is drawn. Cheeks, pale. Her eyes sunken into crevasses of black. She's dressed in a version of the other night's attire. Rin sits next to her, his hand on her bandaged arm. His face filled with concern.

I watch them carefully. The late-afternoon sun shines in through my window.

'I'm so sorry Anna.' Her eyes entreating. 'I've fucked it up, haven't I?' She hangs her head in her hands.

'This isn't what I planned. Please Anna. I've been trying so hard. Please don't tell the psychologist.'

My heart breaks at her expressed powerlessness. At her appeal to me to not take action against that which she believes she's done. I am acutely aware of the control that has been placed in my hands and saddened at how "victim" still imprints itself so deeply in her psyche.

'Rose,' I start softly, 'there is something that I need to tell you.'

She lifts her head, her face a picture of agony.

'Rose. It wasn't you. It was Danny.' Her eyes flinch. Her pupils dilate.

'Danny?' she whispers.

'Yes, Rose. You didn't do it. Danny did.'

Rose's eyes blank over. Her face freezes.

'What do you mean?' She breathes.

'Pa. He was just knocked out. You knocked him out, Rose.'

There's the sharp in-breath.

'He's alive?' She looks at me, terrified.

'No, Rose. Danny made sure he wasn't.'

Rose's hand claps over her mouth as she begins to shake.

'I don't understand.' Her voice is a muffled shriek.

'Danny found him in town that night, looking for you. The witness finally said that Pa went for him. It was self-defence, Rose. Danny did six months before he was fully exonerated.'

I look at Rose. Her face is filled with disbelief.

'Danny? *NO!* He couldn't have,' she whispers. 'Pa wasn't breathing.'

Her eyes are wild.

'Rose. Pa could take much more than you could ever give.' I speak deliberately and slowly.

Rose stares at me. Her face frozen with shock

'You mean. Danny? Danny was in?'

'Yes, Rose. Danny did his time.'

'He never told me.'

'Of course not, Rose. He always wanted to protect you.'

She stares at me.

'How do you know, Anna? How did you figure it all out?'

'You told me. In so many ways. So often. I just didn't put the pieces together until the other night. I confirmed it this morning.'

Rosanna hunches over and begins to rock herself. Then leaps up and paces the floor, door to window and back. Rin watches. His face still.

'Danny… He tried to tell me. More than once. But I… I…' She stops.

'Oh my God, Anna. I've carried this for years. I've loathed myself. Wanted to die. Been terrified that if they… if you… found out… I'd… I'd be thrown into…'

She sits down suddenly. Her hands grip the arms of the chair. She holds on tight as she shakes and then doubles over, her body convulsing. Rin's face is a mask of compassion as he strokes her arm, murmuring softly.

'That was my biggest fear. That I would lose my kids forever.' Her voice is indescribable. My heart yearns to hold her.

I fill her glass. Squatting in front of her I gently place my hand on her arm. She looks at me. Her tear-filled eyes are pools of shadows and light

'And Rose. The posters. Danny put them up.'

She looks at me. Dumbfounded.

'Oh my God… oh my…' Her eyes are spheres of disbelief.

'There is something else too. Can you wait here please?' I say quietly.

I stand and walk to the front door. The tall man and his wife waiting outside the building turn expectantly to me. A slender youth and young girl stand hand in hand next to them.

'Would you like to come in?' I ask.

~

It is eight weeks after Brisbane was annihilated by the cyclone. Rose walks into my room and sits gracefully on the velvet of my new brocaded armchair. She wears a fawn-coloured, knee-length skirt and a soft pink blouse. A turquoise silk scarf drapes her neck. Diamond studded earrings bob in the light and a gold pendant hangs around her neck. Her penetrating eyes shine with a pearlescent shimmer. Her long dark ringlets are swept off her face with a small clasp. A faint peach shine on her lips tells me that, for the first time in her eighteen months of therapy, she is wearing make-up.

Her composure is poised

She smiles as she arranges her skirt and places her handbag on the floor, her recently completed manuscript beside it. I watch her, fascinated with the change in her since her last appointment. She lifts her head; her eyes are tranquil pools of ebony.

'Hi, Anna. Nice to see you again.' A soft light glimmers around her.

'How are you feeling today, Rose?'

She doesn't answer as her mouth curls upwards in that familiar half smile.

'Did I ever tell you about how it all started?' she enquires as she settles.

I watch as she readies herself.

~

'The first time was easy. In fact, it was almost enjoyable.'

'I was hitching north, late in the afternoon. The setting sun burnt me through the windscreen. The country side was dark. I'd been staying with Dad and Mim in Nimbin. Things had gone weird for me in the city. So, I was visiting the kids. Christian was growing up. He loved his life there. But Izzy. She really missed me and her dad.'

She looks out my window as her hand rises gently to her chest, the habitual tightening of her lips reflects her feeling.

'It had been a while since Dan…' She pauses. Her breath deepening.

'He was young. A truck driver. Picked me up just out of town. Headed for Brisbane. We talked into the sunset.' She turns to me.

'I was mad, Anna. Mad as a cut snake. Dad and I had fought. For the first time, ever.' She looks away, lost in her memory. I wait quietly.

'It'd started with us looking at his photos. Dad wanted to chat to me. So, we sat on the couch. Like old times. And turned the pages of the album.'

'He started talking about Dan. At first, I listened. I wanted to know what he was feeling.' She shakes her head.

I make a note.

'And I missed that kind of time with him. It was comforting. Made me feel good. And close to him. But then. Well. I was still so raw.' Her fingers trace the heart-shaped pendant around her neck. I note the gesture. Rose catches my glance and smiles. She turns the locket so gold filigree and tiny studded gems flash in the light.

'Your fourteenth birthday gift?' I ask.

She nods.

'It's beautiful,' I comment. She looks at me. Her face a portrayal of subtle emotion

'Yes. It's an anchor for me. A marker of my life.' She rises and walks slowly to her favourite window and sits on the sill, looking out onto the street.

'You know, I love this view. It's helped me so much to get straight. To feel normal.' Her voice drifts away as she inhales the late afternoon air.

'Remember how I couldn't even look at you?' She turns to me.

'Yes, I do.'

'And how it all blew up so easily?'

I nod.

'It's so different in here now.' She stands tall, gazing back out at the Red Hill streets. Her hand rests on her heart.

'I still wonder about Danny never telling me. I'm still puzzled.' She frowns slightly. 'Dad tried to tell me too.'

'When was that?' I ask.

'That day we had the fight.' Her face clouds over.

'You were talking about that,' I prompt.

'Yeah. I was.' She sits down, rearranges her skirt and folds her hands in her lap.

'I got up and went out to the kitchen. Fixing to make a cuppa. He followed me. "Rose," he said. "There's something I want to tell you." I looked at him. But all I could see was Dan.'

'Then. I couldn't be there anymore. Couldn't speak. Dan was everywhere. Dad reached out to me.' She pauses.

'I pushed him away, Anna. Forced myself past him. The look on his face…' She shakes her head. 'It was split with pain. I grabbed my stuff and took off. He called me. Just once. I ran down the street. I knew he wouldn't follow.'

Her thumb slowly turns the ring on her left hand. She takes a gentle in-breath as her chest tremors.

'I felt so bad. But I couldn't do it anymore. The kids there without me. Him and Mim. Sah. Danny. All of it. My head crashed in with numbness. I wanted them so much. But I had to get out of there.'

She pauses as she takes a shuddering in-breath.

'He told me last week that he wanted to tell me. About Dan and Pa. Things would have been so different if I had listened to him.' She looks up, her face a mask. I hand her a fresh cup of tea.

'What happened then?' I ask.

She smiles broadly.

'Oh, the truckie? He was sort of cute. We drove north, talking about music. And cities. And food. He asked me what I did. I lied. Told him I was a therapist. Like you.' A mischievous light shines in her eyes.

'We pulled up about 10:30 that night. On the outskirts of Mullumbimby. He said he needed to stop. Sleep. Said I could stay with him. I had my sleeping bag so I figured it would be safer up there. I went off to have a pee. And when I clambered back up to the cabin and opened the door. Well…'

Rose smiles.

'The stench of his Brut aftershave was everywhere!' She laughs.

'He looked at me and patted the mattress at the back of the cabin. I don't know what got into me, but I said, "I charge for that!"'

She turns away, watching the crystal light play on the walls of my office. The sun is setting and the light shines on her profile, highlighting the soft touch of her lipstick. Her arms cross loosely, holding her elbows.

She turns to me.

'You know what? I almost enjoyed it. He was young. Vigorous. Quite sexy. And afterwards we lay in each other's arms. But all I could think of was Dan.' A light tremor runs through her.

'But I needed the money. So, all of it seemed to make sense.' She pauses, thinking.

'The next morning, he paid me $100. That was more than I could make in a week in the café. I tucked it into the pocket of my bag. He let me out at South Brisbane. Kissed my cheek and said, "Look after yourself, Rose."'

She stops as her fingers hold her necklace.

'You know. It hasn't been a bad job. I've helped heaps of guys. It's only the way we have to handle it that bothered me in the end. Most of us take drugs. Just to do the job. But I've had some really cool experiences. I think I'm a good listener. Some of them actually never want sex. Just an ear from a woman. So, I've done a bit of what you do.' She grins. 'Except in a very different environment.' Her eyes crinkle as she contemplates me.

I smile back at her.

'I'm not really normal, Anna. Am I?' Her eyes penetrate mine. 'But I understand about sex now. About men. About women. I've made some friends. Some are leaving too.'

I watch her carefully.

'Leaving?' I question.

She nods.

'I'm fully clean. Have been for months. In fact, I haven't worked at all since before the storm. I've been thinking, praying and being with Rin. He's amazing. Such a great mate. He found a house for the kids and me. In Zigzag Street.' She nods her head back towards the Red Hill shops.

'Close to here. So, if I go belly up, you'll be just around the corner.' Her eyes fill with gratitude.

'What about your past, Rosanna? How do you feel about Nimbin? And Ma now?' I ask.

She pauses, then stands and moves to the CDs. She selects one and slots it into the machine, clicking play. Her hand rests on the shelf as the soft strains of 'Clair de Lune' float into the room.

'Dan's favourite,' she murmurs, as she returns to her chair.

She closes her eyes. We sit together in the stillness, light and dark playing in her features as the intensity in Debussy draws to a close. She stands and picks up the rose quartz egg on the coffee table, circling it with her hands.

Her back is turned to me.

'She knew he did it.' Her voice is almost inaudible.

'She was there. That night. She must have known what happened.' Her hands are still, wrapped around the crystal.

'She never did talk about it. Could never face it. Not ever. She was never my mother. I was *bought trouble*. Remember? That was the problem.' She turns to look at me, a curious sweetness and intensity replacing her former hesitancy.

My heartbeat accelerates.

She returns the quartz, sits, and takes a small picture from her bag. Her finger traces the longitudinal crack across its glass. A gesture of tenderness. The woman and child's features are barely visible through the grime. She folds her hands over it, watching me.

Silence fills my office.

'Would you like to continue?' I ask, shakily.

'It was my biggest betrayal.' Her eyes are clear. The lines on her face almost imperceptible.

'She's in a home now. Her memory has gone.'

'Alzheimer's?'

'Yes. Because of what happened in that family.' Rose looks away. 'I did blame her. But now… it's my past. You've taught me how to handle it, Anna. How to walk with it. How to have compassion for my own fate.' She pauses. 'And you know. I look at all my trauma curiously now. It helps me to understand. To accept it.'

She returns the picture to her bag

'Feeling like a victim is a choice, isn't it?'

I wait as she collects her thoughts.

'Every day, I think about the people who've taught me about life. Bruce. Beck.' Her thumb turns the rose gold ring on her finger. 'Sah.

She was my gift from God.' Her voice is hushed. Her face glows with a soft light.

'But I've always had fear. Of what will happen if my happiness runs out. Of stuffing it all up. Even of my own power. Of my ability to destroy things.' Rose stops speaking and slowly sips her tea.

'Didn't Dan say in his diaries that you were strong?' I ask.

'His words were "*a force to be contended with*"...' She smiles wryly.

'He knew me so well.' Her eyes spring with tears.

I reach for the tissues. She blows her nose.

'I'm learning to be in love with my destiny. To not reject it. But to embrace it. And I love my life. Exactly the way it is. That's what's real. That's what's important to me now. I have earnt this, haven't I, Anna?'

Rosanna stops and sits quietly, thinking. Then stands and walks to my mantelpiece. Her fingertips reach up and lightly caress the cool surface of the white marble. She trails her hands over the books. There's a reverence and finality that lingers in her touch.

I watch, entranced, as she quietly returns to her chair.

I go to speak but she interrupts.

'You're going to ask me about my self-respect, aren't you?' She smiles as I nod.

'It's been a terrible thing to lose.' Her voice serious.

'It shrivelled up. Because I've allowed the world to steal it from me.' She reaches for her tea. Her fingers trace the delicate porcelain.

'I've exchanged it for what I thought would give me love and attention. But I chose poorly. That's not love.' Emphasising her words.

'Prostitution?' I clarify.

'And other stuff. Drugs. All the really dumb horrible things I did. The stuff that got me into trouble.' Her voice is sharp.

'And wanting to jump this planet. I can't believe how much self-hatred I had.'

I watch her carefully and make a note.

'I've given my self-respect away, Anna. To gain the approval of others.' She shrugs her shoulders.

'That's what sucks more than anything else.' Her fingers weave through the gold chain of her locket

'Right from the start, Sah tried to teach me that I was beautiful inside. Danny believed in me. Like so many folk did. But I've realised that it's self-approval I've yearned for. More than anything else. That's been my biggest challenge.'

Her chest rises as she takes in a long breath.

'What about your happiness?' I ask.

She turns to me.

'Isn't happiness a decision? One I can make at any time?'

I nod.

'Rin taught me that my happiness is not based in me doing stuff or acting in a certain way. It's about what happens inside of me.' She taps her heart.

'Life is a gift. Every day. And you know, Anna? I haven't made any mistakes. This is my life. My journey. All the crap that happened, was meant to be. I can see that now.' She breathes freely.

'And… I'm learning about forgiveness. About how to release the people who have really hurt me.' Her face is still. Her hands rest in her lap.

I watch her carefully.

'Rose, you have made some huge changes. It's so encouraging to see. Where are you going to take it now?' I ask, my heart in my mouth.

She reaches for the manuscript at her feet.

'Get this memoir published first. And…'

She gazes at me, her mouth turned up at the corners. Her eyes radiate strength. She stands and walks to my desk. Reaching across my papers, she opens my top drawer and takes out my small photo. Returning to her seat she draws hers from her bag. She presses them both to her heart. Then, holding my gaze, she hands the two identical photos to me.

'How long have you known, Anna?' Her eyes are crystal clear.

I look down at the two photos. Then back at her. This woman. The small child that should have squatted on the desert soil. The one who's birth right to be in the embrace of her culture was stolen from us in her first moments. This woman reaches out to me as my tears fall unhindered.

'I have something to ask of you now, Anna.' She leans forward and takes my hands. Her face, filled with love.

'I am going to ask you to sign those forms for me.'

I gaze at my daughter.

We're ready.

~

The distant orb of ochre rose slowly from behind the ocean, reflecting crystal light in the flecks of mica in the sand. Effervescent turquoise and gold danced in the rising sun's rays. The fir trees of the fore-dunes silhouetted the brightening sky. Arms reaching out horizontally. Tufted branches pointing vertically skywards. Tips shaped into the cross of Jesus.

The fine white sand was warm beneath our feet. The sky above the hills behind us scattered with smoky grey clouds, set alight with the luminosity of the dawn. The water's edge encrusted a foaming white. Lapping waves gently bounding and recoiling against the sand in defiance of the previous night's roaring, annihilating storm.

I had watched the sunset that evening before, the pulse of nightfall slowing to a whisper. The endless skyline darkened to the deepest indigo in the approaching storm.

The sun waited to get behind the ocean as above the roaring surf, a sea eagle dropped. A bullet falling, plummeting into the darkened water beyond the breakers. Its wings fanned out. White-tipped fingers grasping the air, steering the final descent onto its prey below.

A school of silver fish leapt into the air around it, before floating, suspended, dancing with the journey of life and death. Then turning, they struck the surface, leaving behind a spray of churning spume. The sea pounded the shore with the thunder of a king tide, sucking sand, kelp, rocks and debris outwards.

In that dusk, all that I had ever felt and thought was suspended in inanimate time. A twilight descended on my past life and my thoughts slipped into the crack between worlds. My memory dropped away as I was immersed into the realm of feeling.

There was truth in my belly. And wrapped around my heart was the love of the woman who had crept into my soul years before. I held my breath in a visceral warp of reality. The enchantment of my life in the forests and gardens of my youth enfolded me as my mind traversed through the watermarks within me.

As the ocean's roar grew, I became witness to that which was infused within me. The forever moments of spirit. The whispering of the faeries. The call of my ancestors' guidance. And the love in the voices of those who had passed before me, holding me steady as I was tossed from one end of my universe to the other.

~

As we watched the sun rise over the far distant line on the horizon, my heart sang into the warm embrace of my life. At my feet stood the urn containing the ashes of my Danny. Around my waist, Rebecca's arms held me close.

Isabella hummed as she rested against us, her head buried into me, her shock of wild red hair lifting gently in the dawn breeze.

'Mummy, he's coming. I can see him in the waves.' She pointed seaward as Christian's surfboard rode the curl of the white foaming surf.

Rebecca bent into me, her breath warm on my neck. I looked into her hazel eyes as they reflected the intensity in her heart. Her hand entwined mine, our matching rose gold rings glinting in the dawn light.

'Are you ready, Rose,' she said, 'to let him go?'

The radiance of her promise shone between us and as Christian strode from the surf, I watched the sun's light cast a golden pathway over the ocean to our feet. And in that eternal beauty and in the presence of grace, my heart came to peace.

THE END

ACKNOWLEDGEMENTS

Endless thanks to Carolyn Martinez and the team at Hawkeye Publishing, Meanjin (Brisbane Australia). Your support and dedication in publishing my debut novel has been a treasured part of my success.

To all the librarians, booksellers and readers who have read this novel, given it a place on your bookshelves, shared it with other readers, and continue to support *Rosanna*, thank you. To Lori-Jay Ellis and the folk at the Queensland Writers Centre, big gratitude for your wonderful literary guidance and instructive programs.

To the 'Fabulous Book Group' Meanjin, where our monthly debates have honed my skills in understanding what makes great literature, I simply cannot do without you! Eternal thanks.

To my writing mentor, Vicki Bennett, for her boundless patience, insight and compassion in growing me as an author. Your belief in me is a priceless gift. To my early readers, Marg Matthews, Joy Porter, Kristina Challands, Kari Didi and Suzie Teo whose incisive and generous feedback guided me.

The biggest gratitude to the friends and family members who have listened to my dreams and encouraged me forward. But especially to Katie McGuire, Conrad Sernia, Amaliah Grace, Sante D'Ettorre, Nici Buirski, and Peter Hope. You all have gotten me here in ways you could not imagine.

To my reviewers and later readers, Nita Delgado, Beth Falzon, Cathy Scully, Cate Sawyer, and Paris Thompson, a big shout out for your skill, diligence and perceptiveness. You have played a vital part in the life of *Rosanna* in multitudinous ways. Thank you!

To all those who shared their lives with me, you are the gift that made this novel possible. From the bottom of my heart, thank you! May your journey forward be filled with love and well-being.

And last but not least, to my beloved son, Miki Clarke, for your patience, wit, humour, and astute feedback. You light my world!

Annie O'Moon-Browning

ABOUT THE AUTHOR

Annie O'Moon-Browning is a Meeanjin-Brisbane author of Australian fiction. She is a counsellor, lecturer, natural health professional, yoga teacher and abstract artist. Annie's love for her fellow humans, her sensitivity to their journeys, and her delight in discovering what emerges, infuses her writing. Her power as storyteller comes from her Celtic heritage and her lifetime of writing. *Rosanna* is a call to arms for change in Australia.

Annie is currently researching her Lutruwita-Tasmanian heritage for her next novel, based on the turbulent private life and political corruption of her ancestors in Nipaluna-Hobart in the 1800s.

Annie is a second-generation author and is a technical writer in Natural Medicine. She loves to dance Tango, couldn't do without her monthly book and film groups, and is addicted to authors of literary genius. Whenever possible she travels to exotic locations to indulge her passion for culture and the inspiration it imparts to her writing.

If you have been or are affected by family violence
please know that the
1800RESPECT (1800 737 732) hotline
is available 24 hours, 7 days a week in Australia.
It is a free, confidential, telephone counselling and online service
for any Australian who is experiencing or has experienced
domestic, family, or sexual violence.

Book reviews can make or break a book. If you liked what you read today,
please do consider posting a review on Goodreads or your favourite forum.

Rosanna is available at hawkeyebooks.com.au
and all good bookstores and libraries.

If you enjoyed *Rosanna*, you'll also enjoy:

www.ingramcontent.com/pod-product-compliance
Lightning Source LLC
Chambersburg PA
CBHW011556190726
48287CB00010B/2921